BLOODY
SEASON

BLOODY SEASON

Loren D. Estleman

BANTAM BOOKS

TORONTO · NEW YORK · LONDON · SYDNEY · AUCKLAND

BLOODY SEASON

A Bantam Book / January 1988

Grateful acknowledgment is made for permission to reprint
the following: Larry Phillips, excerpted from HEMING-
WAY ON WRITING, copyright © 1984, Larry W. Phillips
and Mary Hemingway. Reprinted with permission of
Charles Scribners Sons, a division of Macmillan, Inc.

Library of Congress Cataloging-in-Publication Data

Estleman, Loren D.
  Bloody season.

  I. Title.
PS3555.S84B58 1988   813'.54   87-47573
ISBN 0-553-05231-4

Published simultaneously in the United States and Canada

Bantam Books are published by Bantam Books, Inc. Its trade-
mark, consisting of the words "Bantam Books" and the portrayal
of a rooster, is Registered in U.S. Patent and Trademark Office
and in other countries. Marca Registrada. Bantam Books, Inc.,
666 Fifth Avenue, New York, New York 10103.

PRINTED IN THE UNITED STATES OF AMERICA
DH   0 9 8 7 6 5 4 3 2 1

To Dick Wheeler,
who helped me buck the tiger.

No weather will be found in this book. This is an attempt to pull a book through without weather.
                                    —Mark Twain

Remember to get the weather in your god damned book—weather is very important.
                                    —Ernest Hemingway

PART ONE
FLY'S ALLEY

---

*. . . As a general thing—as far as I could make out—
these murderous adventures were not forays undertaken
to avenge injuries, nor to settle old disputes or sudden
fallings out; no, as a rule they were simply duels between
strangers—duels between people who had never even
been introduced to each other, and between whom existed
no cause of offence whatever.*

—Mark Twain, *A Connecticut Yankee
in King Arthur's Court,* 1889

CHAPTER 1

HE WAS DYING FASTER than usual that morning, striping the sides of the dry sink with bloody sputum and shreds of shattered lung. His ears rang and his head felt hollow.

When the first seizure of the day had passed he remained leaning on his palms on the maple washstand, shoulders gathered into a tent behind his lowered head, the stench of evaporated night-sweat stale in his nostrils. On such mornings his senses were painfully acute and he could not stand to be around himself. He poured blood-tinted liquid into a thick, smeared glass tumbler on the stand, set down the bottle, and drank, not lowering the tumbler until it was as empty as his head. The alcohol spread inside him, burning as it went, cauterizing. He replenished the contents of the glass and drank it more slowly. The sharp barley fumes flushed his own stink from his olfactory system.

A harsh gust skidded around the corner of the frame building and clattered the panes in the window overlooking the narrow lot next door. The room was cold, as it always was in late October when the wind blew mornings, and mornings the wind was always blowing. He filled the basin from the flowered pitcher, stripped off his nightshirt, the cotton peeling away from his armpits with a sucking sound, and stood naked and shivering, blue-white flesh stretched over rib cage, genitals shriveled and plum-colored, while he bathed his chest and crotch and under his arms with icy water. He worked up a pathetic lather from the yellow soap Fly's wife provided the boarders and rinsed himself off. He dressed, ignoring the cross-hatching of old dirt on his long johns, sat down on the edge of the mattress to pull on the trousers of his gray suit, and had to haul himself up with the aid of the brass bedstead to stamp his stockinged feet into black half-boots with lampblack on the toes. The whiskey was echoing in his head now, as hollow and weightless as one of those paste-paper animals the greaser kids in the Mexican quarter busted at Christmastime to get at the candy and trinkets inside. If they busted his head, he reflected, they'd get only bits of a dry-husk brain tobacco-cured and pickled in alcohol. A few memories, orange and wrinkled like tintype, and not one of them worth the breath it took to swing a stick.

He shaved with his braces dangling, supporting himself with one hand on the washstand and working the razor over his scooped-out cheeks and round chin and flicking the lather into the sink. Then he wet his ivory comb, swept his hair into a wave and a curl, smoothed the flowing moustaches. Belatedly he remembered his swollen bladder and emptied it into the chamber pot beside the bed. His urine steamed in the cold room but the smell was not half as offensive to him as that of his sweat. It lacked corruption.

Buttoning his fly, he hawked and spat and contemplated the fresh dark red worm floating in the yellow. Another piece gone.

By the time Kate came in he had found his hickory cane to lean on and was shaking the wrinkles out of a pale green shirt he had taken from a drawer. She saw the high flame on his cheeks and, when he turned at her entrance drawing the pearl-handled knife from the lanyard around his neck, the luminosity in his gray eyes, and knew that his morning had been no better than the night before. At such times he was hellish handsome, with his ash-blond hair shining wet and his slightly darker moustaches lying flat and feline and his complexion all roses and milk like a girl's. When he saw it was she, he resheathed the knife.

"You all right?" she asked.

He put on a grin with the shirt and said nothing. Long

white fingers slipped the bone buttons through hand-stitched eyelets.

"Doc, Ike Clanton was here looking for you. He had a rifle with him."

"If God will let me live long enough to get my clothes on, he will see me." His Georgian drawl often made his words sound gentler than they were. He tucked in the shirt, smoothing it with his palms, and broke a fresh collar out of the box on the bureau.

She watched him slide the braces up over his nearly nonexistent shoulders, a painfully thin man in his late twenties, several inches taller than she but barely half as wide, with his ears turning out. For all her superior bulk Kate was not fat by the standards of that place and time, merely generous, full in the hips and bosom and corseted narrow in the waist under the calicos and ginghams befitting a woman no longer on the line. She was not wearing a bonnet and her short black hair emphasized a large round head and the broad nose that had earned her a nickname to set her apart from all the other Kates on the circuit. A big, not-handsome woman with a pleasant smile stamped indelibly on her pink face.

"What are you fixing to do?"

"Eat breakfast." He unslung his cartridge belt from the chair and buckled it around his waist so that the Colt's Lightning in the scabbard swung short of the hem of his gray frock coat when he put it on. The cane barely creaked as he swayed toward the door to the hallway. He weighed scarcely more than a full horse rig.

"Watch out for that Ike."

"I scraped better dogshit than him off my left bootheel."

Mrs. Fly was coming in from her husband's photograph gallery behind the house when he closed the door behind him, his breath whistling. She was small and young with dark hair in braids and the braids pinned on top of her head.

"Ike Clanton was looking for you."

"I heard. They're singing it in the Bird Cage."

The dining room was warm, with a barrel stove going in the corner. He sat alone at the big table. It was past noon now and the other boarders were out, eating lunch downtown or inspecting their claims. While he was sipping coffee and grinning at the *Daily Epitaph,* Kate came out of their room wearing a bonnet as long as a shotgun and left without a word. Mrs. Fly brought his breakfast and he ate part of it, dealt a hand of patience on the oilcloth, went bust his third time through the deck, and returned to the room for his long gray overcoat and gray felt hat.

Outside, the wind shoved at his coattails and lifted his collar. When he turned the corner onto Fourth Street it struck him full force, rocking him. He leaned into it, gripping the crook of the cane tightly, one hand on his hat. The wind carried dust from the street and a metallic smell of early snow off the Dragoons.

Wyatt and Morgan were standing on the corner of Fourth and Allen in front of Hafford's Saloon. They had on black hats and mackinaws over their black suits and boiled white shirts. Their pistol butts altered the hang of their clothes.

"Ike Clanton was looking for me," Doc said.

Morgan's moustaches lifted. "I can't feature it. You never got around to calling him horseshit last night."

"I think I must have. The yellow son of a bitch wouldn't fight."

Wyatt said, "Well, he wanted to fight today, and has got a busted head to lick because of it."

"You?"

"Virgil. Ike was on the rut this morning with a Colt's and a Winchester, squawking how he was fixing to have all our balls for breakfast, and him and Morg just kind of slid up behind him on Fourth and Virge buffaloed him."

"Dropped him like a turd," Morgan said, his eyes crinkling. "We took him up to Judge Wallace's and got him fined."

Doc glanced from one Earp to the other. They looked enough alike to be twins in spite of the difference in their ages, both of them lean and long and blue-eyed, fair of hair and drooping moustaches. Their linen was always white and their trousers carefully brushed, thanks to Morgan's woman Lou and Wyatt's Mattie—or Sadie, whichever one he was being domestic with at the time. Doc depended for his own haberdashery on a Chinawoman who waited tables at the Can Can

Chop House; Kate wouldn't know a washboard from a singletree.

Of the two brothers, Morgan looked less on top of the weather, red-eyed and sallow. He and Doc had drunk most of the sting out of a chill night. Wyatt drank beer only and little enough of that. His eyes were clear, watering some in the wind that rouged his cheeks.

"Where is Virge?" Doc asked.

Wyatt gestured up Allen just as the eldest of the three Earps emerged from the Wells Fargo office, head down and carrying a shotgun with the muzzles pointed at the boardwalk. Built along more stately lines than either of his brothers, he looked as big as a front porch in his mackinaw, his black hatbrim turning up on the left side in the wind, heavy handlebars underscoring his jowls. From time to time a gust exposed the plain deputy U.S. marshal's star on his vest under the coat. His heels struck pistol shots off the boards.

Wyatt saw Doc eyeing the shotgun and said, "I had a set-to with Tom McLaury this morning. Frank's in town too, and that Billy the Kid."

"Bonney's dead, I heard."

"Billy Claiborne, then. I buffaloed Tom and called him a damn dirty cow thief and some other things. We had some more words there in front of Spangenberg's. Him and Frank and Ike and Ike's brother Billy was looking over the six-shooters inside."

"Where are they now?"

"Dunbar's, as of about ten minutes ago."

"All of them heeled?"

"Enough to disincline me to ask the others."

"I never knew the place to be so livesome of a morning," Doc said. "I will have to start getting up earlier."

Morgan grinned. The expression plainly hurt him and he stopped.

"Billy Clanton and Frank are wearing their irons too high and wide for town," said Virgil in his phlegmy baritone. "They are looking to make a fight or claim we showed the white feather."

He stopped talking. Doc and the others followed his gaze

across Fourth to the west end of Allen, where five men were coming out of the Dexter Livery & Feed stables owned by John Dunbar and Sheriff John Behan. Doc spotted Ike's brother Billy first, a full head taller than any of his companions and as wide as Virgil Earp but more oxlike in the chest and shoulders, leading a dun horse with a white blaze. He alone among the party was clean-shaven. Frank McLaury, moving with the cocky swinging stride of a small man, had a hand on a bit chain belonging to a strawberry roan. Long-jawed Billy Claiborne was there, picking his teeth with a pine splinter. He and Frank and Frank's brother Tom, trailing the pack, wore moustaches and Ike Clanton up front had red chin-whiskers streaked brown with tobacco juice. Doc saw a splash of white bandage showing under Ike's hat and laughed out loud. Billy Clanton turned his head to glare at the men assembled in front of Hafford's, then accompanied the others across Allen into Ed Benson and John Montgomery's O.K. Corral. A pistol scabbard flapped on his right hip. All the men were coated except Tom McLaury, who wore a vest over a dark blue shirt with the tail out. Winchester butts stuck up above both horses' saddles.

"Maybe they're leaving," said Virgil. Morgan snorted.

Wyatt said, "Here comes the law in Cochise County."

Johnny Behan paused in front of the Alhambra to touch his hat and say something to one of the women from the Bird Cage Theater coming out through the batwings, then continued on to the Earps's corner. He was trim and looked taller than he was in a flat-brimmed sombrero and light topcoat and dark trousers, a fresh shine on his boots with designs on the toes. His slim moustaches were newly clipped and as he drew near, Doc caught a scent of lavender water and pomade.

"Marshal, the talk in Barron's is you're prodding these boys into a fight." He was looking up at Virgil, Doc noted, with the quick brown eyes that made nuns and virgins drip.

Virgil said, "They are the ones making the fight talk. Why don't you come with us and disarm them. They just went into Benson's corral."

Behan glanced in that direction, touched one of his moustaches to make sure he hadn't left it on the hardwood floor in Barron's barbershop and bath, looked across Allen in the direction of the Occidental Hotel. He was proud of his Roman-coin profile. "I won't do that. If they see any of you Earps they will fight sure."

Doc said, "If you like we will cover you while you run home and change drawers."

Virgil said quickly, "I mean to disarm them, with or without your help. If it comes to a fight it will be on them to start it."

"They won't fight with me," Behan said, glaring at Doc, whose gray gaze had no humor in it. "I will go down alone and see if I can disarm them."

Virgil stroked his throat with his free hand. "All I want them to do is lay off their arms while they're in town."

The sheriff nodded. During the conversation he and Wyatt had not exchanged so much as a glance.

Doc and Morgan were standing in the intersection of Fourth and Allen. Behan started around them and stopped in front of a bearded man in miner's overalls crusted with silver clay, who had come up Allen Street from the direction of the corral. They spoke for a few seconds, then Behan walked away up Fourth toward Fremont. The bearded man mounted the boardwalk and addressed Virgil, who was leaning in Hafford's doorway with the muzzles of his shotgun resting on the sill.

"Marshal, these men mean trouble. They are all down there on Fremont Street, all armed, and I think you had better go and disarm them." His coastal British accent was as thick as a core sample.

"What a Cornish Jack thinks you could stick up an ant's ass," said Wyatt.

"*Who's* there?" Virgil asked.

"Tom and Frank McLaury and two of the Clantons. That Billy the Kid was there too and another man I don't know. He's drunk as a lord."

"Ringo?"

"No, I know Ringo and this was not him."

"Wes Fuller, I bet," said Wyatt.

"All armed, you say?" Virgil pressed.

"Well, Billy Clanton and Frank McLaury. I can't say about the rest."

Morgan had moved in close to the boardwalk. "They have horses. Hadn't we better get mounted ourselves in case they want to make a running fight of it?"

Wyatt said, "No, if they want to make a running fight we can kill their horses."

The miner had gone back the way he had come, walking with his knees bent and his toes pointed out. Virgil stretched, bones cracking, and stepped out of the doorway balancing the shotgun. "Well, I guess we had better go do it."

Virgil and Wyatt stepped into the street and started along Fourth toward Fremont, trailing the third Earp. Doc fell into step beside Morgan. Wyatt stopped and turned. The wind uncovered the star on his vest engraved SPECIAL POLICE.

"Doc, this is our fight. There is no call for you to mix in."

"That's a hell of a thing for you to say to me."

They stared. Virgil cleared his throat and extended the shotgun to Doc. It was a full-length Stevens ten-gauge with a brass frame. "Hand me that cane and hide this under your coat. Don't let them see it until we come within range."

Doc slid his left arm out of the sleeve of his ankle-length greatcoat, traded Virgil the cane for the shotgun, and snugged the butt under his arm with the muzzles hanging down, pulling the coat closed over it. The procession continued in column of twos.

Fremont Street, home of the *Epitaph* office and the Cochise County courthouse, was much quieter than saloon-lined Allen Street, and nearly deserted at that hour. Clumps of panicum grass twitched down the center. At the corner the party turned west. Someone said, "Here they come," and Doc was aware of a crowd watching from the doorway of Bauer's butcher shop. He pursed his lips and whistled a tune he had heard in Fort Griffin. Playing the rubes.

"Son of a bitch pisses icicles."

Nearing Bauer's they spread out four abreast with ten feet between each man and his neighbor. Morgan and Virgil took the outside while Doc moved to Wyatt's right. Gusts pulled at the flap of Doc's coat, exposing the shotgun in teasing glimpses like white thigh on a variety girl. "Let's try and disarm these jackasses," Virgil said.

Morgan caught Doc's eye. "Let them have it."

"All right."

They were within sight of the fifteen-foot-wide lot between Fly's boardinghouse and a private residence belonging to W. A. Harwood, where a group of men stood, two of them holding horses, thirty yards west of the O.K. Corral. Doc spotted John Behan's sombrero just as the sheriff separated himself from the others and came trotting up Fremont with his palms stretched out in front of him.

"Earp, for God's sake don't go down there," he told Virgil. "You'll all be murdered."

"I mean to disarm them, Johnny." He passed Behan, accompanied by the others.

"I have disarmed them all."

Virgil had his big Army thrust inside his trousers on the right side and was holding Doc's cane in his left hand. Now he rotated the pistol to his left hip and shifted the cane to his right hand. He did these things without breaking stride.

The group gathered in the lot had withdrawn inside, out of sight from the street. Entering the lot slowly, the Earps and Doc closed ranks. Out of the corner of his eye Doc glimpsed Wesley Fuller's lanky coated length weaving into the passage between Fly's boardinghouse and the skylit photograph gallery behind it. The gallery door swung to with a clatter.

The newcomers were facing Frank McLaury and Ike Clanton on the outside of a tight group with Billy Clanton and Tom McLaury in the center and the whitewashed wall of the Harwood house at their backs. Billy was standing in front of his blaze-face with his hand on the Frontier Colt's on his hip. Frank McLaury was armed similarly, his fingers on the stag handle, and his brother Tom stood a little behind Frank's strawberry roan, resting a hand on the Winchester butt showing above the saddle. Ike's hands hung empty at his sides. Apart from the group, near the gallery, slouched Billy Claiborne's insolent young frame with his thumbs hooked inside his cartridge belt.

At Fourth and Allen Doc had transferred his nickel-plated Colt's Lightning from its scabbard to his right coat pocket. Now it was in his hand. His left was still holding the shotgun under the gray coat. A sweetish warm stink of fresh manure filled his nostrils from the corral three doors down.

Wyatt's knuckles showed yellow around the cedar handle of his big American. He said, "You sons of bitches have been looking for a fight."

Billy Claiborne took his thumbs out of his belt and broke for the gallery. Sheriff Behan, having passed around the other side of the boardinghouse, held the door for him.

Virgil lifted Doc's cane high in his right hand, looking like a giant shepherd in town clothes. "Throw up your hands!"

Doc and Morgan rolled back the hammers on their pistols, the double-crunch dry and loud in the silence.

"Hold on, I don't want that!" Virgil said, pushing his free hand behind him. Simultaneously Tom McLaury threw open his vest and said, "I have nothing!" Both exclamations were lost in the broken bark of two pistols discharging at almost the same instant. Frank McLaury staggered, clawing at his belly with blood showing black between his fingers. His Colt's came out in his other hand. Billy Clanton, a hole in his chest, hunched and threw his pistol above his head, turning to clutch at the edge of Harwood's window with the hand holding the weapon. He began to slide. His horse reared, wheeled, pawed the air, and bolted for the street.

Frank McLaury's horse was plunging and whinnying, its eyes rolling white. Tom, attempting to use the animal for cover, lunged for the bit chain and missed. Ike fled from the raking hooves and found himself heading straight for Wyatt. He stumbled, caught his balance on the run, and grasped Wyatt's left arm in both hands, trying to turn him. His breath was raw with whiskey.

Wyatt flung him back. "This fight has commenced. Get to fighting or get away."

Behan was motioning from the door to the gallery. Ike wheeled with the momentum of the shove and sprinted through the opening. Doc rapped off two quick shots at his heels, chucking dirt and splintering the doorsill.

"Why didn't you cut the son of a bitch down?" Doc shouted.

"He wouldn't jerk a pistol."

When the firing started Virgil had switched hands on the cane again and drawn his Army. He sent a ball at Billy Clanton, already reeling from the wound in his chest, and shattered his right wrist. Billy border-shifted on his way down and fired wild.

There was a lull.

Shots coughed from the direction of the gallery. Wyatt and Doc returned fire through clouds of spent powder. Morgan spun and fell. "I've got it!"

"Get behind me and keep quiet!" Wyatt said.

The lot was filled with thick gray smoke like soiled batting, hanging on a doldrum between gusts. Doc backed out into the street, his eyes stinging. Inside the lot the screaming roan bucked and plunged through haze, concealing Frank McLaury momentarily as he tried for the Winchester in the boot but exposing his brother Tom, who jerked his head right and left like a deer caught between hunters and made a dash for the street.

Doc scabbarded his pistol and swung the shotgun level with his hip, palming back the hammers and squeezing both triggers. The muzzles roared. Tom slipped, then recovered himself and swept in a crouch past Doc, who said, "Mother-fucking—" and hurled away the shotgun to redraw his Colt's. But by then Tom had rounded the corner of Harwood's house and was lost to sight.

Billy Clanton was sitting cross-legged on the ground with his back against the wall of the house, steadying his pistol across his broken right arm. His shirt was soaked through with blood. A ball slapped Virgil in the calf and he went down, releasing Doc's cane at last. He rolled onto his left elbow and, using his right knee to support his Army, shot Billy in the abdomen.

The rest of the fight had spilled into the street. Frank McLaury's horse had dragged him out of the lot with one hand grasping the saddle latigo and the other clawing frantically for the carbine in the scabbard. Wyatt threw a shot at him that missed and branded a slash across the horse's rump. It shrieked, threw its head, and hauled hooves toward Fifth Street, tearing loose its master's grip. Frank landed running and made for the other side of Fremont, rebel-yelling and spraying pistol lead across his left arm at Morgan Earp, who had regained his feet and was bleeding down the back of his mackinaw from a ball behind his right shoulder. He returned fire. Doc wheeled from the path of Tom McLaury's retreat to find himself face to face with a wheezing, wild-eyed Frank slicked with blood from belt to boots. "I've got you this time!" Frank sobbed.

"You're a good one if you have." Doc turned sideways into target stance, flinging out his right arm at shoulder height with his Colt's in his hand just as Frank's pistol barked. Something struck Doc's right hip like a blow from a willow stick. He winced and fired. Morgan Earp's pistol exploded at the same instant—all three going *bammity-bam*. A blue hole slapped Frank's neck under his left ear and another ball knocked more blood out of his belly and he sat down in the street and soiled himself.

Sobbing now too, Billy Clanton tried to recock his Colt's, but his thumb kept sliding off the hammer. Just then Camilius Fly's wiry figure in striped shirtsleeves and black vest emerged from the passage between his two buildings and reached down and took hold of the pistol and pulled it from Billy's bloody grasp.

"Give me some more cartridges," said Billy.

The sudden silence boxed Doc's ears. Then the crowd in Bauer's doorway boiled out into the street, talking manically and mingling with others come up Fourth and Third. Tom McLaury had collapsed into a pile at the corner of Third with most of the middle of him gone, although he was still flopping. Wyatt bent over a cursing Virgil with his pistol still out and a couple of bystanders were helping support Morgan, whose legs were failing him. Pairs of newcomers got Tom McLaury and Billy Clanton into a cradle-carry and shuffled toward the house on the corner of Third, the wind spreading their coats and exposing white shirts and scarlet braces in gaps between vests and trousers.

"Murder!" Billy was bellowing and struggling with his attendants. "Them damn Earps have went and murdered us!"

Belatedly, Doc leathered his Colt's and pulled aside his own coattails and peeled down his trousers to inspect his hip, where Frank McLaury's pistol ball had gouged a furrow through his long johns after taking a piece off his pistol scabbard. The graze stung like tanglefoot on a raw morning.

John Behan came out of the gallery, looking small now under his broad brim. As he approached Wyatt his eyes were like cigarette holes in gray ticking.

"Earp, I am placing you under arrest for murder."

CHAPTER 2

ALVIRA SULLIVAN, CALLED ALLIE Earp in Tombstone although no record of a marriage to Virgil Earp existed, ran up Fremont from the house she shared with him on the corner of First, toward the clatter of guns. She was a small, plain woman with short curling auburn hair who looked far older than her thirty-four years in a sunbonnet and old dress with the skirt gathered in both hands. At the start of the noise she had been sewing a patch onto a miner's canvas coat, and the sailmaker's palm she had fashioned from one of Virgil's old tobacco pouches was still on her hand, looped to her thumb and ring finger. Pillows of dust erupted around her feet and blew away in snatches.

Long before she reached the scene, the last shot had finished echoing in the Huachucas to the southwest. Voices jangled on its heels.

The block between Third and Fourth was jammed with people. The wind was warm with them and shotgun barrels caught the afternoon sun in bronze stripes. Allie inserted herself in the crowd, got turned around, and for a moment became disoriented among the belt buckles and overall-clad bellies reeking of sweat and clay. Panic rose.

A gap opened then and she darted inside, then had to retreat while a boy with dust on his coat and trousers and what she thought at first was red clay caked on his shirt was carried through it, shrieking murder and calling for someone to pull his boots off. Dark spots the size of pennies pattered the earth under his hammocked frame.

The crowd was splintering into sections now, a section to a body. She hurried to the next one. Before she got there she could see that the man being carried was dead, his head swaying with the hair hanging straight down from his scalp, mouth and eyes open, the whites glittering. Her bonnet slipped back from her head as she pushed in fighting for a closer look at his face. Male hands crushed her upper arms, turning her away. She was facing a platinum watch chain strung across a brown pinstriped vest. She struggled, spraining a wrist.

"My God, Mrs. Earp, get away! There has been an awful fight."

Now she looked up into the long yellow face of Harry Jones, a lawyer. "I am looking for Virge," she said. "Take me to him."

"He's all right, Mrs. Earp."

But he was pulling her through the crowd by one arm toward Fly's boardinghouse. She pushed her bonnet back onto her head with one hand.

Another crowd was gathered inside the narrow lot next to Fly's. The air there was foul with spent powder. "Make room," Jones was saying. "This is Mrs. Earp."

"Stand back, boys," bellowed a big man in a dirty sheepskin. "Let his old mother get in."

She glared at the man, but he had turned away to open a path.

She knelt beside Virgil. He was sitting on the ground with his back against Fly's wall, red in the face and chewing his moustaches and cursing. Dr. George Goodfellow, small and round with a full beard and his cuffs pushed back past his wrists, had slit open Virgil's trousers leg and was probing inside a gory hole with silver forceps. The calf was fishbelly white and without hair above the ankle.

"Forget it, Doc," someone said. "The ball went clean through."

Goodfellow paused, turned the leg to examine the exit hole on the other side, causing Virgil to take in his breath, said,

"Huh," and returned the forceps to his leather bag after a perfunctory wipe. He poured alcohol into both wounds, releasing a fresh flood of evil language, and bandaged them, rolling the gauze around and around the leg and securing it with a big safety pin. Throughout this operation Virgil held Allie's hand tightly.

"Virge, what happened?"

"Morg lost his head."

She had been raised in Nebraska by immigrant Irish parents and met Virgil in Council Bluffs when she was a waitress and he drove a stagecoach. They were not married in the religious or legal sense but behaved as if they were, not an uncommon occurrence on the Great Plains where clergy was rare and spread as thin as prairie dust. She took in sewing, told fortunes with cards, and although she distrusted all of the Earp brothers except Virgil, whom she loved with the considerable energy of an Irishwoman raised in Nebraska, she had been traveling with the clan for seven years, attempting all the while to persuade Virgil to break away. When she met his younger brother Wyatt he was a deacon in the Union Church at Dodge City and an officer on the police force, and she knew that he had used both these positions to make safe the whorehouse he ran there with James, eldest of the five full brothers. She liked Morgan, the third brother, without trusting him, and she seldom thought about the baby, Warren, who was out wandering the territory just now in search of a game or a bar to keep. Daylight work was anathema to the nocturnal Earps, particularly Wyatt, whom she held responsible for most of the clan's trespasses and despised for the way he treated his woman, Mattie.

Someone had brought around a hack. Virgil squeezed the blood out of Allie's hand as Goodfellow and Jones helped him onto the front seat. As she got in behind, Jones supporting her elbow, the doctor went back to supervise a similar operation involving another carriage half a block down Fremont. Allie glimpsed a tall man in a mackinaw like Virgil's leaning on John Clum and Colonel William Herring. Then Jones climbed up beside Virgil and flipped the reins and their team started forward with a jerk and a "son of a bitch!" from Virgil, and the wounded man in the second hack was lost to view.

She hoped it was Wyatt.

Dr. Harry M. Matthews, the Cochise County coroner, was gray and balding, stoop-shouldered from many hours spent hunched over riddled corpses with their pockets turned out in alleys on Allen Street and slashed corpses smelling of violets and spilled stomach contents in cribs on Toughnut Street and flayed corpses bound upside-down with rawhide thongs to palos verde outside Geronimo's stronghold in the Dragoons. He had thick forearms with the hair scrubbed off and a facial tic that from time to time made him turn his head and wink as if someone had just told a lewd joke. He was not yet fifty.

With the aid of an Irish carpenter who had helped carry the bodies into the house he stripped Tom and Frank McLaury, removing buckskin breeches stiff with gore from the latter and a second pair of trousers underneath and using alcohol and cotton to sponge the jelled blood from blue puckered holes and probing inside with his fingers for the lead balls that had made them. Tom McLaury's trousers thumped when they landed on the floor and the carpenter removed a flat cowhide wallet from the right hip pocket and peeled apart $2,923 in damp bank notes and laid them on an ivory lace shawl covering a table with a brass lamp on it. Billy Clanton, subdued by an injection of morphine, lay quietly on the carpet with an embroidered pillow under his head and his shirt open and a folded towel growing dark on his torso, his lips forming the word *murder*. His eyes had taken on a glassy sheen behind the lashes.

Robert Finley McLaury—Frank—had been shot twice in the abdomen and once in the head. The first ball had penetrated the small intestine and burrowed into the lumbar muscles in the arch of the back. The second had deflected off the ninth rib on the left side, separated into six fragments, and perforated the stomach, colon, and large and small intestines and nicked the pancreas. The ball in the brain, after entering half an inch below the left ear between the temporal and inferior maxillary bones of the skull, had tunneled through both hemispheres, transfix-

ing the carvenous sinus and superior petrosal sinus, and come to
rest among the epithelial cells in the subdural space at the rear of
the brain case on the right side. Death from the first injury was
probable, given the loss of blood due to internal hemorrhage
and the threat of general peritonitis from the contamination of
the bloodstream by the feces; certain from the second, because
of the extent of the trauma and lack of sophisticated medical
equipment that far from Chicago in that year of Christ 1881;
from the third, instantaneous.

Thomas Clark McLaury had been struck by twelve
buckshot pellets on the right side discharged at close range,
splintering the humerus in the upper right arm, perforating
both lungs and the liver and obliterating the gall bladder,
stomach, and colon; shredding the large and small intestines,
fracturing the pelvis, and lodging in the sartorius and gastroc-
nemius muscles in the right thigh and calf. All of the wounds
sustained in the abdomen and lower thorax were fatal.

"Drive the crowd away!" said Billy, his voice rising. "Oh,
drive them away!"

The windows were a smear of flattened faces. Billy tried to
sit up, then subsided just as the carpenter stepped forward with
his horned hands out to restrain him. He coughed, staining his
lips, and his head rolled to one side. His chest rose and fell
automatically and stopped.

William Clanton had been shot through the right wrist, the
ball entering two inches behind the metacarpus and describing
an oblique trajectory, missing the radius but parting the ulna as
it exited five inches farther back on the outside of the arm.
Another ball had penetrated two inches left of the left nipple
and slightly below, puncturing the pectoral muscle and missing
the heart but tearing the pericardial sac and collapsing the left
lung, flattened against the scapula on that side. Yet a third ball
had entered beneath the twelfth rib on the right side, chipped
the intercostal artery, passed through both intestines, and lay
pressing against the spinal cord. Both were fatal injuries.

Having finished his preliminary examination, Matthews
washed his hands in a basin of lukewarm water provided for
that purpose, toweled off, drew two cigars from the inside
breast pocket of his coat hanging on the back of a chair, gave

one to the carpenter, and lit them both with a sulfur match. His fingers smelled of alcohol despite the washing. Clouds of smoke deadened the blood-and-excrement stink in the room.

"Should I fetch the undertaker?" The carpenter sounded eager.

"Ritter's ears are better than yours or mine when it comes to gunfire." He rotated the cigar between his lips, wetting the end. "You may leave, and thank you."

Gratefully the other man let himself out the front door. Alone, the coroner contemplated the Frontier model Colt's he had picked up from the floor near Frank McLaury's body and placed on the table next to the bank notes. He was a collector and carried a Schofield pistol in his instrument bag for his own protection. The Colt's was blue-black with a stag handle, a twin of the popular Peacemaker but chambered for the .44-40 centerfire cartridge employed by the Model 1873 Winchester rifle and carbine. The mechanism appealed to his medical mind. When drawn back, the hammer advanced the cylinder to the next chamber, where once the trigger was released the nose of the hammer snapped down on the cartridge, igniting the powder and expelling the ball from the barrel at the approximate speed of eight hundred feet per second. A simple engine, really. He winked.

It was not Wyatt but Morgan, with his shirt off and his coat draped over his shoulders, a patch on each where the ball had gone in from behind and where Goodfellow had cut it out and then wrapped gauze around his chest and over his left shoulder toga-fashion. Morgan's helpers tracked dirt in through Allie's door and tipped him into bed beside his brother. He lay face down, grunting.

Virgil looked up at Goodfellow, who had followed the party inside.

"He has lost some blood," the doctor said. "I will be in every day." To Allie: "Change the dressings twice daily and send someone around for me if either of them takes on fever. That will mean infection."

He handed her a blue bottle of laudanum and left after
drilling her in its application. John Clum and Colonel Herring
remained. Clum, the slight, slope-shouldered young mayor of
Tombstone and founder-publisher of the *Daily Epitaph,* stood
with his hat in his hands and his tan ending where his fringe of
dark hair began. His handlebars and naked scalp heaped ten
years onto his appearance. Beside him the huge attorney with
muttonchops resembled an erect walrus in a charcoal suit and
wing collar. Snuff clung to his whiskers and hammocked in the
creases of his vest. Both men had pistols stuck in their belts and
Herring had a shotgun broken over his right arm in clear
violation of the city antifirearms ordinance.

Virgil said, "John, can we count on the Citizens' Safety
Committee to watch the place and see we are not both
murdered in our sleep?"

"We will post guards outside on a rotating system," said
Clum. "But I think you have taken the fight out of Ike for
now."

"It ain't Ike I'm concerned about."

"Even a mob respects a show of arms," Herring said.

Clum was sober. "A coroner's inquest is setting up now.
Wyatt would not be arrested by Behan but there will be
warrants issued. I will put the best face I can on the business in
the *Epitaph.*"

"I'd feel easier about that if you had the *Nugget*'s circulation."

"It would be simpler if you had not deputized Doc
Holliday," Clum said.

"Doc is like a puppy. Where Wyatt goes he follows."

"I guess Wyatt will be retaining Tom Fitch," said Herring.
"He is a good man for this kind of thing."

"It is a hell of a note when a peace officer cannot carry out
his sworn duty without getting arrested for it."

Clum said, "Sworn duty had nothing to do with this
business."

"Don't forget that guard," Virgil said.

The two men nodded at Allie and departed, walking stiffly
with the long barrels nudging their groins. They pulled the

door shut against a flat gust that strained the pegs holding the house together.

"Allie, give me some of that laudanum." Morgan's voice was thick in his pillow.

"Suffer some," Virgil said. "I made it clear going in I never wanted any killing stuff. Wyatt and I have interests to look out for here. Some of us don't admire to be shotgun messengers our whole lives."

"Well, you would have had a good view of them from up on the hill." The nearest hill of consequence was Tombstone's cemetery. Allie prevented Morgan from adding anything by sliding the spoon into his mouth. A fly lighted on his bandage and she brushed it away with her free hand.

"They never wanted to make a fight in that blind alley. We could have buffaloed them."

Morgan swallowed, pulled a face. "You would have gone to buffalo Crazy Horse at the Little Big Horn."

Corking the blue bottle, Allie spotted the sheriff's sombrero through the window. "It is Johnny come to see how you are getting on," she said.

Virgil said shit. "Hand me that gun." He stretched an arm toward his Winchester leaning in a corner.

"I said it was only Johnny Behan."

"And I said hand me that gun!"

Moving hastily, she leaned the rifle against the bed and picked up Morgan's big pistol from the table where John Clum had put it and laid it on the chair by the bed inside Morgan's long reach.

Behan's rapping jiggled the door in its board frame. Virgil told her not to answer. He had drawn the Winchester across his lap.

The rapping came again. They waited. Wind razored the corner boards outside. After a long moment the sheriff's footsteps retreated off the little front porch. He passed the window heading back up Fremont without looking in.

"Stack that spare mattress against the window," Virgil said.

The room was gray with the feather mattress blocking the light. Allie lit a lamp, stood around, then sat down and took the

cover off the black-and-silver Singer sewing machine she had
fought the Earp brothers to bring with her down the Santa Fe
trail from Dodge City. For a moment she sat without moving,
then began to work the treadle. She discovered she was still
wearing the leather palm designed for hand work and put it
aside. The thumping and whirring of the machinery gentled
Virgil and Morgan to sleep, interrupted at intervals by one or
the other's snoring and muttered curses when a shift in
positions sent fresh pain to torn flesh and muscle. Steam
whistles brayed in the Dragoon foothills to the northeast and in
the San Pedro Valley to the southwest, a sound not heard that
early in the day since the big fire in June; it meant the miners
were being called in to help maintain order. Now and again one
of John Clum's vigilantes cried out to another outside the
window.

Presently the three were joined by Morgan's wife, Louisa,
a dark, pretty woman in her middle twenties who like Allie had
been on the scene following the shooting but had gone from
there to be with Mattie Blaylock, alone in the house she shared
with Wyatt across from Virgil and Allie's. Lou touched
Morgan's sleeping forehead, then spelled Allie at the sewing
machine. The income from their mending and dressmaking
supplemented that from the Earps' investments and gambling;
during the lean time after Wyatt had been let go as a sheriff's
deputy and before their interests began to pay off, it had
supported them all. The oil burned down to a coppery glow
and then the porch boards whimpered under a man's weight.
Virgil was awake instantly, thumbing the Winchester's hammer
to full cock.

"Al, it's me."

She recognized Wyatt's voice and undid the latch. He
swept in along with a draft of early-evening cold, took the door
from her, and set the latch behind him. He still had on his
mackinaw but his vest was unbuttoned and under it his white
shirt, sweat through, clung like wet tissue to his chest.

"What are they saying?" Virgil let the hammer down
gently.

"Johnny has put in for warrants on all of us," Wyatt said.

"Shit."

Morgan said, "He will see us lynched."

"Or shot resisting," Wyatt said.

Virgil said, "Well, I mean to resist."

Allie said, "Johnny *Behan?*"

"Stay out of it," snapped Wyatt. "Virge, that was not Fred White's ghost lobbing shots at us from Fly's."

"Johnny seen his chance and bit on it," Virgil said.

"Or Wes Fuller or Billy the Kid. Either way it is the same, for Johnny was there and could have stopped it."

"Or Billy Allen," Morgan said. "I seen him in the gallery when Claiborne hauled his freight inside."

"How are you, Morg?"

"Dandy. I am thinking of leaving the holes open so I have a place to carry my studs."

Virgil said, "My leg hurts like hell. Thank you kindly for asking."

Wyatt smiled for the first time that day. "That Billy Clanton had him some sand, all right."

"The bastard."

"How's Doc?" asked Morgan.

"Dealing faro at the Alhambra and doctoring a wounded pistol scabbard. His luck is holding and I would not want to be Johnny and go to arrest him while he is riding the tiger."

Morgan said, "I hope to hell he tries. I want to be there and see it."

"You will stay in bed," said Lou. She was still sitting at the machine with a yard of broadcloth in her hands.

Wyatt looked at Allie for the first time, his thumb on the door latch. He had a smudge of spent powder on his right cheek. "Don't let anybody in but me or Jim or Doc. I don't trust Clum's storekeepers not to fall asleep."

"Mattie?" she asked.

His ice-blue eyes fogged over, and she knew that he had not thought about his woman until that moment. "Mattie stays inside, same as always." He left.

Morgan said, "Al."

She glanced at Lou, then fixed the latch and went over, carrying the laudanum and spoon. But when she proffered the yellow-tinted liquid he jerked his head negatively. One blue eye watched her with his fair hair down in his face.

"If they come, Al, you will know they got Wyatt. Take my six-shooter and kill me and Virge before they get us. We'll not be strung up like geese."

Lou helped Allie stack furniture against the door and the remaining windows. They took turns sleeping in chairs and standing guard with Morgan's pistol between them. Allen Street ran wide open that night with all the miners in town and eyewitnesses reliving the fight in saloons and on streetcorners for those who would claim to be eyewitnesses later. Whenever glass shattered or a door banged in that direction the two women jumped.

CHAPTER 3

"PLEASE STATE YOUR NAME, current place of residence, and occupation at present."

"John Harris Behan. I reside currently in the City of Tombstone, County of Cochise, Arizona Territory. I am sheriff of Cochise County and I own a half-interest in the Dexter Livery and Feed on Allen Street."

Dr. Harry M. Matthews winked. He had on the salt-and-pepper tweed he wore to funerals and inquests, and with his hands folded atop the bench in the adobe courthouse on Fremont he seemed not as bent as he did when he was standing. The witness, in a black morning coat and bow tie, sat with his hands on his knees and sunlight glistening on his advancing forehead. His moustaches were waxed lightly. The room smelled of dried mud and sawdust and of mesquite burning in the parlor stove opposite the gilt-framed portrait of Governor Fremont.

Someone in the jury box coughed, a dry-stick sound in the silence following the sheriff's formal statement. The ten jurors, Tombstone businessmen all, were wrapped in dark wool and wore softly shining cravats tucked into their vests. The recorder's pen scratched over foolscap.

"What did you observe when you came upon the Clantons

and McLaurys in the vacant lot next to Fly's photograph gallery?" asked Matthews.

Behan wet his lips and slid his palms up and down his thighs and addressed the portrait of George Washington.

"When I went down to disarm them, I put my hands around Ike Clanton and found he had no arms. He showed me that he had nothing on him. Ike Clanton said that they were just getting ready to go out of town. Frank McLaury and Billy Clanton were armed. Frank McLaury had his horse, holding him down there. I think Billy Clanton had his horse with him. I am not positive."

"Who started shooting?"

"I cannot say who fired the first shot. It appeared to me that it was fired from a nickel-plated pistol. There was two shots very close together. I know that the nickel-plated pistol was on the side of the Earps. I won't say which one of the Earp crowd fired it."

"Did any of the Clanton and McLaury party draw their weapons when the order was given to throw up their hands?"

"The only thing I saw was Tom McLaury throwing open his coat, taking hold of the lapels of his coat and holding it back." He demonstrated, uncovering the sheriff's star pinned to his vest.

"Did you see a shotgun?"

"There was a shotgun in the Earp party. Holliday had it. He was putting it under his coat, so as to get it more effectively concealed. That was when they were coming down the street."

"Did you see it fired?"

"I cannot say that I saw the shotgun go off. There was a scramble. I don't know whether the shotgun was fired or not. I think it was; I did not see it."

"Did you see the deceased fall?"

"I saw Billy Clanton fall first and then I saw Frank McLaury fall, on the north side of Fremont Street, almost exactly opposite Fly's place, after the fight commenced."

"Did you see Tom McLaury fall?"

"No, I did not see him until the fight was over. Then I saw him on the ground."

"You are satisfied that he was unarmed?"

"I am satisfied that two of the parties were not armed—I mean Ike Clanton and Tom McLaury."

"State again your reasons for attempting to disarm the party."

"When I went to disarm them I understood that there was likely to be a row between the Earp brothers and Holliday and the Clanton crowd."

"Did they refuse to give up their arms?"

"No one refused except Frank McLaury. He said that he came on business and did not want any row. He never refused to go to my office."

"When you met the Earp party before the fight, did you tell them that you had disarmed the other party?"

"I did not. I did tell them that there would be trouble if they went down. I told them I did not want any trouble, and would not allow it if I could help it, and not to go down."

"Did Frank McLaury have his pistol drawn when Marshal Earp told him to throw up his hands?"

"He did not."

"Did you consider the Clantons and McLaurys under arrest at the time?"

Behan touched the knot of his bow tie. "At the time I left the McLaurys and Clantons and met the Earps, I considered the Clanton party under arrest, but I doubt whether they considered themselves under arrest or not."

A sound came from among the jury that might have been another cough. Matthews winked irritably and shot the men in the box a withering look. Then he folded his hands under his chin. His fingers still smelled of methyl alcohol.

"I ask you to remember if anything was said to you by either party before the fight that would indicate the Earp party was not acting in an official capacity when they went to meet the Clantons and McLaurys."

"Nothing was said to me to make me believe they were acting in an official capacity. After the fight was over, Wyatt Earp said, 'We went there to disarm that party.' I think I heard Virgil say the same thing. The horses were saddled, but Frank McLaury and Billy Clanton had just come into town. During my conversation with them, Ike Clanton said, 'We are going out of town.' But Frank McLaury said, 'I am not. I am here on business.'"

"Thank you, Sheriff. I have no further questions."

"My name is Joseph Isaac Clanton. I live on the San Pedro near Charleston. I deal in cattle."

Ike's head was sunk between his shoulders, minimizing his almost nonexistent neck and lending him the hunkered look of a bear cornered in its lair. His big horned black-nailed hands lay palms up between his knees with his forearms resting on his thighs and his hooded yellow eyes quartered the room as if calculating the distance of a charge. In reality he was looking for a place to get rid of the tobacco bulging his right cheek. He had on a black suit with worn velvet facings and a gold double eagle for a fob.

"Were you present on Fremont Street on October twenty-sixth, eighteen eighty-one, at the time of the deaths of William Clanton, Robert Finley McLaury, and Thomas Clark McLaury?" Matthews asked.

"I was present. I am the brother of William Clanton who was killed that day. I saw the whole transaction."

"Please state what happened."

He swallowed the bitter juice and shifted the plug to his other cheek. "The night before the shooting, I went into the Alhambra lunch room for a lunch, and while there, Doc Holliday come in and commenced to abuse me. He had his hand on his pistol and called me a damned son of a bitch and told me to get my gun out. I told him I did not have any gun. I looked around and I seen Morg sitting at the bar behind me with his hand on his gun. Doc Holliday kept on abusing me. I then went out the door.

"Virgil Earp, Wyatt, and Morg were all out there. Morg Earp told me if I wanted a fight to turn myself loose. They all had their hands on their pistols while they were talking to me. I told them again I was not armed. Doc Holliday said, 'You son of a bitch, go arm yourself then!' I did go off and heel myself. I came back and played poker with Virge Earp, Tom McLaury, and other parties until daylight. Virge Earp played poker with his pistol in his lap the whole time. At daylight he got up and quit the game. We were playing in the Occidental. I followed Virge Earp out when he quit. I told him that I was abused the night before and I was in town. Then he told me he was going to bed."

Deputy Billy Breakenridge set a cuspidor at Ike's feet and he used it, splattering brown juice into the polished brass interior. He drew the back of a hand across his lips and resumed chewing. A neglected streak glistened in his chin whiskers.

"I came back and cashed in my chips and stood around town until about eight o'clock. I then went and got my Winchester, expecting to meet Doc Holliday on the street, but never saw him until after Virge and Morgan slipped up behind me and knocked me down with a six-shooter. Shortly afterwards I met my brother Billy. He asked me to go out of town. I just about that time met the corral man where my team was and asked him to harness up the team. We then went to the O.K. Corral in company with the McLaury brothers. We met the sheriff there. He told us that he would have to arrest us and take our arms off. I told him that we were just going to leave town and that I had no arms on. He then searched my waist. He told my brother and Frank McLaury to take their arms up to his office.

"Tom opened his coat and showed him and said, 'Johnny, I have no arms on.' Frank McLaury said he would keep his arms unless the sheriff disarmed the Earps. He said that if he would disarm them, he would lay off his, as he had business to attend to in town before he left.

"Just at that time I seen Doc Holliday and three of the Earps coming down the sidewalk. The sheriff stepped forward to meet them and told them that he had these parties in charge, and to stop, that he did not want any trouble. They walked right by him.

"I stepped two or three steps from the crowd and met Wyatt Earp right at the corner of the building. He stuck his six-shooter at me and said, 'Throw up your hands!' The marshal also told the other boys to throw their hands up. Tom McLaury opened his coat and said that he had no arms. They said, 'You sons of bitches, you ought to make a fight!' At the same instant, Doc Holliday and Morg shot. Morgan shot my brother and I don't know which of the other boys that Doc Holliday shot. I saw Virge shooting at the same time. I grabbed Wyatt Earp and pushed him around the corner of the house and jumped into the gallery. As I jumped, I saw Billy falling. I ran through the gallery and got away."

He spat. The cuspidor bonged. "Billy Clanton, Frank McLaury, and myself threw up our hands at the order from the Earp party, and Tom McLaury threw his coat open and said, 'I have got no arms.'"

Matthews rubbed his left eye, the one with the tic. "Did you have any trouble with the Earps previous to the day in question?"

"Doc Holliday came into the Alhambra Saloon and said I had been using his name. I said, 'I have not.' I never had any previous trouble with the Earps. They don't like me. We had a transaction—I mean, myself and the Earps—but it had nothing to do with the killing of these three men. There was no threats made by the McLaury boys and Billy Clanton against the Earp boys that day, not that I know of. They had ordered me to heel myself, and I told them I would be there."

Matthews asked some more questions, which Clanton answered with his chin on his chest and his hands folded loosely between his spread knees, turning his head occasionally to use the cuspidor.

"I did not expect any trouble from Wyatt Earp but from Virge and Morg Earp and Doc Holliday. The boys expected no attack until somebody told them just before they were leaving town, and they never left. . . . I did not have any arms on when the Earp party came down and ordered us to throw up our hands. Virge Earp had my arms, a Winchester and six-shooter. . . . I had not seen Frank McLaury or my brother for two days before the shooting. I never had a conversation with the McLaury boys and Billy as to making a fight in my life. . . . When the firing commenced, Virge and Doc Holliday were about six feet from the McLaury boys and Morg Earp's pistol was about three or four feet from Billy when he commenced firing. I did not see my brother or either of the McLaurys fire a shot."

Matthews thanked him.

". . . Martha J. King. I live in the City of Tombstone. I am a housekeeper."

In her late thirties, the woman looked a few years older, with most of her dark hair pinned back and the rest falling in sausage curls behind her ears, a style too young for her that accentuated the lines in her neck and from her nostrils to the corners of her mouth. She wore a black dress still gleaming from the brush, with a white lace collar secured at the throat by an ivory brooch. Her hands were red and peeling and clutched a rose-embroidered handkerchief in her lap. She nodded when Matthews, his tone low and funereally solicitous so that the recorder had to strain to hear him, asked her if she was present on Fremont Street at the time of the trouble, then said yes so that her answer could be taken down.

"I was coming from my house to Bauer's meat market to get some meat for dinner," she said. "I saw quite a number of men standing in a group together on the sidewalk by the door of the market, and I passed on into the shop to get what I went for, and the parties in the shop were excited and did not seem to want to wait upon me. I inquired what was the matter, and they said there was about to be a fuss between the Earp boys and the cowboys. I was standing back at the time they said it. I stepped to the door of the market and I heard someone talking but did not understand at first what they said.

"Then the party seemed to separate, and this man who was standing with the horse—he was in the act of leading his horse—turned to the other man who was talking to him and looked up to the man and said, 'If you wish to find us, you will find us just below here.' That is all I saw at this time. The tall man who was talking to the man with the horse went down the street. Then I stepped back into the shop again."

She twisted the handkerchief. "The butcher was in the act of cutting the meat when someone at the door said, 'There they come!' and I stepped to the door and looked up the sidewalk and I saw four men coming down the sidewalk. I only knew one of the party and that was Mr. Holliday. And there were three other gentlemen, who someone told me were the Earps. Mr. Holliday was next to the buildings, on the inside. He had a gun under his coat. The way I noticed the gun was his coat would blow open and he tried to keep it covered.

"I stood in the door until these gentlemen passed and until they got to the second door. And what frightened me and made me run back, I heard him say, 'Let them have it!' and Doc Holliday said, 'All right.' Then I thought I would run, and ran towards the back of the shop, but before I reached the middle of the shop, I heard shots; I don't know how many. I don't know who said, 'Let them have it.' I cannot describe the party. It was one of them that was with Holliday."

". . . C. H. Light. I reside in the City of Tombstone. I'm a minin' man."

The young miner wore a stiff brown suit with shelf creases in the trousers and a clean gray workshirt buttoned at the throat without a cravat. He had a pink, girlish mouth and his fair hair was parted to the right of center and swept down over his right eyebrow. His Cornish accent was so thick that Matthews had to ask him several times to repeat himself more slowly. He sat on the edge of the chair with his elbows on his knees and his palms sliding against each other with a rasping sound, his body twitching with nervous energy.

"There seemed to be six parties firin', four in the middle of the street and one on the south side of the street, and the one with the horse. Afterwards, I recognized the man with the gray clothes to be Doc Holliday. I think there were about twenty-five or thirty shots fired altogether. I did not see any of the parties have a shotgun. The fight occurred about one hundred and thirty or forty feet away from where I was. I think, from the reports, that the first two were pistol shots. I think that there was one report from a shotgun. I do not think the whole of it occupied over ten or fifteen seconds."

★ ★ ★

"Your name is William F. Claiborne and you reside in the City of Tombstone, County of Cochise, Arizona Territory, and you are a driver in the employ of the Neptune Mining Company?"

"That's right."

Claiborne, who had gotten some people to start calling him Billy the Kid once William Bonney had relinquished both the nickname and his life in New Mexico the previous summer, slouched on his spine in the chair, his long bony legs thrust out in front of him with his spurs marking the floor. He had sandy hair cropped close, exaggerating his long jaw and saillike ears and the puppy hairs on his lip that vanished when sunlight struck them. He was just twenty-one and wore striped pants and a new shirt buttoned all the way up.

"The day this thing happened," he said, "I went down with Ike Clanton to Dr. Gillingham's office to assist him in getting his head dressed, and then I walked up Fourth Street and met Billy Clanton and Frank McLaury, and Billy axed me where was Ike. He said, 'I want to get him to go home.' He said he did not come here to fight anyone 'and no one didn't want to fight me.' Then he axed me to go down to Johnny Behan's stable with him, and we went down there and through the O.K. Corral.

"Then Mr. Behan come up and was talking to the boys. I did not hear what he said to them. I was talking to Billy, and Behan was talking to Ike Clanton and Frank and Tom McLaury. And then, shortly afterwards, Mr. Behan turned his back and walked up the street and the next thing I saw was Morgan Earp and his two brothers and Doc Holliday. And Marshal Earp said, 'You sons of bitches, you have been looking for a fight and now you can get it!' They both said the same thing at the same time, and Marshal Earp said, 'Throw up your hands!' which Billy Clanton, Ike Clanton, and Frank McLaury did, and Tom McLaury took holdt of the lapels of his coat and threw it open and said, 'I have not got anything.'

"And at the same instant the shooting commenced by Doc Holliday and Morgan Earp. The first shot taking Tom McLaury was fired by Doc Holliday, and the next one was fired by Morgan Earp, taking Billy Clanton. And Billy Clanton was

shot with his hands in this position." He sat up, raising his long
callused palms level with his eyebrows. "Billy Clanton said,
'Don't shoot me, I don't want to fight!' And that was the last I
seen of Billy alive."

Matthews was idly drawing a human rib cage in the right-
hand margin of his notes with a pencil. "At what point were
weapons drawn?"

"When the Earp party come up they had their pistols in
their hands. I saw Billy Clanton draw his pistol after he was
shot down. I saw Frank McLaury draw his pistol after about six
shots had been fired by the Earps. Tom McLaury did not have a
weapon of any kind."

The jury deliberated for two hours and returned to the
hearing room murmuring among themselves and trailing cigar
fumes. For the first time since the inquest was convened, all of
the witnesses who had testified were assembled on the benches.
Outside the window the shadows had lengthened to encompass
the scene of the killings under examination.

Conversation sloped off as the jurors took their seats in the
box. Matthews waited for complete silence, then turned to
address saloonkeeper R. F. Hafford, seated in the corner nearest
him.

"Has the coroner's jury reached a verdict?"

Hafford rose, a tall, teamster-shouldered man with a round
beard and his fingers curled under the hem of his black frock
coat. "We have."

"Please state it for the record."

Hafford drew a folded sheet from an inside breast pocket
and opened it, coughing into a pudgy fist to clear away phlegm.
Ike Clanton, watching, stopped chewing.

"We the jury find that William Clanton, Frank and Thomas
McLaury came to their deaths in the town of Tombstone on
October twenty-sixth, eighteen eighty-one, from the effects of
pistol and gunshot wounds inflicted by Virgil Earp, Morgan
Earp, Wyatt Earp, and one Holliday, commonly called Doc
Holliday."

Ike resumed chewing. He leaned over toward Billy Claiborne, close enough for the latter to smell Levi Garrett's on his breath. "Well, who in hell never knew that?" he whispered. "What's it signify?"

Claiborne said, "I ain't sure. I think it means the Earps and Doc are as good as hung."

CHAPTER 4

THE UNDERTAKING FIRM OF Ritter and Eyan scrubbed down the bodies with lye and drained them of blood, pumped formaldehyde and glycerin in through the carotid and femoral arteries, and sewed shut the mouths with needles drawn between the upper lips and gums and out through the nostrils. They scoured and waxed Billy Clanton's buck teeth, plugged the hole under Frank McLaury's ear with flesh-colored wax, and pomaded the hair of all three corpses, finally applying rouge to the faces. From a fund pledged by Ike Clanton and Billy Claiborne and contributed to by cowboys still trickling in from San Pedro and Charleston, good suits of clothes were purchased from Myer Brothers at Fifth and Allen and stitched and pinned to fit as snugly as any Vanderbilt's. At last their hands were folded on their breasts and powdered lightly and their cuffs were buttoned together to prevent the hands from sliding apart.

The day after the shooting the bodies were inserted in mahogany caskets with glass windows and silver trim and placed in the window of a general merchandise and hardware store on the south side of Allen between Fifth and Sixth with a wooden sign strung over them reading MURDERED IN THE STREETS OF TOMBSTONE. Camilius Fly captured the tableau in a whump and flash of magnesium powder.

The bodies were returned to the undertaking parlor the

following afternoon. There, miners and townsmen come too late for seats lined walls ambuscaded with plaster cupids and death-angels and divided their attention between the service and the families and friends occupying the benches. These included cowboys in new denims and clean bandannas and too-tight boots and ranchers in store suits smelling of camphor and naphtha. Ike Clanton attended in his black inquest suit. With his chin whiskers trimmed and waxed and his hair arranged in a curl on his forehead he looked slightly less lifelike than his brother Billy; only the tobacco lump under his right ear moved. His sister Mary sat equally motionless beside him in the front row in the same black dress she had worn to bury their father three months earlier. Ike's brother Phin sat on the other side of her in a stiff collar, and Billy Claiborne occupied a seat farther back wearing a calico shirt with striped braces and garters, his hands resting on his pinch hat in his lap. All three men sported black armbands.

The Tombstone-trained eye might have spotted Charleston notables Frank Stilwell and John Ringo among the cowboys standing in the rear with their hats in front of them, but for the most part the mourners were strangers to the deceased. Proper funerals were rare entertainments in an area whose cemetery contained more nameless corpses than Gettysburg's.

The procession down Allen Street and north to the hill bore more spectacular distractions. The Tombstone brass band, plumed shakos and gold frogs on red velvet, led off with tubas, a trumpet, a bass drum, and a slide trombone, followed by twin eight-thousand-dollar hearses with glass sides and glowing side-lanterns and hard rubber tires; Ike and Mary in a hired trap with Phin Clanton riding the axle; Billy Claiborne following in a buckboard; and others strung out behind in buggies and on foot, the rest of the column deteriorating into a rabble with children kicking apart green horse-apples at the end and mongrel dogs snapping at heels and stopping to urinate against the boardwalk. Strings of firecrackers snapped and spat sparks, shying horses and starting small fires in the chaparral that were quickly tramped out. A bow-tied Sheriff Behan, Undersheriff (and *Nugget* editor) Harry Woods, and Deputy Billy Breaken-

ridge accompanied the procession on foot with shotguns
cradled.

On the rocky slope studded with Spanish bayonet overlooking town, two gravediggers in overalls with cuds in their
cheeks leaned on their shovels and watched as the caskets were
lowered by ropes into a hole twelve by eight by six and the last
handful of earth thumped the lids. Then they came over and
began tipping sand and gravel and clumps of yucca into the
cavity. The wind pasted their brims to the crowns of their hats
and caught and carried smoking dust from the disturbed earth,
spreading it across the graves farther down. A shovelful landed
in the middle of Tom McLaury's face and skidded over the
glass.

Ike Clanton shook hands and supported his sister's elbow
as Phin helped her up to the crest of the hill where the carriage
waited. Ike hung back a little, watching the laborers. The hole
was half-filled now.

"Well, Billy, good-bye," he said. "You never did have the
sense God gave a lofer wolf, to run when you're outmanned
and outgunned." He pulled on his hat and turned away.

The band, playing "Tenting Tonight" as it left town,
sounded tinny in the Oriental, where Wyatt Earp sat at the faro
table in the gaming room dealing to Tom Fitch and flicking
long white fingers at the sliding counters in the cue box to keep
track of the cards dealt. He had on a black Prince Albert and an
empty beer glass stood at his right elbow. Blue smoke from his
cigar haloed his head and curled in the shaft of sunlight slanting
through the leaded-glass windows.

Fitch bet and lost the last of a modest stack of chips. "Is
there a room where we can discuss your case in private?" he
asked then.

Wyatt waved his cigar around the room, appointed in brass
and varnished mahogany with a Brussels carpet. "It does not
get a deal more private than this." At that hour they shared the
establishment with a bartender polishing the white china beer
pulls in the main room and a miner with his arm in a sling
feeding coins into a bronze baroque slot machine in the corner.
Little Egypt, clad in veils and beads monitored his luck from a
gilt-framed painting mounted high on the wall.

Fitch rolled his shoulders. Thickening in middle age, his complexion darkened and cracked from years of stumping for office on the Utah salt flats, the attorney had gray hairs like steel shavings in his impressive black handlebars but none in his heavy brows, which moved independently of the rest of his face and each other. They fascinated judges and distracted juries and he would sooner lop off an arm than pluck a hair from either of them.

"Spicer has set the hearing for the thirtieth," he said. "It fixes to be a long one."

"How long is long?"

"Two or three weeks. I have never known one to last longer than a month."

"That won't do. I and Virge have placed all our mining and water interests on the block to stand this ten thousand bail. We cannot live on what the women take in sewing."

"You have the gambling concession here, and your brother Jim has his saloon."

"Lou Rickabaugh has the concession. I have a quarter interest. And no one is tripping over his spurs just now to play with me. They are all afraid that a ball with my name on it will smear their brains across my board."

"That will pass."

"I will tell Lou you said so."

"How are Virgil and Morgan coming along?"

"Virge is walking some. Goodfellow says Morg will make out fine if Virge doesn't kill him first." Wyatt played with his chips, riffling them in the stack. His fair hair lay flat on his scalp and curled at his collar with red glinting in it. "Tom, how's our chances of walking out of this hearing without chains on?"

"I don't know. When this town was more adobe than timber the business would have been just a formality. A year ago it would not even have come to a hearing. Then it would have been judged a fair fight because all the holes were in front, and if you were not lynched first, no one would have volunteered to ride you all the way into Tucson for trial. But now that Tombstone is a county seat you are skidding pretty close to the mouth of the law."

"I was under the apprehension that we are the law. Or was until Clum took away Virgil's post." The last words were bitten off.

"That was the council. You still have his support in the *Epitaph*."

Wyatt belched.

"You have few enough friends here without throwing him off," Fitch said. "As long as Behan and the cowboys have the *Nugget* you will need the vigilante sheet."

"I am a businessman."

Fitch brushed tobacco off his vest. "I approve of your attitude, about the four of you representing the law. If you keep to it I can get you through this. And it's good news about Virgil walking. I'll want him on the stand to back up your testimony."

"What about Doc?"

"No."

"They will bring him into it anyway. I was fixed to study the law once and took to spending time around lawyers. I know how it's done."

"Let them. We will play down Holliday's participation in the fight so that it won't mean anything." Aware of the clicking and whirring from the slot machine, Fitch leaned forward and dropped his voice. "You will testify that the first shot on your side came from your pistol. Billy Clanton shot first and you returned fire and those were the first two reports."

"There will be others testifying different."

"They will be sufficiently confused among themselves because it all happened so fast."

"Thirty seconds by my count."

"The strategy is that you and Virgil and the other two were acting in your authority as city peace officers. That will be easier to sustain if two temporary deputies did not start the shooting. Particularly two with their reputation for belligerence."

"I never wanted things to come to that pass. Virge didn't neither."

"There is no help for that now."

Wyatt's cigar had gone out. He relit it, turning the end in

the match flame. "I guess you know what you're about," he said, puffing. "I was not born in Illinois to hang in Arizona."

"Stop by the office later. Your statement is being transcribed and I want to go over it with you before you sign it. I am planning to introduce a motion—"

Wyatt was looking past him. Fitch turned in his chair and saw Billy Breakenridge entering, blinking a little in the dimness after the bright sunlight outside. He was slender, and the skyward tilt of his hat on the back of his head and the upsweep of his dark handlebars lent him a joviality he didn't possess. Two points of his deputy's star showed past his coat. He looked around, nodded at Wyatt, then turned and took a seat in the main room, leaning his shotgun against the table. The bartender brought him a beer.

"Services must be over." Fitch turned back, hoisting his brows. "Is that true what they tell about Breakenridge?"

"He is some tight with that Charleston crowd just like his boss."

"No, I mean the other."

Wyatt blew a ring and tapped some ash into his beer glass. "Leaves that many more women to go around."

"That is what comes of bunking with cowboys, I suppose." The attorney stood. "Shall I accompany you back to your house?"

"No, business will be picking up now that the planting is finished."

"My advice is not to go out on the street alone."

"I won't be." Wyatt gestured with his cigar toward the man at the slot machine, who turned and showed Fitch a blue muzzle resting inside his sling. The lawyer looked up then and recognized the ruddy face and red chin-whiskers, not of a miner, but of Sherman McMasters, a friend of the Earps who rode shotgun for Wells Fargo.

"I am a gambler," Wyatt said. "Not some woolly-headed nigger."

Fitch traded the muted opulence of the Oriental for the puckered street and its brassy sunshine. The wind was blowing from the direction of the Mexican quarter and brought with it a hot smell of tacos and guacamole to mingle with the manure stench on Allen and sour mash fumes from the alleys behind Hatch's and the Eagle Brewery. It was a ripe town, stinking of prosperity. He touched his hat to Kate Fisher, who was lifting her skirt above a surprisingly trim ankle to mount the boardwalk. She nodded and continued up Fourth to Fremont and let herself into Fly's boardinghouse.

Doc was sitting at the cramped writing table in their room when she came in, using a steel card-cutter to trim the blurred edges off a deck he had been carrying since Prescott. He had won forty thousand dollars there, although most of it playing faro with someone else's deck; but the town itself was lucky for him. Kate hung up her cape and bonnet.

"You ought to have come out and watched," she said. "It was a sight."

He took his fingers off the nickel-plated Colt's on the corner of the table and returned to his labor. The pistol lay on an envelope addressed in his elegant hand to Atlanta, Georgia. "I intend to miss every funeral but my own," he said.

"You talk as if you were dead already."

"It will save me the trouble of adjusting later."

She hesitated. "I am going to Globe."

He sheared a hairline strip off the pasteboard in the clamp, then replaced the card with another and lined up the edge with the heel of his hand.

"I thought you might want to come with me," she said.

"The sheriff would just take me off the stage and stick me in jail." He worked the scissors again.

"He won't do that. He is afraid of you like everyone else in town except that Wyatt Earp."

He clamped in another card.

"Your streak has gone cold here," she said.

"Wyatt would lose his bail money."

"What do you care? He almost got you killed."

"Almost is a crime, all right." He inspected the last card, then laid it down and selected another.

"Stand clear of him, Doc." She was leaning over him now, a hand on the table. He smelled lilac water. "He will get you shot or hanged and that Fort Griffin fire trick won't work twice."

"I have bets laid from here to Valdosta that a ball or a rope will do for me before the cough." The card moved as the blade came down and he ruined it. "Shit!" He shoved the cutter away and reached for the open bottle on the table. She grabbed his arm.

"There is no good talking to you. That goddamn foxy con man has cast an evil spell over a poor sick man that has to drink to stay alive!"

He jerked the arm free, slopping whiskey over the deck of cards and his pink shirtsleeve. A flush climbed his face then and she saw it and tried to back away, but he swept the bottle around by the neck and laid the side of it along her temple with a thud. She lost her balance and fell. He was up before her, backhanding her across the face with his free hand and then reversing directions and slapping her with his open palm so that it stung clear to his elbow. She sprawled on her side and started crawling. He followed her and bent over her and went to work on her with his fist. When she crossed her arms over her head he kicked her in the ribs. He upended the bottle, shaking out the contents, plastering her hair and darkening her dress. When it was empty he threw it at her and it struck her forearm with a clunk, slid down her hip, and rolled on the floor. The air swam with ferment. He kicked at her again, but missed this time and stumbled forward, almost falling on top of her. He was wheezing, legs bent, arms hanging, his vest ridden up his narrow back, and inside of him the old familiar sensation of feral cats shredding the wall of his chest. He was bleeding through his trousers where the scab on his right hip had broken open.

The room was quiet then, except for his whistling breaths and her sniffling and sucking down blood and snot. She had voided her bladder; he could smell it. Sitting there on the floor soaked and bleeding and stinking of piss and bad whiskey and lilac water she made him feel ashamed, the only person on earth who could do that except maybe Wyatt and one other. He started to apologize and help her up. She wrenched her arm out of his grasp.

"Beat a woman!" she shrieked. Her left eye was closing and when she swept the back of a hand across her nose it came away smeared. "Kill an unarmed man! Where is your decency?"

"I coughed all that up with my lungs years ago," he said, and went down on one knee, his eyes glazing over.

PART TWO
THE
TRANSACTION

Bad local government is certainly a great evil which ought to be prevented, but to violate the freedom and sanctity of the suffrage is more than an evil. It is a crime which if persisted in will destroy the government itself. Suicide is not a remedy.

—James A. Garfield, Inaugural
Address, 1881

CHAPTER 5

RAISE THE DEAD. TURN the earth out of their pockets, strip them, scrub off the paint and powder and flush the yellow juice from their veins and stand them up in good Tucson boots scarred at the toes and running down a little on the outside of the heels. Spin the clock in the other direction. Stuff the blood back into the holes and the balls and smoke back into the barrels and sit the risen dead on their mounts and wagon seats and reverse them out of town. Day to night to day to night to day, flashing like Camilius Fly's magnesium powder, day to night, Wednesday to Tuesday to Monday, faster and faster, day to night, October to September to August and the rainy season back to the heat and then the thaw and then snow. Make it March on the night the trouble started and let the dead tell their side.

Bud Philpot had the cramps. His stomach would gurgle and clench and bend him double so that he lost sight of the road except for the pale patch blurring between the traces. Worse, his fingers were frozen thick as sash weights and he couldn't feel the reins between them. Driving a six-hitch team was like playing a piano and a man required his sense of touch. The lines would go slack in his hands and the team would slow down.

The sky was skittle-black, without stars, and the coach's yellow side-lanterns reflected flatly off the flakes turning and tumbling out of it to the white tenting below. Snow clung fuzzily to the dormant mesquite bushes lining the road like heaps of bone. The horses panted and billowed white steam.

"Rein up, Bud, and go take a dump."

The cramps were loosening a little. Philpot cracked his face enough to cock a grin at Bob Paul, the big clean-shaven man riding next to him with a Stevens ten-gauge across his blanketed lap. It was a young face with an old man's mobility, the muscles underneath worn smooth and loose like the mechanism of a broken-in Winchester. "It's a temptation," he said, "but if I was to commence shitting now I won't never stop and likely freeze to the ground and you'll have to bust me loose with the butt of that splattergun."

"Well, give me your seat then. I would just as soon die in a stage wreck as anyplace, but I would not want folks saying that Bob died of Bud's runs."

Philpot drew rein and leaned back on the brake. His fingers were too stiff to tie off and he handed both sets to Paul and let him climb over, sliding sideways into the messenger's seat with a twinge in his bowels that made him curse.

Paul was an old driver and handled the horses by varying tension on the reins and with a series of vocalizations elaborate enough to signify language. He kept the shotgun across his thighs, adjusting its position now and again with an elbow when the vibration threatened to pitch it off. The coach was hauling seven passengers inside with the freight and an eighth in the dickey seat on top in the rear, huddled into a company bearskin with his hat pulled low. His name was Peter Roerig.

The Benson road, two ruts in the iron earth between the Dragoons to the east and the Whetstones to the west, was a succession of bootjacks and inclines lined with desert growth and rough as a slag heap. Philpot swore and clenched his sphincter at the jogs and lurches. It felt like he had a rock jammed up him.

A mile outside of Contention, Paul slowed down to climb a grade. The horses smelled woodsmoke from Drew's Station and he fought them, bracing his heels against the footboard and applying and releasing the brake. The wheels jerked and pulled and slid on snow pounded flat and slick by the team's hooves.

"Whoa, boys!"

In the light of the side-lanterns coming off the snow on the ground, a group of men in big hats and bandannas with yellow beards spilling out around them moved out from behind a skeletal clump of chaparral on the shoulder. Snow dusted their brims and the shoulders of their oilskins and their rifle barrels glistened black and wet.

At the shout, Bob Paul let the reins fall slack and swept up the shotgun. One of the rifles crashed. Philpot grunted, slapped his chest, and slid off the seat. Paul shot out his left hand with three lines in it to snatch Philpot's collar and heaved him back up. The stink of excrement washed over him in a wave. Other rifles had opened fire; balls were splitting the air around him. Feeling no pressure on the reins, the horses bolted up the grade, whinnying and splattering mud and snow into Paul's face. He shouted at them and let Philpot slump to free both hands and stood on the footboard and worked the brake. Behind him the clattering reports faded, deadened by snow and distance, then stopped.

The lighted windows of the station were hanging ahead when he got the animals down to a canter. He reined in before the adobe building.

"Bud?"

Philpot was sitting with his chin inside his rough collar and his hat canted down in front of his face. Paul tore off the hat. The driver's head drifted toward his shoulder and his body leaned over sideways. The front of his coat glittered with blood from a ragged hole over his heart. Paul left him there and climbed down. He was surrounded by a crowd, the station having emptied out at the noise of gunfire. It grew as the passengers helped one another down, everyone talking at once.

"Stand away!" Paul jerked his shotgun at the newcomers. The coach contained eighty thousand in silver bullion bound for the railhead at Benson.

"Who's dead?" someone asked. "Is that Bob Paul?"

He recognized the station keeper's pockmarked face. "No, I'm Paul. Bud Philpot got it." He started counting heads among the passengers. "Everybody all of a piece?"

Someone said, "That fellow on top fell off back there."

Paul said, "I caught him. Not that the favor did him any kindness."

"Not him. The one in back."

He glanced up at the empty dickey seat.

"He wasn't moving when we left him." The passenger speaking was an angular young man in a checked suit and chesterfield splashed with mud.

"Christ." Paul told the station keeper to watch the coach and started back on foot.

"They'll cut you down," the keeper called.

"Do I look like I'm carrying bullion? They are horseshit and pony tracks by now."

Snow fell with a sizzling noise. The big clean-faced man was a shadow, then a sensation of movement behind a curtain. After five minutes he returned, the shotgun dangling. The lights of the station shadowed the pouches in his broad face.

"Wire Tombstone," he told the station keeper. "Tell them the shipment is safe but we got two dead."

The snow slacked off after midnight. It had stopped falling when seven horsemen approached the station at a walk, iron shoes creaking on the fresh fall. At the base of the grade Bob Paul swung a lantern and they drew rein. He recognized Sheriff Behan's big sombrero and greeted Billy Breakenridge, shook hands with Virgil Earp when he swung down with a grunt, and nodded to Wyatt and Morgan, both part-time fellow shotgun messengers. Marshall Williams, the Wells Fargo agent in Tombstone and a sunny entity by nature, smiled a greeting and rolled a cigarette. Paul didn't know the seventh man, medium-built under a buffalo coat and slouch hat, with a round face, moustaches curled down on the ends, and kindly blue eyes that glinted in the lantern light as if hunting mischief. He was not thirty. All the men wore big hats and heavy coats and clanked when they moved. They had brought two pack horses with them. The fellow in the buffalo coat had a Sharps rifle in his scabbard.

Virgil said, "Bob, this here is Bat Masterson. He is a good man to have on the road if you keep an eye on him and see he does not tie any tin cans to your tail."

Masterson pulled a small hand out of its glove to accept the shotgun messenger's big paw. "Adobe Walls," Paul said. "I heard about you. I thought you'd be older."

The glint deepened. "I came near to not getting that way on that occasion."

"Well, I cannot promise you Comanches, but there are four or five white men I would admire to turn over a mesquite flame. They murdered a good Wells Fargo man and a paying passenger."

"Where are they?"

"Laid out up at the station. Coyotes this winter are thick as mosquito wigglers."

"What have you found?" Behan remained in the saddle with his arms folded on the pommel.

Paul stepped off the road and raised his lantern. A scattering of brass cartridge shells caught fire in the glow. Wyatt picked one up and flicked snow off the flanged end. "Winchester short. They used up enough of them to kill just two."

"I count seventeen," Paul said. "Here is where one of them waited with the horses." He carried the light into the mesquite. The new snow lay bowl-shaped in depressions where the earlier fall had been trampled. He hooked something out of the brush and held it out.

Virgil turned the item over and handed it to Wyatt. It was a triangle of black cloth with lengths of frayed rope sewed around the edges.

Paul said, "I thought they was yellow whiskers. They each was wearing one."

"The trail is hours old," said Behan, when the men returned to their animals. "The snow will melt come morning and we will have nothing but lathered horses to show for our trailing."

Wyatt mounted. "Bat can read sign like an Apache. I am no poor shakes at it myself and neither is Virgil."

First light was a metallic sliver over the Dragoons. Bob Paul swung a leg over the black he had brought back from Benson after delivering the stagecoach and the party set out, the horses shuddering and snorting milky vapor.

The sky cleared at dawn. The sun warmed the earth and drew forth a fog that burned off by mid-morning, the droplets prisming into brilliant colors in the moment of dissipation. The snow dissolved into patches that became brown puddles in the afternoon. By then all of the riders except Behan, hanging back with Breakenridge, had shucked their coats and rolled them behind their cantles.

Now and then they stopped while Masterson rode his paint around in a circle, leaning out of the saddle, or dismounted and went ahead on foot to study the ground. Sometimes he was joined by Wyatt.

"These fellows are not new to life on the scout," said Masterson, stepping into leather. "Doubling back and using riverbeds and rock face. Johnny would have lost this one thirty miles back."

Wyatt showed his teeth. "Johnny would lose his ass in a washtub unless it had a county ballot tattoed on it."

"You are still chewing over that appointment?"

"He promised me undersheriff and then turned around and gave it to Harry Woods. The difference comes to twenty thousand a year. I guess I am still chewing over it."

They camped in the Dragoon foothills, where Masterson served Billy Breakenridge a plateful of beans and curled bacon with a hibernating scorpion on top of it and smiled when the deputy squealed and dropped the plate. The others howled, all except a scowling Behan. After supper Morgan shared a bottle with Masterson and Virgil, who offered it to Bob Paul, but it was declined. Wyatt smoked a pipe. Behan took off his sombrero and combed his spidery hair forward over his dome. They banked the fire and slept. Marshall Williams snored loudest.

In the morning the trail bent north and then west past Tres Alamos, following the swollen San Pedro River up the valley. There it mingled with other, older tracks at sundown and Masterson lost it.

"Rancher named Wheaton went bust sometime back," Wyatt told him, separating a prickly pear from his chaparreras between thumb and forefinger. "His place is a day and a half upriver. If I was planning a holdup in the snow and wanted a place to shelter fresh mounts it would be there."

"It's worth looking. That San Pedro crowd has pushed too

many stole cattle through this country to track an ammo wagon after them."

Part of Wheaton's roof had tipped in, the adobe beaten down to rubble on that side and the windows gaping. The barn, a solider construction, stood swaybacked a hundred yards away with sunlight streaming between leaden gray sideboards not yet carried off by scavengers in a region starved for wood. They rode down on the shack out of a lifting sun, six men unshaven and mortared from crowns to rowels with three days of dust and dried mud and their horses throwing lather. The two county men trailed behind. Dismounting before the door, Morgan Earp fisted his pistol and kicked apart the latch. But there was nothing inside to shoot except a huddled armadillo and he followed the others to the barn. It contained four caked saddle horses with their heads hanging on a floor of ammonia-smelling straw. Masterson let his rifle droop.

"Well, we did not figure to beat them here."

"Any of them look familiar?" Virgil asked Paul.

He shook his head. "I never saw their mounts."

Wyatt laid a hand on a shivering cow pony's hollow flank. "I know this one. I saw Luther King riding it down Allen Street a week ago."

Masterson said, "It does not look to stand out that much."

"I'm telling you it's King's."

Virgil found a tick in his clothes and squashed it. "King is tight with Len Redfield, ain't he?"

"That is scarcely evidence." Behan had just caught up, with Breakenridge behind. The sheriff's gelding tried to pry loose a patch of trampled alfalfa from the bare earth with its muzzle.

"I am a deputy U.S. marshal, not a judge." Virgil mounted.

"Stage robbery is county jurisdiction."

"Murder in the territory is federal. Hold your water, Johnny. You will get your slab of the glory."

"Johnny don't want it," Morgan said, grinning. "Him and the Redfields are old poker partners."

Len Redfield was a big man, yoke-shouldered, and balloon-knuckled from fights in the pasture and in town. He wore braces over a red-and-white-checked shirt gone pink from wearing and washing and gray dungarees glazed with dirt at the knees. He closed the door on his wife inside their whitewashed house in the lower valley and stepped off the porch to meet the riders. Wyatt got down without asking leave and the others watched Redfield's square face darken.

"We are looking for Luther King and the other men who tried to rob the Benson stage," Wyatt said. "The trail leads here."

"Like hell it does."

"You are calling me a liar?"

Redfield said, "You're trespassing."

"This here is law business, Len." Virgil stretched himself on his saddle horn.

"I don't know nothing about no holdups and I ain't seen Luther this month."

Wyatt said, "You're a liar."

The rancher's face congested deeper and his right shoulder dropped. Wyatt turned his head, taking most of the blow along his jawline, scooped his big American out of his trousers, and laid the barrel behind Redfield's left ear. Redfield went down, shying Virgil's horse. Landing on his hands and knees, he started to push himself up. Virgil took his boot out of its stirrup and planted it against Redfield's chest and shoved. The rancher sprawled on his back. Wyatt kicked him in the ribs. The snap was brittle in the clear air. He placed his foot across the fallen man's throat and rolled back the pistol's hammer and pointed the muzzle at his face.

"Where is Luther King or I'll blow your brains clear to China."

"Wyatt."

He kept his shooting arm straight and turned his head slightly. Morgan, astride his chestnut, was approaching from the corral. He had a hand wrapped around his Colt's resting on his thigh and he was herding forward a lumpy-looking man in overalls and a dirty duster, shoving him stumbling ahead with the horse's shoulder when he hesitated. Finally Morgan turned the horse hard and the man fell on his face with a rattling noise.

"He clumb the far side of the corral when he saw me coming," Morgan said. "He almost made it."

"Morning, Luther." Wyatt elevated the Smith & Wesson's muzzle and seated the hammer gently. Redfield breathed, catching his breath when his cracked rib pinched him.

Bob Paul spurred his black in a wide loop around the corral, milling the horses around inside, and came back. "There's two badly used animals in there," he said.

Belting his pistol, Wyatt left Redfield to place a heel against Luther King's shoulder and rolled him over. Virgil said, "Look out," and Wyatt kicked a Colt's Navy out of the man's hand. Then he kicked him in the face.

Behan said, "There is no call for that."

"Luther, you're putting on weight." Wyatt took hold of the bib of the stunned man's overalls and tore it loose from the buttons. Red-and-white cartridge boxes spilled out. He threw the boxes after the Navy, unbuckled two cartridge belts from around King's waist and added them to the pile, found a short-barreled Colt's Thunderer in a duster pocket and got rid of that. King looked a lot less lumpy now. "Luther, what if you fell in the San Pedro? I have saved you from drowning."

"Company." Marshall Williams, one stovepipe-booted leg resting across his pommel, paused in the midst of building a cigarette to loosen his Winchester in its scabbard.

Behan shielded his eyes and squinted at the rider coming in out of the sun. "It is Len's brother Hank."

Wyatt said, "Bat."

Masterson quirted his mount and cantered out to intercept the rider. The other man drew rein and they conversed across ten feet of ground, gesturing. Finally they rode in. Hank was as tall as his brother but not as wide and wore big sad moustaches under a black pinch hat with a Spanish brim.

Len was sitting on the porch steps now, a hand on his side. His wife had come out and squatted next to him with her skirt in the dust of the yard. She was bareheaded and her skin and dress and tied-back hair were all the same sand color. Her face was long and simian and she had large ears that stuck out.

Virgil stepped down and told Masterson and Williams to search the outbuildings. "We will have a talk with Luther indoors."

Wyatt twisted a hand inside the collar of King's duster and heaved him to his feet. He had to clutch his overalls with one hand to keep them from sliding down.

Dismounting, Bob Paul followed the Earps and their prisoner into the house, leaving Behan and Breakenridge to watch the Redfields. Inside the small parlor Wyatt hurled King into a horsehair armchair pinned all over with doilies and antimacassars. An oval-framed picture fell off a wall, cracking the thick glass.

"You are some bad road agent, Luther," Wyatt said. "You should seek another line of work, the others too."

"I ain't no road agent."

Wyatt backhanded him across the face. The noise was like a pistol shot in the room.

"Why'd you run, Luther?" Virgil lowered himself onto a davenport that sighed under his weight. Troughs of dust curled up around him and settled on the flowered upholstery.

"Fthzlwz." King's lip was swelling.

"Talk plain." Wyatt slapped him again.

"I thought you was outlaws." He grimaced out each word. "This country is full of them."

"Marsh Williams and Bat have guns to your friends' heads," Wyatt said. "They will shoot the woman first and then it is up to you whether Len or Hank gets it next."

King said nothing and Wyatt cocked his hand a third time. Virgil interrupted him.

"You don't want to be in Yuma with summer coming on." He sat back with his knees spread and his hands on them and the palm-polished handle of his Army Colt's turning out past his open greatcoat. "They stick you in a tin box in the sun like a sourdough biscuit and don't let you out until you are baked down to skin and skeleton."

Bob Paul said, "He won't see Yuma. When Doc Holliday hears about it he will be lucky to see a rope."

"Wzdk—" He pinched his torn lip. "What's Holliday to do with it?"

"Hell, his woman Kate was riding on that stage. All that hare-assed shooting got her killed. Doc is some taken with that Kate."

Wyatt snatched at it. "Three of you stood by the road, stuck up the stage and killed Philpot and Roerig and Kate Fisher. The other one held the horses in the brush. I don't know which one he was, but whoever he was he is lucky. Doc will run down the others and cut off their wedding-tackles with that pig-sticker he carries and shove them down their craws and then shoot them for mumbling."

"Jesus."

"Doc is mean but fair," Virgil said. "He will have no truck with whoever held the horses."

"I held the horses!"

Wyatt, big and lean and sunburned and needing a shave, his jaw purpling where Len Redfield's knuckles had raked it, looked at his brother. Virgil plucked a fresh tick off his neck and contemplated it before cracking it between thumb and forefinger. "Let's get the others in here."

Morgan went out. Minutes later the room was crowded with three Earps, Bob Paul, Marshall Williams, Sheriff Behan, and Deputy Breakenridge. Masterson stayed outside with the Redfields. A sour-sweet mix of sweat and leather and horse and gun oil filled the house.

Luther King spoke, pressing his lip at times to make his words clear and playing with a cigarette Williams had rolled for him. No one had given him a match.

"It was Billy Leonard, Jim Crane, and Harry Head done the shooting. I held the horses like I said. I rid with them to Wheaton's for fresh mounts and left them at Hank Redfield's to get cartridges and money from Len. I was fixing to meet up with them when Morg catched me."

"They changed horses at Hank's?" Wyatt asked. King nodded. "Where are they camped?"

The prisoner smiled. Blood trickled down his chin. He had a bowl haircut and no hair on his face and the grin made him look like a schoolboy. "You won't get them. I have talked all I am fixed to."

Wyatt said, "You will talk a blue streak when Doc commences to sawing on the family jewels."

King paled a shade but said nothing.

Virgil stood, stretching and cracking some bones. "Doc's

woman was never on that stage, Luther," he said. "Bob snookered you."

Before the other could react, Behan cleared his throat loudly. The sheriff's sombrero was dusty and his neck had broken out in an angry rash under several days' growth of beard. "King is my prisoner, Earp. I am arresting him for complicity in attempted stage robbery. That's a county offense, not federal. I am taking him to Tombstone."

"I will go with you," said Williams.

"That won't be necessary."

"It is a long ride. You and Billy might fall asleep."

The silence was spoiled by Morgan's singing. "Can you bake a cherry pie, Billy-girl?"

Breakenridge glared.

CHAPTER 6

WYATT EARP AND HIS brothers and their women called her Mattie. She had been christened Celia Ann Blaylock, a mannish-looking strawberry blonde with iron-curled hair and deep-set eyes that seemed always in shadow. She did fancy sewing, took in laundry, and had a temper that was slow to blow and then impossible to cap when it did. She had been with Wyatt since 1870, shortly after his first wife Urilla died delivering his stillborn child. Mattie and he had traveled together to Deadwood and Dodge City and all the other places on the circuit, and although like Virgil and Allie they had never taken vows, she had been known as Mattie Earp in all of them.

When word reached Tombstone that the Earps were returning from their manhunt, she peeled hurriedly out of her faded calico and brushed and put on the one good dress she had brought from Dodge, a black velvet brocade with a high ivory-lace collar. She fretted over the trunk creases in the skirt, brushed her hair, pinched color into her cheeks, and put a drop of vanilla extract behind each ear. Wyatt hated scents of any kind and never knew the true source of the fresh natural smell he admired in Mattie, or had admired until recently. Morgan's woman Lou arrived in time to help her with the buttons in back. Lou was wearing a shift made from leaf-print percale that looked as good as new calico with a close row of bone buttons down the front.

Heavy boots struck the porch boards while Lou was adjusting Mattie's collar. The three brothers came in carrying their saddlebags and carbines, looking more alike than ever under skins of brown dust with clumps of mescal stuck to their coats and their hats sweat through at the crowns. Morgan kissed Lou and curled an arm around her waist, grinning like a young boy. Virgil said, "I don't smell nothing cooking."

"The food is across the street, and is that all you have to say to me after seventeen days?"

He swung around, swept Allie out of the doorway in both arms, and kissed her hard, his whiskers rasping. "Ouch."

Mattie hugged Wyatt, smearing the front of her dress. He leaned his Winchester in a corner and tossed his saddlebags into his leather easy chair, the best piece of furniture in the little house. Dust rolled off them in a thick cloud. "Where are the papers?"

She detached herself and lifted the stack from the table. "I saved them all."

He transferred his bags to the carpet and sat down with the newspapers in his lap. "Get the water boiling and dig out my best shirt."

She hesitated. Allie's frank gaze met hers, then moved away. Mattie went out after the washtub.

Wyatt felt Allie watching him and looked up. "You'd best go home and fix a bath for Virge too."

"I don't take orders from any man but my husband," she said, her chin tilting.

Virgil said, "Go home then, goddamn it. I want a bath."

She looked at him quickly, then hugged Lou and left.

"Taking up with that little Irish mick was the worst mistake you ever made," said Wyatt.

"At least I take mine one at a time."

Morgan laughed. When Wyatt looked at him he took Lou and went out.

Wyatt read the close print swiftly while the kettle on the cookstove bubbled, refolding each paper cracklingly when he was finished with it and laying it on the floor. Virgil smoked a cigar from a box of General Arthurs on the table, his first since they had all run out of tobacco on the trail. They had been out two weeks and three days and had given up on Leonard, Head, and Crane when their tracks crossed the Mexican border and disintegrated among the rocks south of it. By that time they had lost Bat Masterson when his horse pulled a tendon and he turned back.

"What do they say about Luther King?" Virgil asked, when Wyatt flung aside the Tucson *Weekly Star*.

"Nothing we never heard on the way here. Walked out the side door bold as Sam Grant while his honor Undersheriff Harry Woods was letting Johnny Dunbar draw up a bill of sale for Luther's horse. Harry Jones was there overseeing the transaction."

"We can get the lay from Jones. The talk is Johnny Behan's galloping his wife."

"Meantime Woods is fixing the stage holdup on Doc in the *Nugget*."

Virgil blew a ring. "Doc and Billy Leonard was some tight in New Mexico."

"Woods is saying Bob Paul had an oar in too. He changed seats with Philpot so Philpot would die in his place."

"That is crazy talk. If Paul was tied in they would have just not shot at him and took the bullion peaceable as you please."

"It's Behan's doing. He knows I am running against him next year and everyone knows I backed Paul in the last election. It is no secret that Doc and I are friendly. They are the same as claiming I tried to hold up that stage."

"You think Doc done it?"

"I quit trying to think for Doc in Dodge."

Mattie was pouring water into the steel washtub. Steam rolled out and clouded the flaking mirror nailed over the dry sink. Wyatt stood and undid the buttons on his shirt. The limp material came away from his underwear with a peeling sound. Virgil squashed out his cigar in a china saucer.

"I will meet you later in the Oriental," he said.

His brother glanced at Mattie, who was busy arranging one of his good white shirts on the ironing board, and lowered his voice. "I might be someplace else."

Virgil nodded.

★ ★ ★

Virgil emerged from his white porcelain tub scrubbed pink all over except for the brown ending in a V at his collarbone and across the tops of his wrists and the darker turnip color of his genitals. Allie was in bed already. She complained when he joined her without toweling off first, soaking the sheets and her flannel nightdress as he pushed the garment up under her arms and took her, fumbling first for her breasts and then her crotch and then driving himself up inside her, hot and bursting, his skin smelling of soap. His pace quickened, he exploded with a shudder, and then he rolled off and went to sleep with his broad hairy back to her.

She lay awake, waiting.

The first raised voice she heard was Mattie's, thin and harsh and carrying, the words indecipherable from across Fremont. Wyatt's was deep, slower, edged. Crockery crashed.

Virgil was snoring. Allie slid out from under the counterpane and stood, pulling down her nightdress. The floor was clammy under her bare feet. She padded to the window in time to see Wyatt bang his front door behind him. He had on his gambler's black broadcloth over a white shirt starched plank-stiff, and his stovepipe boots gleamed with grease and lampblack. Pounding along the boardwalk he almost collided with his friend Fred Dodge rounding the corner of First and swept on past without stopping. Soon he was out of sight.

Allie used Virgil's tepid bathwater to scrub away the stickiness between her legs and dressed quietly. Her breath frosted in the crisp air of twilight as she crossed the street. She rapped on the front door and waited. After a minute she pulled the latchstring and let herself inside.

She was alone in the house. Something crunched underfoot and she looked down at the scattered shards of a Wedgwood platter she had seen Mattie wrapping carefully in white muslin before leaving Kansas. The back door sagged open on its leather hinges. She went that way, passing a tub full of stagnant water and Wyatt's trail clothes in a muddy heap on the floor next to it. Through the open door she heard a slapping noise, as of someone beating a thin rug. A breathless feminine grunt accompanied each blow.

Allie stepped into the backyard and watched Mattie, still in the black dress with her hair in her face, whipping the rusted pump, disused now that pipe had been lain from the Chiricahuas in the east, with something white.

"Mattie." Allie lunged and caught the thing on the backswing, tugging it from Mattie's grasp. It was one of Wyatt's good dress shirts, crusty from starch but smeared now with orange rust.

"It had a spot!" Mattie was shrieking. Her eyes were feral in her horsey face. "He tore it off because it had this little spot on it after I washed and starched it so careful!"

"Mattie."

"Me washing and ironing shirts for him to show off in for that whore!" She fell to her knees, beating the base of the shuddering pump with both fists.

After a while Allie helped her up and into the house, leaving the spoiled shirt waving on the end of the pump handle.

The woman's name was Josephine Sarah Marcus. She had been called Josie in Brooklyn and San Francisco and still signed herself that way in letters to friends back home; but the Earps, who named everything from scratch and so made it theirs, called her Sadie. She was tall and wasp-waisted and wore her dark hair straight down her back to her seat in a time when most women of marriageable age pinned theirs up. Her eyes were large and sleepy-lidded in a dark oval face and she walked with her chin elevated, calling attention to her long neck. She spoke with a stage inflection that effectively disguised her native Brooklyn accent and did not correct people who assumed she had been born in England. She was nineteen.

She had moved to California with her parents, been seduced by an actor with the Pauline Markham theatrical troupe during its San Francisco engagement, and run away from home to join the troupe on its tour of the territories. The romance had faded quickly, but she stayed on and came to Arizona with the company in 1879, appearing as the cabin boy in *H.M.S.*

Pinafore. There she had fallen in love again and left the show to live for a time with Harry and Kitty Jones, but was now residing in a house of her own on one of the sites that the Townlot Company under Mayor Alder Randall had sold several times without regard to who held the original papers. To date, no attempt had been made to dispossess her. The reason was standing outside her door.

When Wyatt knocked she was expecting him. Tombstone was a close neighborhood for all its population bloat, and the return of the Earps, after the excitement of the attack on the Benson stage and Luther King's escape and the rumors about Wyatt's friend Doc Holliday, crackled up and down Allen Street like telegraph. She had hooked herself into a blue silk dress that left her bosom uncovered, and before opening the door she tied on a yellow crepe bonnet and drew a yellow open-weave shawl over her shoulders.

Wyatt's face was sunburned, gunmetal-colored where he had just shaved, and the rush of air when she opened the door brought with it a crisp tingle of lime-water and starch. His whiskers tickled when he kissed her and his embrace strained her ribs, but she held him almost as tight, nuzzling her cheek against his stiff shirt. When they separated she took his arm and they went out into the Tombstone twilight.

On Allen Street the piano music coming from the Eagle Brewery and the Oriental collided with a clatter and someone in the Alhambra whooped when his lot came up in keno. The couple entered the Maison Doree Restaurant in the Cosmopolitan Hotel, where the Creole waiter who showed them to a corner table scowled at a fork and ordered the entire setting taken away and replaced down to the linen tablecloth. When that was done, by a Chinese busboy in his fifties, the waiter turned down the gas flame over the table and ghosted away until they were ready to order. The violinist played "Mollie Malone."

"Virgil's horse dropped dead from under him in old Mexico," said Wyatt, opening his menu. "That's when we turned back. The both of them was too much weight for Morg's horse and when Bob Paul's gave out too we footed it leading the rest. After two days without water or food we wished we never left those carcasses behind."

"How ever did you manage your way back?" Sadie's lids weren't sleepy now. She laced her long-nailed fingers under her chin.

"We have all of us been in tighter scrapes. It is a question of keeping your head."

"You are too modest."

"It's a fault," he agreed.

"Well, I think it is like a play. Antony pursuing Brutus."

"Antony never had to worry about what was going on in Rome while he was away."

"What happened was not your doing."

"I never said it was. The plan was to have Luther King behind bars and not down there cutting the bear loose with Leonardhead and Crane by now." It had become common practice locally to run the names together like a variety act.

"The *Nugget* says Doc Holliday helped him escape so he would not give him away."

"The *Nugget* is a pack and parcel of lies and has been since Johnny made Woods his little Mary. A lady like you should be reading *Ben-Hur*."

"I am a divorced woman and no lady."

"You have to be married before you can be divorced."

"Are you and Mattie married?"

"Leave her out of it."

The harsh edge in his voice made her draw back. "Look out for Johnny," she said. "He is more dangerous than any road agent."

"Johnny will shoot off his own foot someday."

"He is too clever for that."

"Being too clever is Johnny's long suit."

It was for love of Johnny Behan that she had left the Markham troupe and lived with him as his wife after moving out of the Jones house. She smiled; the cabin boy once again. "Are you going to avenge Doc's good name? Like MacDuff?"

"Doc is no King Duncan."

The waiter returned and Wyatt ordered ham in champagne sauce for himself and Gulf of Mexico shrimp for Sadie. She always ate lightly when she was with him. A dusty bottle of French wine was brought and he went through the tasting

ritual and pronounced it satisfactory. The waiter filled their
glasses, set down the bottle, and was gone.

The restaurant was filling up. John Clum arrived with his
wife on his arm and nodded to Wyatt on the way to their table.
A group of San Pedro cowboys in freshly brushed suits sat
scratching the rungs of their chairs with their Mexican spurs
before heading over to the Bird Cage, and a waiter startled a
couple seated near the kitchen when he set fire to a brisket of
beef swimming in brandy. Luke Short, Wyatt's friend from
Dodge City, dined alone in a corner with his ubiquitous straw
hat hung on the back of his chair and his right hand out of sight
under the table with likely a pistol in it. His gaze held Wyatt's
just long enough to acknowledge his presence. He moved
around town in his own bubble since shooting down Charlie
Storms in front of the Oriental in February.

Wyatt spotted Harry Jones threading his way between
tables and hailed him over. As always the lawyer resembled a
professional pallbearer in black swallowtail and a frayed white
collar curling up at the points. He shook Wyatt's hand and
leaned down to kiss Sadie's cheek and borrowed a chair from an
adjoining table, folding himself into it like a jointed toy on a
stick. His long yellow face looked tragic under the gaslight. At
that point Sadie lost interest. The talk was about to become
political.

"What happened in Johnny's office?" Wyatt asked.

"I was all caught up in that bill of sale," Jones said.
"Dunbar was there and Woods, and either one of them could
have swung the door for King and drawn him a map out of
town for all I saw of it."

Wyatt watched him, not believing a word. Jones had
supported Behan's appointment to sheriff earlier that year. But
politics came easily to a gambler and he played the hand as
dealt.

"Dunbar is Johnny's partner. You should have seen you
was outmanned."

"I didn't know that there was anything to it but a man
selling his horse to make bail. I thought all of Behan's vices
were contained to women."

His bitterness excited Wyatt, but he retained his gambler's

mask. He wondered how much of the talk about the sheriff and Kitty Jones was gossip. He wondered if it mattered. "I hear you are thinking of turning Republican."

"Not while that senile old bastard is sitting in Prescott. Sorry, Sadie," he added. She nodded absently. She wasn't listening.

Wyatt said, "Fremont won't live forever."

"He already has."

"Who will you support for sheriff next year if not Johnny?"

"Who said I had to support anyone?"

"This territory is full of lawyers. I never met one that wouldn't rather be governor."

"Is that what you want?"

"I am no lawyer. Sheriff is good enough for me. Johnny fancies himself higher."

"Little cock-of-the-walk," Jones said.

The waiter brought the dinners. Jones started to excuse himself, but Wyatt touched his arm. When the waiter left: "Harry, who put up that story about Doc and the Benson stage?"

"It is no story. Holliday is as guilty as Cain."

"That is your answer?"

"It is the truth. He left town that day at four o'clock with a Henry rifle and a six-shooter and did not come back until past ten. His horse was badly done."

"That is thin."

"Doc never leaves Tombstone unless he has a better game somewhere else."

Wyatt sat back. "Thank you for coming over, Harry."

The lawyer didn't rise. "You should know they are saying that you failed to find Leonardhead and Crane because you didn't want to."

"Who is?"

"There is talk."

"Where do you stand?"

"If I gave it any credit I would not have come over."

Wyatt looked at his ham. "Are you seeing Billy Breakenridge anytime soon?"

"Why?"

"It isn't important. I will talk with him myself."

Jones got up, bending again to kiss Sadie. She asked him to give her love to Kitty.

"Johnny will take care of that," said Wyatt.

The skin tightened across the lawyer's cheeks. He hovered a moment, his hands twitching at his sides. Then he left the restaurant.

"I cannot feature a cuckold." Wyatt picked up his fork. "He is always the wild card."

Sadie said, "Kitty told me Johnny has offered to deputize him. What does that mean?"

"It means he gets a cut off every dollar he collects in county taxes. Billy Blab packs Curly Bill with him when he visits the ranches so he doesn't come back with his own pockets turned out."

"Is that why you want to talk with him?"

"I will tell you if it comes to anything."

"It is too bad about Harry."

Wyatt ate. "I cannot feature a cuckold."

CHAPTER 7

"MARIA, *ES EL DIENTE oro,*" Doc said.

"No esta el diente oro. Toma un otro."

"I cannot pull one of the others. The gold one is the one that's impacted. Shit, what's the word? *Decaimiento.* It must come out."

"No esta decaimiento. Mucho dinero."

"It will cost you a lot more if I don't pull it now. Do you want to lose your whole jaw? *Mandíbula?*"

They were in one of the gilded boxes that had given the Bird Cage its name. The curtains were open to let in sunlight and Doc half-straddled a fat Mexican woman in pale green taffeta sprawled with a swollen jaw in one of the cigarette-stung seats. His rose-colored shirtsleeves were rolled up his thin sinewy arms and he had a pair of iron pliers in one hand. She clamped her mouth shut. Her eyes were murderous in her brown face.

"Damn it! Lottie!"

A moment later the curtains at the back of the box moved and a large woman in charcoal broadcloth and black lace entered. Her hair was caught with silver combs and she had enough paint on her face to make it seem as if there were no paint on it at all. Doc said, "I could shoot her and pry her mouth apart, but pulling the tooth would not do her much good in that condition."

The woman turned to Maria and spoke to her in rapid Spanish. The Mexican woman listened with her eyes stony on Doc. As Lottie continued, the woman's expression thawed. "*Sí, esta bien,*" she said after a short silence. She closed her eyes and opened a mouth with more spaces inside it than teeth.

"What did you say to her?" Doc asked.

"I said I would have the gold filling melted and made into earrings for her. I will, too."

"Lottie, you have always had a way with whores."

"So have you. But Mr. Hutchinson's and my living depends on it." She went out through the back, carrying her skirts.

Doc settled himself firmly astride Maria's broad lap, spread the fingers of his left hand across her face, bracing himself, and clamped the offending molar between the pliers.

The rafters were still ringing with her screams when he clanked the pliers and raw tooth into the shallow basin Lottie Hutchinson had provided. This event drew furious whistles and hand-smacking from the boxes across the room, where some off-duty whores had gathered to watch the show with their ruffled dressing-gowns hanging open. Doc bowed gracefully, filled a tumbler with gin from a bottle on the box's little table, drank off part of it, and handed the rest to his patient.

"*Enjuaga y escupi.*" It was the only phrase in Spanish he could deliver without hesitating.

She chugged the gin around inside her mouth and spat a bright pink stream into the basin as he held it. Then she drained the glass and swallowed.

"*Gracias, Señor Doctor. Quiere usted paga ahora?*"

"Pay me later. I have climbed on you all I care to for one day."

He was losing his audience. He handed her the basin, then tugged down the points of his vest and put on his frock coat and gray hat.

He descended the stairs carrying his dusty black bag and found Morgan Earp slouched in the third row of seats in the auditorium. His long arms rested across the shoulders of a redhead and a brunette hooked into dresses as tight as sausage casings. Neither of the women looked less than forty under the powder. Morgan himself was in his late twenties, his face boyishly good-looking under peeling sunburned skin and the trademark Earp whiskers. One loop of his string tie hung below its mate, tied carelessly in a manner that always infuriated Wyatt. Doc believed that this was Morgan's purpose.

"I thought you throwed away your shingle after Dodge," said Morgan.

"I keep my hand in for when my luck goes sour. And a lady requested."

"You better give a thought to closing that cut before Kate sees it and takes the wrong meaning from it."

Doc touched a hand to the scratch leaking blood on his left cheek. "I think I will leave it open until she gets back. She has been taking me for granted lately." Kate had carried two black eyes and some loose teeth into the red-light district south of town a few days earlier and he hadn't seen her since. He couldn't remember what they had fought about this time. "I heard you fellows ran out of trail down in Mexico."

"It was that Buckskin Frank Leslie," Morgan said. "Johnny brung him back from Tombstone and after Bat's horse pulled lame and he left us Leslie put his muckety injun scout know-how to work getting us lost. I don't trust him any farther than Johnny and I don't trust Johnny as far as I can pick him up and throw him."

"You should have brought me."

"No one could find you, Doc."

"I had a poker game in Charleston that night."

Morgan goosed the redhead and rose. Both women took the hint then and left through the side door, bustles swaying. Morgan regarded Doc.

"They are saying you came back late on a fagged horse and got a fresh one from Dunbar and left it hitched outside all night, like you was expecting to have to light out in a Missouri hurry."

"They were discussing the holdup in Charleston. I thought Wyatt might need me to ride posse, but he never."

"You don't usually play poker with a Henry rifle."

"I do when I play in Charleston."

Morgan chewed on that, shrugged. "O.K." He put his hat on the back of his head. "You drinking?"

"Damn it, Morg, you know if I pulled that job I would have got the eighty thousand. Whoever shot Philpot never knew his gun from his bunghole. He should have dropped a horse."

"Maybe he missed."

"I shoot well enough sober and I wouldn't stick up anything drunk."

"I wouldn't know you sober. Hell, Doc, I'm just asking because Wyatt is too polite to. I wasn't riding shotgun on that shipment. It don't swing no freight with me if you stuck up King Alexander of Russia."

Doc said, "I *sure* would not have stuck it up with you riding it."

After a moment Morgan took that the good way and grinned. They repaired to the Alhambra.

The spring rains came, pounding the last of the snow out of the Whetstones northwest of Tombstone and bringing out the desert blooms in broad streaks of orange and white and blue that withered quickly in the sun and were taken away as brown dust by the wind. The San Pedro spilled over its banks and began to recede. In May a prospector sifting dirt near Contention spotted a shaggy buffalo bull summering north of the border and it was getting to be such a rare sight that some miners left their claims to look at it and a few families came out from town in buggies and spring wagons so the children would have something to remember and tell about. For a time they watched it chewing unconcernedly on the spring grass, a big blade-humped graybeard with horn scars as thick as snakes on its shoulders and flanks and a yellow eye. Finally somebody shot it and everyone went back to what he was doing before.

Joseph Isaac Clanton rode up from Charleston on the last day of May but one, his skin burned brown and his hair and chin-whiskers gone red-gold driving herds north from Sonora. In Tombstone he caught a bath and a bottle and checked into the Grand Hotel on Allen wearing the suit he had carried rolled up with his gear. In the Eagle Brewery Saloon he was seen talking and sharing another bottle with Billy Breakenridge, who got up and left him with a slap on his shoulder when San Pedro regular Frank Stilwell came over carrying a beer and trailing smoke from a short cigar. Ike laughed and pretended to shield his eyes from the glare off the new deputy's star on Stilwell's vest. Behan did most of his recruiting in the lower valley. Later Ike shot pool behind Hatch's and played poker with Virgil Earp and some others at Hafford's. Tombstone was a good old place and the law was friendly.

He had come west with his mother and father to pan gold in California, worked cattle in Texas with the old man and his younger brother Phineas when Billy was still nursing and his sister Mary was in school, and migrated to the territory after his mother's death when Texas cattle were being quarantined for the tick fever and couldn't be driven north where the money was because the army and the Rangers were waiting at the border to turn them back. In those days Ike's father was a hell-driven man, black-bearded and hard and as quick with his fists as he was with a quotation from Scripture, not white and cranky and stove-in as he was now. That Clanton wouldn't have treated a peckerwood section hand like Curly Bill Brocius as a full partner while ordering his own eldest son around like a nigger.

They got the cattle wild below the border, and if some domestic Mexican ranch beef got caught up in the drive there was no help for it, a man couldn't stop to weed out brands from naked stock. There was no help for it either when the wild ones became scarce and grandee stock was all there was, in numbers so big no greaser don would miss a few hundred head, even if he had the vaqueros to prevent them from wandering all over Sonora and into American territory where they belonged to whoever spotted them first. Up here the clan ran off small parties of Apaches looking to steal the herds, and they'd been fighting them and the Mexicans when Tombstone's first adobe was still yellow mud on the floor of the San Pedro. Like the cattle the place was as much theirs as anyone's.

Ike spent the next few days loafing around town. He

ordered a pair of Mexican boots at Tappanier's, priced a
Centennial Winchester with silver mountings at Spangenberg's
gun shop, bet on a Toughnut Street cockfight and lost, met
with some cattle buyers in from Tucson at Dolan's Saloon who
were not very interested in purchasing stolen Mexican beef, ate
in the Can Can Chop House and in the lunch room at the
Alhambra, and bucked the tiger at Luke Short's faro table in the
Oriental. Short was a sour-faced, dapper man who dealt with
his straw hat tilted forward over his eyes and wouldn't say what
had prompted the late Charlie Storms to challenge him last
winter. He carried a short pistol in a special pocket sewn into
the lining of his suitcoat.

Ike's poke was getting light, and he had still to catch Wyatt
Earp alone.

On June 2, Ike was back in the Eagle Brewery drinking
without help when Wyatt came in and shook his hand. The
gambler's palm was smooth but for a ridge of callus across the
base of his fingers, and strung with piano wire. He asked what
Ike was drinking and bought another tall whiskey for him and a
beer for himself. The bartender wiped off a table and set down a
mug and a glass with moisture beading the outsides.

"Seen Frank McLaury lately?" Wyatt asked.

Ike hesitated, then nodded. "Up in Galeyville." He wondered if Frank was what this was about. It was a matter of some
local talk that Hattie Earp, stepdaughter of James, the oldest of
the brothers, was sneaking around with one of the McLaurys;
although Ike supposed it was Tom and not his sawed-off, short-
fused older brother. James, displaying considerable indignation
for a retired whoremaster who had married one of his girls, had
sprained his good arm birching Hattie within the hearing of
neighbors.

"Did Billy Breakenridge tell you I wanted to talk with
you?" Wyatt asked.

"Yes, but he never said what about."

"If you are close to Frank you might want to bring him
in."

It wasn't about Hattie. "Well, it depends on your
direction."

"It is involved and private."

"Sounds like money."

"Thirty-six hundred dollars."

Ike sipped at his whiskey. Above them the big ceiling fan swished as it turned. He waited for the breeze to reach them. "Frank's brother Tom is the range banker."

"I am not looking to buy any greaser cattle."

"Well, what then?"

"Meet me out front and I will tell you." Wyatt got up, leaving his beer untouched.

Ike drained his glass and joined him on the boardwalk fishing for his plug of Levi Garrett's. Wyatt charged his black pipe. The light was dying around them. A match flared yellow in the window of the Oriental across Fifth, then softened into the butter color of a lamp burning.

Wyatt got his tobacco going finally and flipped his match into the street. "You are aware that Wells Fargo has put up twelve hundred a head for the men who tried to hold up the Benson stage?"

"The shinplasters are all over the country." Ike used his tongue to turn the chew around inside his mouth.

"Help me catch Leonardhead and Crane and you can have every cent of the reward."

"Riding posse is nigger work."

"Charleston is a small town. Everybody knows everybody else. It is common talk there that these three men stop at your ranches, the McLaurys's and yours."

"I am an honest cattleman."

Nellie Cashman passed them in a white blouse and dark skirt and jacket. They took off their hats and she inclined her head, lowering her startling eyes. Wyatt pulled on his pipe and admired her trim figure from behind. "I do not think that it can be as tight as all that," he said, out of her earshot.

Ike put his hat back on. "What good are them three to you without the reward?"

"I am running for sheriff."

"Arrest Doc Holliday then. He killed Philpot."

Wyatt got out his watch and popped open the face. "I guess I should be talking to Frank or Tom."

"I never said I wasn't thinking on it."

Wyatt nodded and put away the watch.

Ike spat, baptizing the base of an awning post. "Billy Leonard and me are claiming the same ranch," he said. "It would be a ripe one on him if he got put out of the way of it and I get paid besides."

"He will laugh right up until they stretch his neck."

"I will need Frank's help."

"Cut any deal that suits you. My terms are the same for one or a hundred."

"His spread is in Sulphur Springs Valley. I can go talk with him and be back here Monday."

Wyatt nodded again and walked away smoking.

On Monday, June 6, they met again in the lot behind the Oriental. The puckered yard smelled sharply of sour mash mixed with leather and sizing from Glover & Company Clothiers and the shoe store next to it. Ike was in the company of two men. One was a ruddy bantam in his early thirties with brown hair and tufted chin-whiskers. The second was blade-thin and of middle height and had light merry eyes set in a face the color of shale. All three were dressed in faded flannel shirts and bandannas and leather chaparreras worn shiny in the knees.

"Earp, this here is Frank McLaury."

"We met." McLaury's twang was pure pioneer hard-scrabble, short and nasty. He looked at Wyatt, then away. The two had squared off over a string of stolen army mules some months earlier when Wyatt was a deputy sheriff and hard words had fallen.

"Joe Hill," said the thin man, grasping Wyatt's hand. A white grin gashed the dark face.

Ike said, "Joe was there when I put it to Frank, so I brung him in."

"Split it up as you please," said Wyatt. "It is still thirty-six hundred for the three or twelve hundred for each."

"I'm concerned about the strings on it," Hill said.

"You need not be. All I require from it is Leonardhead and Crane. As sheriff my first year's salary will be ten times the reward."

Ike grinned around a fresh plug. "Hell, we might could

turn them in our own selves and run for office. I guess I can wear a tailcoat."

Wyatt knocked out his pipe against his heel and made no response.

"What's to stop this rooster from arresting us all for knowing where to find them?"

Wyatt didn't look at McLaury. "Honest Johnny Behan would just lay all your guns and cartridge belts and truck on his desk and walk out of the room leaving the door open. I would trip over my spurs some night soon after and shoot myself in the back."

"If the rest of the crowd ever learns who turned up those fellows we would do the same," McLaury said.

"They will not learn of it from me."

McLaury snapped his tongue off his teeth and looked away.

Wyatt went on. "You move Leonardhead and Crane where I can drop the lariat around them and then I will collect the reward and hand it over to you in cash. You need not appear in the transaction."

Ike said, "I know Billy Leonard. You won't take them in kicking. Does that money go dead or alive?"

"It would be my guess."

"Guesses and promises," McLaury said. "That is how you Earps work."

Ike took aim at a dung-beetle and missed. The tobacco juice left a stain on the ground. He wiped his mouth. "Well, I will put no man's head in the noose for free gratis. You find out if that bounty goes both ways."

"I will have Marsh Williams wire Wells Fargo and ask."

SAN FRANCISCO CALIF

JUNE 7, 1881

MARSHALL WILLIAMS

TOMBSTONE ARIZONA

YES WE WILL PAY REWARDS FOR THEM DEAD OR ALIVE

L F ROWELL

"Who the hell is L. F. Rowell?" Ike handed the yellow flimsy to Frank McLaury.

"Assistant to John J. Valentine," Wyatt said, "president of Wells Fargo."

The four shared the shade under the awning in front of Dave Cohen's cigar store on Allen along with a four-foot wooden chief scarred all over with match-tracks. The day was dry and hot and the cattlemen, in town clothes now, had all shed their coats. Wyatt was sweating slightly under his Prince Albert. Across the street, James Earp's Sampling Room saloon and the office of the *Nugget* seemed to shimmer in the heat. A row of horses hung their heads at the hitching rail.

McLaury moved his lips as he read and gave the telegram to Joe Hill. "You did not give us up to Williams and this fellow Rowell?"

"I said I would not."

Ike said, "They are hid across the New Mexico line in Yreka. We can get them to come as far as Frank and Tom's ranch. We would take it as a kindness if you would jump them before they get there so it will look more proper. Soldier's Holes would be a place."

"What story will you tell them?"

"Frank come up with it."

"We will say a paymaster is on his way from Tombstone to Bisbee by that route to pay off the miners," McLaury said. "The devil will have them by the balls when they hear of it. They need the stake."

Ike shifted his plug. "Joe will carry the message. Folks trust Joe."

"It is my eyes." Grinning, Hill returned the flimsy to Wyatt.

He folded it twice and poked it into his vest pocket. "Let me know when you arrive at a date. I will have a posse on hand at Rabbit Springs on the Bisbee road. Naturally the reward will be less expenses for outfitting and horse hire."

"Hold on, we never said that."

"Ike, you still owe for that horse your brother Billy stole from me."

"You got that horse back!"

Hill said, "Let it go. How much can it come to?"

"Cross us up on this and next time it won't be just your horse," McLaury rapped.

Ike shrugged into his coat, flipping down the lapels. "Pleasure doing business with you, Marshal."

"I am a city police officer."

"Soon it will be sheriff."

Joe Hill unsnapped his fob and ran the chain through the buttonhole in his coat. "Who can I leave my watch and chain with before I ride out?" he asked Wyatt. "This town is full of thieves."

Wyatt took them, and didn't see the three again until after Tombstone burned to the ground.

CHAPTER 8

THE FIRE BEGAN WITH a barrel of whiskey and ended under several thousand gallons of water; and when it was over, the four blocks bounded to the north and south by Fremont and Toughnut streets and to the west and east by Fourth and Sixth streets had ceased to exist.

Talk had it that a number of customer complaints had caused a saloon keeper on Allen Street to take a barrel of Thistle Dew out of service. While measuring the amount he was returning to the distributor he lost his notched stick through the bunghole and called for his bartender to help fish it out. The bartender came over, forgetting about the lighted stump of cigar clamped in his teeth.

The sheet of flame singed both men's moustaches, scaled a brown muslin curtain, and spread across the pitch-smeared ceiling with a whump. From there it battered out a window to leap the alley to the hardware next door. Most of the buildings on Allen were board and batten, with common walls, and the fire rolled in an orange ball across the rooftops in front of a dry wind, limning windows until the panes tipped out and blistering the paint on suspended signs pushed horizontal by the heat. A case of cartridges went off in a gun shop with a crackle and a twang of bouncing lead and a stack of powder kegs exploded, lifting the roof and splaying the sideboards like a barrel bursting. But even that roar was lost in the rumble of the firestorm cartwheeling through the heart of town. A column of smoke as black and thick as a muckslide poured into the sky, leaving a stain visible from as far away as Tucson and Prescott. The bell in the firehouse clanged, steam whistles bellowed in the silver mountains, and Tombstone twisted and blackened like a scorpion in a skillet.

The town's pride was brought around, a fourth-class Jeffers Jigsaw steam fire engine, thirty-five hundred pounds of polished brass mounted on circus-wagon wheels with blurring flywheel and a seven-and-a-half-inch piston stroke that sounded like a cow pulling its feet out of a river bottom. But while the horses in the four-hitch team were broken to the racket, no one had thought or else known how to train them to behave around a conflagration, and four men in miners' helmets and dampened slickers were required to hold the plunging leaders while their companions socketed the pump to the main. The gauges measured, the pump began drawing, and then the limp canvas hose grew erect and ejaculated a blue-white geyser in a high spreading arch over the wall of fire.

The miracle was flawed. The pipeline from the Chiricahua springs was too long and poorly graduated, and the little pump was unequal to the pressure required. The geyser towered and fell and squirted and spluttered and the flames marched on. Men formed brigades, filling from the horse troughs and passing and offering bucketfuls to the blaze. Women sluiced down blankets and plunged smoldering brooms into the troughs and slapped the flames off awning posts and out of one another's skirts when they got too close. Eye-whites glittered in faces carved from soot and masked with bandannas from the noses down. Riderless horses set free from the corrals galloped up and down Allen whinnying and blowing.

By nightfall the devastated blocks formed right triangles of charred and fallen framework against a smudged sky, glowing in jointed sections like snakeweed. The homeless slept under friends' roofs and on the floor of Nellie Cashman's Russ House and crews stood watch outside in two-hour shifts for gusts and smoldering straw. In lighted kitchens firefighters applied axle grease to blistered hands and faces. No one had died, and when the sun rose over a gutted settlement the next day, the survivors would pluck that knowledge smoking from the ashes and polish it with self-congratulation until it gleamed.

At first light the Mexicans who followed that trade were pouring and baking adobe bricks at five times the usual speed and the first wagons departed for the Huachucas with axes and bucksaws for the materials required to raise Tombstone from its ashes. Saloon keepers sifted the remains of their establishments for undamaged fixtures, and men armed with pinch bars and sledgehammers knocked apart foundations and chimneys weakened by the flames and carted away charred beams and furniture in wheelbarrows.

Other individuals just as enterprising were at work.

Virgil Earp jangled shut the door of the *Epitaph* office on Fremont and crossed the sun-patched floor to take the hands of John Clum, standing behind his desk, and bank cashier Milton Clapp, who struggled up out of the depths of a horsehair armchair to put his feet on the floor and look up at the newcomer. Clapp was short and scarecrow-lean, all elbows and angles under his black suit, and wore large gold-rimmed spectacles whose thick lenses made his eyes appear swollen. Virgil nodded at Colonel William Herring, a man as large as himself but considerably broader across the middle, who kept his seat. The three men led the Citizens Safety Committee.

"Marshal, I am happy to see you are not a casualty." Clum retook his high-backed swivel and indicated an empty chair between the other two visitors with a hand swathed in bandages.

Virgil accepted the seat, sweeping his coat-frock behind the handle of his Army. "I took firebreak duty on Fourth. I got a blister off the axe handle." He showed his palm.

"George Parsons appears to have sustained the only injury worth noting," Clum said. "A balcony collapsed under him and he smashed his nose. I find it amazing that no one was hurt more seriously or killed. The Apaches would say that the sun and moon were smiling on us all yesterday."

"Except George," Virgil said.

"Except George." Clum frowned as the conversation

turned away from one of his favorite subjects, his three years as agent in charge of the San Carlos Apache reservation. "In any case we are presented with the opportunity to rebuild Tombstone along the lines of a proper city instead of a ramshackle arrangement of canvas and clapboard. To do that we must first smoke out the vermin."

"Lot jumpers," Virgil said.

"You are aware of them."

"You can't not be. Some of them have been squatting on what's left of the better saloons and sporting houses since before sunup. They are commencing to put up tents."

"It is a shabby business. The consensus, Clapp's and Colonel Herring's and mine, is that the man who was in possession of the lot when the fire broke out is the lot's legal owner, and that the courts will establish that in time. However, the process could take months."

"Meanwhile the lot jumpers are free to throw up their buildings as they please and the devil take aesthetics and the rights of the owner," Herring said.

Virgil stood. "Give me twenty-four hours."

Clum said, "Don't go off half-cocked."

"I am always at full cock."

"Propriety must be observed. This committee has only local sanction and we cannot afford to have Governor Fremont and the United States Army come haring in here on the pretense of establishing order. Cochise County is scarcely five months old and already they are blathering about us on the floor of Congress. A body count at this stage would undo all our fine intentions."

"Blame it on the fire."

"Some of these jumpers are supposed to be gun men," Clapp pointed out.

"Some of them are sure enough gun men," Virgil said. "I cannot tell my boys to leave their arms at home. A fine intention like that would make for a dandy body count and all of it on our side."

Clum ran a hand back over his bald head. His hair had begun to fall out before he was twenty and his political enemies considered the statesmanlike dearth responsible for his victory in the last election. "Concentrate upon putting the fear of God into them short of killing."

"That is night work."

"So long as it is done soon we don't care what time you do it," said Colonel Herring.

"Give me twenty-four hours."

By sunset the charred rubble on Fremont and Toughnut and at the upper end of Allen had produced a heavy crop of tents made from sticks and wagon sheeting in rounded heaps like mushrooms. In front of them the claimants prepared dinner in pots over fires built from the unburned debris, turning the air greasy with beans and bacon and prairie onions, the long barrels of horse pistols hugging their thighs. They tossed one another tobacco pouches and plugs and exchanged Cornish Jack jokes that grew steadily more coarse with the loss of light.

At dark the flames flickered in scattered bits like shreds of bright cloth. Nearing midnight they began to die out singly, then in clusters, and by the time the horsemen appeared on Allen there was not a spark in sight. The jumpers were dead asleep in their tents.

The first lasso whirled twice around with a low whistle, shot out straight, and landed with a plop around a tentpole on the corner of Sixth. Instantly the noose closed and the horse on the other end snorted at the bite of a rowel and galloped west bearing its rider. The tent fluttered off, exposing to starlight its occupant wrestling with his blanket. The pale light whitened further a sleepy frightened face surrounded by tousled hair.

"Lot jumper, you *git!*"

The sepulchral shout, coming from the darkness above him, tore the man to his feet and he bounded into the night, stumbling over the blanket tangled around his legs.

"Lot jumper, you *git!*"

It was a warm night and the second victim was clad only in long johns. He snatched up his boots and clothing and hobbled for cover, cursing shrilly when he stepped in the hot ashes of his own campfire. One of the riders laughed, a high-pitched bray.

"Lot jumper, you *git!*"

The third man tripped over a foundation stone and fell skidding into a pile of fresh horse-apples. He scrambled up smeared and ran, narrowly avoiding collision as another rider galloped past towing another collapsed tent. The man in the saddle cut loose with a rebel yell.

"*Git!*"

The operation swept north, placing the Milky Way at the marauders' backs and giving aroused sleepers glimpses of men in big hats and bandanna masks mounted on tall horses loaded down with iron. But few took the trouble to pause in their flight and look.

"*Git,* lot jumper!"

By Fremont Street, surprise was forfeit. The horsemen fired their pistols into the air and at uninhabited ruins, shattering panes not burst by the fire and letting water out of the troughs. Their lassos snatched away empty tents. They reared and wheeled and punched holes in the clouds and called upon God to bless the Union and upon God-fearing men to vote for Wyatt Earp for sheriff. The tents were flung into a pile on Allen and doused with coal oil and set to the match in a towering pyre. When the sun rose it found no canvas between Fremont and Toughnut and only the deed holders in possession of the burned lots.

That day's number of the *Epitaph* contained an editorial by John Clum denouncing this lawless method of foiling lawbreakers by undisciplined nightriders and commending the efforts of Police Chief Virgil Earp and his deputies to restore order.

On July 2, President James Abram Garfield was shot in the back while standing on the platform at the Baltimore & Potomac Station in Washington, D.C., waiting for a train to New England. His assailant was the Reverend Charles J. Guiteau, a failed office hopeful who claimed that God had commanded him to kill the President. Garfield was taken from the heat and malaria of Washington in summer to Elberon, New Jersey, where doctors were confident of his recovery.

While readers of the *Epitaph, Nugget,* and *Prospector* followed wire information on the President's condition, rumors reached Tombstone of a massacre in Skeleton Canyon in the Guadalupes near the Mexican border involving the Apaches and a party of Mexican muleskinners. Nineteen skinners had been slaughtered and seventy-five thousand dollars in silver bullion spirited away.

"Geronimo, you figure?" Doc Holliday, seated at his favorite drinking table in the Alhambra, drained the quart bottle into his glass and ordered another and a second beer for Wyatt. The place smelled of char from the fire damage to the gaming room and sawdust from the repairs. Hammers rattled and saws wheezed day and night as the town rebuilt itself like a cirrhoded liver.

Wyatt shook his head. "A mad dog like him has no need for bullion. He would have cut the packs off and taken the mules. Mule meat is worth more than silver to an Apache, Clum says."

"Who if not him?"

"Your friend Billy Leonard needs a stake."

"It requires more hands than he is comfortable using."

"Stilwell, then," Wyatt said. "Or Curly Bill."

"Stilwell is in town playing deputy. When you say Curly Bill you are also saying Ike Clanton, and Ike is a cow thief."

"*Mexican* cows. Dry-gulching greasers is not the same as killing white men. I have not seen Ike since before the fire."

Doc thumbed the cork out of the fresh bottle. "He has not got the brains nor the sand. It was the old man if it was anyone in that clan."

"The old man is too old and stiff for that work. His boys done it for him."

"I have not seen Ringo or Rattlesnake Bill Johnson in a month of Sundays." Doc sucked whiskey off his moustaches.

"One bad chip is pretty much like all the rest in the stack."

"If it was Ike we will know it soon enough. He will try to buy every pot on Allen and bed every whore betwixt here and Benson. Before Tombstone came along I bet there isn't a knothole in the territory he didn't bugger."

Wyatt said, "It is no worry of ours either way."

"Worrying isn't in my nature."

"No, you crap rabbit ice."

Doc topped off his glass. "The poor dumb fornicating greasers. If the President is not safe they don't none of them stand a snowball's chance on an alkali flat."

"We are living in a hard time."

"It has been all hard times since Honest Ape got inaugurated."

"You seceshes will keep on fighting that war." Wyatt finished his beer and hauled out his watch.

"Set a spell," Doc said.

"I promised Sadie I would go riding with her in the morning."

"She'll keep."

Wyatt closed the face. "Kate isn't home?"

"She got a straw up her ass over something and is selling it down Toughnut again."

"Christ, Doc."

"She will be back. No one else will put up with her."

"I don't know why you do."

"She is the only one who will put up with the cough. If she has not caught it by now she never will. Most like." He got out his handkerchief, spat in it, looked at it, folded it, and put it away. He drank. His Adam's apple bobbed twice and he set down the glass empty.

"Colorado is the country for you," Wyatt said.

"My luck is here."

Kate wasn't on Toughnut, but in the Arcade Saloon a block up Allen with her chins resting on her arms on a table in one of the curtained rooms in back that had not been touched by the fire. Her shoulders were bare above a lavender dress she had just bought from Glover's because Doc had burned all the others except her ginghams and she sat with her feet hooked under the rung of her chair and the toes turned inward. She was making a chain across the tabletop with rings from her glass.

"That goddamn foxy con man has cast a wicked spell over Doc that's been his ruin." She mumbled and sucked spittle out of the way of her tongue. "Not that Doc's bound for heaven in a brass buggy. But he's a sick man drinking to stay alive and can't help himself. Wyatt drove him to this like he drove him to the doings at Dodge and every place else since Fort Griffin."

"Drove him to what?"

She focused on the dapper small man seated across from her wearing a sombrero. She'd forgotten she was sharing the table with Sheriff Behan. She smiled crookedly and waggled a finger above the smeared glass.

"You're just sore mad at Wyatt on account of he stole that stuck-up little tart Sadie Marcus right off your little cock. I bet it is little like the rest of you. Little Johnny Behan with his big hat and his little cock. I bet you have to take off the hat when you piss or it gets lost in the shadow."

Milt Joyce, the Cochise County supervisor, grinned. A narrow man with a black mariner's beard and round-nailed clerk's hands, he stood near the curtained entrance twirling an elk's tooth on the end of his watch chain.

"Bring us another bottle," Behan rapped.

When the cork was pulled Kate brightened, extending her glass for refilling. A purple-blue welt showed along the line of her right cheekbone. Behan said, "Swine beat women."

She touched the welt. "He don't mean to, it is just the whiskey. When the cough gets to sawing at his insides he has to drink to make them numb. It is like when you have a tooth pulled." Her face twisted into a comic mask of pity. "He was an honest dentist before the cough and before he took up with that Earp crowd."

"It is painful to see a fine man brought so low," Joyce offered.

Behan wrapped a hand around his glass and pretended to drink. "I heard he shot a nigger in a swimming hole and that's why he had to leave Georgia."

"You heard a lie. Doc never killed anyone in his life." She took a long swallow.

"Maybe it was Leonard killed Philpot and that passenger."

She almost choked for laughing and Joyce had to come forward and clap her on the back. She sat with her bosom heaving and drank again. A nipple peeped above the ruffled top of her dress.

"Are you all right?" asked Joyce.

Behan told him to shut up. He was staring hard at Kate.

"Billy Leonard could not get out of his own way with a rifle," she said. "Doc can shoot rings around him sober."

"Did he shoot Philpot?"

She looked at him again and smiled, breathing through her mouth. "Little Johnny. You got any hair left at all under that big hat?"

"Sloppy-titted whore." He slumped back in his seat and took a drink in earnest.

Joyce topped off her glass. "Tombstone is no place for the gentlefolk," he said. "They make one mistake and then they must keep on making them until they stretch a rope."

"A woman does not count for horseshit here. If she did I would have left that goddamn whiskey-soaked tooth-pulling shotgun killer years ago."

"You said he never killed anyone."

She wasn't listening. "A woman does not count for horseshit. Ask Mattie Earp, scrubbing Wyatt's drawers just so Sadie can pull them down."

"Rum old twat," said Behan.

Joyce said, "What Doc needs is time behind bars to think about his past life and how he has treated you."

"He was behind bars in Fort Griffin," she said. "I set fire to the livery and got him out when everyone was off fighting the fire. He has forgotten that, I bet."

"He needs reminding."

"We had like a honeymoon after that in Dodge. We was Dr. and Mrs. Holliday there."

"Have another snort."

Behan took the deposition out of his inside breast pocket and spread it out on the table facing her.

"I can't read them words," she said.

"It is a statement saying you were present when Holliday confessed to the attempted robbery of the Benson stage and the killing of Bud Philpot," said Joyce. He pulled the stopper out of a bottle of India ink and dipped a horsehair pen inside. "He cannot ignore you once he has seen this."

"He will kill me."

"Sheriff Behan will see he does not." He shook off the extra drops and held out the pen.

She took it, swaying. "Johnny has lost his woman and his hair. It's no comfort."

"Well, if you would prefer going back to Doc."

She shrugged and signed her name all over the bottom of the sheet.

CHAPTER 9

"THEY ARE ALL DEAD," said Morgan.

"Who is?"

"Leonard, Crane, and Head. Old Man Clanton too."

Wyatt resumed blacking his boot. He had one shirtsleeved arm inside it to the shoulder and a horsehair brush in his other hand. "You see them?"

"Seen their graves. Leonard and Head's, anyway. Jim Crane and the old man are buried clear out in Guadalupe Canyon where the greasers left them." Morgan had on a filthy duster and his pinch hat had lost all shape. His boots were caked with mud and red clay; it was the rainy season out on the desert. His stubble had grown out red.

"Tell it."

"It is like Joe Hill said. Crane and the old man and some others got bushwhacked by friends of them Mexican muleskinners they killed for bullion and Bill and Ike Haslett gunned Leonard and Head when they tried sticking up the Hasletts's store in Huachita."

"Hill said it was horse thieves killed Leonard and Head."

"It was his only lie."

"They die instant?"

"Leonard hung on for a spell, they told me."

"Say anything?"

"Nothing we can use."

For a time the whisking of Wyatt's brush was the only sound. They had been conversing in murmurs because Sadie was in the next room dressing for dinner and a play at Schieffelin Hall. Wyatt had moved his things out of the house on Fremont into the building Sadie had shared with Johnny Behan when they were living as man and wife. Of late she had begun signing for parcels as Mrs. Wyatt Earp. This was a source of no small embarrassment when Mattie's parcels started showing up at Sadie's door.

"The Hasletts?" Wyatt asked.

Morgan moved a shoulder. "Curly Bill has swore to get them. He will be taking over as head of that San Pedro outfit now that the old man is gone. Ike Clanton is as dumb as a fencepost."

"If Curly Bill says he will get them they are as good as in the ground. He will take Ringo and half of Galeyville and Charleston with him."

"That is how Bill generally does things," Morgan said. He stood stock still on the carpet, afraid of shedding dust on Sadie's fine things from San Francisco. The room was crammed with tables and shawls and tassled pillows and fat vases and lamps with fringed shades and a portable pump organ and a phonograph with a big daisy horn and conch shells holding down stacks of songsheets on every available surface. Wyatt was sitting on a floral mohair davenport with an apron around the legs and doilies pinned to the arms. A man couldn't turn around or fart without knocking over something he couldn't afford to replace.

"Leonard squawked like a caponed rooster." Wyatt pulled on the gleaming boot and stood up, supporting himself with a hand on Morgan's shoulder while he stamped his heel home. A cut-crystal lamp wobbled on a pedestal table with a base smaller than its top. "Named Luther King and Jim Crane and Harry Head as his only associates in the holdup. Old Curly Bill will do us a kindness yet by gunning the only two who could contradict it."

"It won't get Doc off. I heard about that paper Kate put her name to."

"You let me and Doc see to that. You did your part." He put on his Prince Albert and smoothed the skirt over his American. "There is food in the kitchen if you care to rustle yourself something while we're out."

"Thanks, I'll go home where if I break something it is already paid for."

White teeth showed behind Wyatt's handlebars. "First morning I woke up here I thought I was back in Jim's whorehouse in Dodge."

"Jim's place was never like this."

"Jim's girls were never like Sadie."

The play was about a girl who was in love with a boy accused of being a thief. At the end the detective who had been following him since the first act took pity on his story and let him go. Wyatt preferred Shakespeare, but Sadie admired the girl's ruffled pink dress. After the curtain he saw Sadie home and walked from there to James Earp's house on Fremont. There, the oldest of the five brothers, forty and thinning on top, with neat horseshoe moustaches laid over a round beard, opened the back door and stood aside in his vest to let Wyatt enter. James's left arm, crippled by Confederate grapeshot at Fredericktown, hung stiff at his side. Of the Earps he was the only one shorter than six feet.

"I sent Nellie and Hattie over to spend the night with Allie," he said.

Wyatt nodded. The big kitchen was full of family and two outsiders. Virgil was there with his cravat undone, and Warren, the youngest, slumped in a ladder chair with one arm hooked over the back and his right ankle resting on his left knee in a pose Wyatt recognized as one of his own. Warren was smoking a General Arthur and when he turned his head to greet the brother he most admired, lamplight glistened on his downy upper lip.

Doc sat at the bare table dealing himself blackjack from his lucky Prescott deck. Across from him, sideways to the table, sat Kate with her hair plastered flat to her big skull and a cape over her shoulders, looking a good ten years older than the last

time Wyatt had seen her. Both of her hands were wrapped
around a thick white china mug.

"Drink it," Virgil said. "Don't warm your hands on it."

"I am up to here with coffee." Her voice creaked.

"That is the idea."

She made no effort to raise the mug. Her nose and eyes
were running.

"Warren."

Warren arose with primal grace and scooped a blue
stoneware bath pitcher off the table and upended it over the
woman's head in the same movement. She squealed and
spluttered and absorbed more of the icy water in her hair and
clothes than reached the washtub at her feet. Virgil caught the
mug before she dropped it, dumped its diluted contents into the
tub, and refilled it from the pot boiling on the stove. He thrust
it into her hands. "Drink."

Her teeth chattered a full five seconds before she could get
the word out. "B-bastard."

"Bitch. Drink."

She raised the mug in both hands and gulped.

"How long?" Wyatt asked.

"Better part of an hour," said James. "I'm running out of
coffee."

"Salt?"

Virgil belched. "Shit. I forgot."

James caught Warren's eye. "In the shed."

Warren set down the empty pitcher and went out. He
returned carrying a five-pound canvas sack and chunked it in
the center of the table.

James said, "We aren't curing a side of beef."

"If you wanted it in handfuls you should of said." Warren
sat down.

Virgil pried the mug out of Kate's hands, tipped a handful
of caked salt from the sack inside, and leveled it off with coffee
from the pot. Kate glared at the mixture with eyes shot pink.

"I won't drink that."

He struck her ear with the heel of his hand. She reeled and
would have fallen off the chair, but he hooked his fingers in the
matted hair at the back of her head and pulled back hard and

jammed the mug against her teeth. "Drink it or I'll shove it up your wobbly ass, cup and all."

She struggled, but he had her braced over the back of the chair, starting her eyes and exposing the whole of the blurred line of her throat. When she opened her mouth to gasp he tilted the mug. Coffee streamed down her chin and stained the front of her dress. Her throat worked and she coughed like a swimmer inhaling water but he slanted the mug until it was empty and stood back, releasing her hair. She choked and sprayed snot. A sound like a steam pump drawing began deep inside her. "Watch your boots," warned Virgil, retreating another step himself just as Kate bent forward and spewed into the washtub between her feet.

When it was over she remained in that position, head hanging, hands dangling between her knees, vomit dripping off her chin. Warren made a disgusted sound and got up and opened the door to let in fresh air.

Virgil scooped a towel off the back of the chair Warren had vacated and threw it at her. "Clean up."

A minute went by before she stirred. Then she picked up the towel and began mopping her face mechanically. By then the Earps were gathered in the corner by the cookstove. Doc pocketed his cards and got up to join them.

"What do you think?" Wyatt asked.

Virgil said, "I think she is going to be one sick whore."

"Not that."

James lit a cigar one-handed and flipped the match atop the stove among the curled corpses of its ancestors. "A whore is what she is. Whores always know what's best for whores."

"When they are sober," Doc said. "I sure am sorry about this, Wyatt."

Wyatt said, "The best way you can show it is to fire her out of town as soon as this thing is done. She has already cost Virge and me five thousand in bail money that is not doing either of us good sitting in the courthouse safe."

"I have been in jail before. I could have stood it."

"Billy Blab would be out back taking a leak when the stranglers came for you. And I would be a sorry sheriff's candidate with a friend in jail for murder."

"Think Billy squats to make water?" Warren was grinning.

Virgil rubbed at a coffee stain on his shirtcuff. "I talked with old man Fuller today, Doc. You caught up with him hauling water into town at four o'clock the day of the Benson stage thing. You hitched your horse to the back of the water wagon and rode in with him, got in about six."

Doc had paused to tip up a pocket flask whose silver plate had begun to flake off, exposing dull tin beneath. He heeled the cork back in. "Did I stop for a drink?"

"The stage was in the valley by six and you could not have got to Drew's in time to stick it up at ten," Virgil said. "Fuller will swear to it in court."

"His boy Wes is no friend." He put away the flask.

"He is less of a friend to the old man. Others remember that you were dealing faro at the Alhambra that night. Kate is the only witness to say different."

"And we have Kate," said Wyatt.

"Yes," Doc said. "We have Kate."

They kept Kate through the night. The coffee ran out by midnight and after that they flushed her out with warm water and salt and rewarded her afterward with a glass of brandy that she picked up once in both hands and set down empty. Virgil and Wyatt took turns talking to her in low voices and occasionally cuffing her while Doc skinned Warren at monte and James read George McClellan's memoirs in the parlor. He fell asleep with the lamp burning. Kate made three trips to the outhouse while Warren stood guard outside. At dawn James's wife, Nellie, returned with her daughter Hattie and helped Kate clean herself up and lent her an old dress and shawl for the walk to the jail to finish sobering up. Nellie, herself a former prostitute, was a big woman and she scrubbed her down and buttoned her up with masculine thoroughness and a minimum of sympathy. She had overseen Hattie's whipping for her indiscretion with one of the McLaurys with similar detachment.

Doc touched Virgil's arm as the latter was escorting Kate out. Her face was bloated and blotchy and her eyes were smudges, but she was steady.

"She has no need to be locked up. She will stick now that she has seen the elephant. She always does."

Wyatt said, "We cannot count on that. Virgil will see to her comfort."

Virgil opened the back door. "Let's go, Kate. I am arresting you for public drunkenness and throwing up in the tub that Nellie boils Jim's shirts in."

Doc told her good night.

The bloat had gone down and she was dressed in new calico and a bustle, with a lace handkerchief in her sleeve, when she laid her hand on the Bible in Justice Wells Spicer's courtroom on Fremont a few days later. She took her seat in the maple chair beside the bench and identified her signature sprawled on the bottom of a whiskey-stained square of paper for the county prosecutor, a wide man with a hangman's noose of brown beard spilling to his watch chain. He asked her if she was aware of the contents of the document.

She brushed lint off her skirt. "I remember signing some sort of paper when I was out tossing drinks with little Johnny Behan and Milt Joyce. I disremember what was written on it or if there was anything written on it at all."

Spicer, rumpled and balding with unremarkable features crowded into the center of a spoon-shaped face, gaveled the room to silence, warned Sheriff Behan against uttering obscenities in a court of law, and eventually dismissed the case against John Henry Holliday for attempted stage robbery and murder.

Back at Fly's boardinghouse, Kate found her carpetbag by the door and Doc stretched out in his vest on the bed. His eyes were open and especially luminous, always a sign of imminent seizure. A bottle stood on the floor near his hand.

"Look around for anything I missed," he said. "You have two hours before the Kinnear stage leaves for Benson. You can take the train anywhere from there."

"I have friends in Globe." She didn't move.

"Go to Globe then."

"I haven't money for a ticket."

"Your gloves are there on the table."

After a moment she stepped to the writing table and picked

up the kid leather gloves, stained at the fingertips now and missing a pearl button, that she had ordered from Chicago after Doc's big score in Prescott. A thick sheaf of crisp paper currency slid out of one.

"It is another five hundred I owe Wyatt," he said.

She put the gloves and the bills in her reticule. "I will write when I get settled."

"If you want."

At the door she turned. "Who will look after you when you are in a bad way? Not Wyatt."

"The same person who did it before you."

"You were not so bad then."

"Nothing was."

"You and Morgan are always talking about Billy Breakenridge." Color climbed her cheeks. "If people knew about you and Wyatt maybe they would talk about you."

Another time he would have been off the bed and clouting her. He didn't move. She knew then that he was sick. Emboldened, she said, "You will write asking me to come back."

He said nothing.

She let herself out carrying her carpetbag.

And she would come back.

Late-summer heat lapped at the puddles left by the monsoons and cracked their beds when they were gone. On its heels came the winds of autumn, hot and dry when they blew up from old Mexico and coldly carnivorous when they swept down from the snow peaks of the Rincons, pushing icy rain before them. It stitched up the sand and brought an odor of scorched earth and rusty iron. In the mud near Hereford on September 8, four men stopped the Bisbee stage in an arroyo, removed the Wells Fargo strongbox and a mail sack containing $2,500, and took $750 in cash and jewelry from the four passengers. The driver was a weatherworn intimate of the saloons in Tombstone and Charleston who identified two of the robbers as Pete Spence, a neighbor of the Earps on Fremont, and Frank Stilwell, lately Deputy Stilwell of Cochise County.

Sheriff Behan placed Billy Breakenridge in charge of a posse made up of Deputy Dave Neagle, local Wells Fargo agent Marshall Williams, Fred Dodge, and, at Williams's insistence, Wyatt and Morgan Earp. They followed tracks sunk deep in gray mud through the Mule Mountains to Bisbee, a miners' sprawl of adobe dugouts and frame shacks pegged into the side of a hill, where Breakenridge dismounted first, muttering something about catching a bite.

Morgan said, "Don't let us find you catching it with Stilwell."

Breakenridge turned, opened his mouth, then closed it and moved off.

"Little cunt," Morgan said.

The remaining group broke into two parties. After twenty minutes, Wyatt, Williams, and Dodge entered a saloon with clay walls and a mud floor, where Wyatt sat down at Stilwell's table, laid his American on top of it, and told the man sitting there he was under arrest.

"What for?" Stilwell refilled his glass from the clear bottle on the table.

"For losing your bootheel back there on the trail and having a new one put on here. Fred found the old heel in the Mules and we just came from the bootmaker's."

Stilwell bent his mouth into a smile. He was clean-shaven—an anomaly on the frontier—but for a brown stubble, and wore a slouch hat on the back of his head and one of his trademark short cigars screwed into a corner of his mouth. The cigar was a prop; he was scarcely older than young Warren. He wasn't wearing his star but the holes were plain in his vest.

"I collect taxes for the county," he said. "I have no need to go around throwing down on stages."

Fred Dodge, a gambler acquaintance of Wyatt's who looked uncannily like Morgan Earp in his slicker and parlor handlebars, lit a cigarette and dropped the match sizzling into Stilwell's glass. "Who said anything about a stage robbery?"

Wyatt said, "Frank, everyone knows you have throwed down on so many the horses gee up to your voice quicker than they do to the drivers'."

"Why trouble over it, Wyatt? You know I will be cut loose

ten minutes after I see Johnny." He frowned at the match
floating in his whiskey.

"Troubling over things is what I do best, Frank."

"Don't get tight-ass with me. You are just out to make
Johnny look small."

"He doesn't need help."

"I count that raw talk for a friend of that stage-robbing
tinhorning whore's-son of a lunger Doc Holliday."

"He is standing behind you, Frank." Wyatt sounded
dreamy.

Stilwell's color started to change. Then the bent smile
flickered back and he crooked a finger to flip ash off the end of
the cigar without taking it from his mouth. The column fell to
the table. "The place is backed into a hill and even he is not
skinny enough to slide down the stovepipe."

"I lied, Frank. It was worth it to see you unload in your
drawers."

"The trouble with you men after office is you disremember
who your friends are."

"If I did that we would have come in shooting. There may
be shooting yet."

Dodge was standing by the table with his gun handle
showing and Marshall Williams was cradling a Winchester in
the doorway. Stilwell let out his breath and presented his Colt's
pocket Navy by the barrel with the butt pointed up.

Wyatt made no move to accept it. Lamplight lay flat on his
blue eyes. Stilwell smiled again and rotated the pistol so that the
butt faced down. Wyatt took it.

"Curly Bill taught me the border roll," Stilwell said. "He
used it on Fred White."

"I heard it Fred shot himself when he went to disarm Bill."
Wyatt handed the weapon to Dodge, who spun the cylinder
with a noise like a snake's rattle and stuck it in his belt.

"Maybe. I never featured that circus shit to work on a real
lawman anyway."

"I am a businessman." Wyatt stood, picking up the
American. "Let's go see how Morg and Neagle are coming
along with your pard."

"What about my drink? Dodge spoiled it."

Wyatt stuck his fingers inside the glass and plucked out the match. "Drink up, Frank."

Stilwell swept the glass bumping and splashing across the floor.

"You Earps are high now," he said, rising. "The sun don't shine on the same dog's ass all day."

"That's real original, Frank. I learn something new every time I arrest you."

Pete Spence, a man nearly as thin as Doc, with animal eyes and no chin, was surprised in his bedroll outside Bisbee by Morgan Earp and Dave Neagle and taken into custody without a shot fired on either side. The two parties backtracked through the Mules with a prisoner to each and Billy Breakenridge riding liaison between them.

"Don't worry, Billy," Morgan told him. "If we have to shoot them we will save their assholes for you."

In Tombstone, Sheriff Behan claimed county jurisdiction over Stilwell and Spence, but Williams swore out federal warrants with Virgil Earp as deputy United States marshal for robbery of the mails. Virgil and Wyatt had the pair manacled and trundled them onto the Tucson stage and rode along to see them bound over for trial.

In Elberon, New Jersey, on September 19, James A. Garfield drew his last breath, a big one. Chester Alan Arthur, a fifty-year-old Vermont native, was sworn in as twenty-first President of the United States. Wyatt saw a sketch of him in the Tucson paper and thought he looked like a buffalo bull he had shot topping a cow in Kansas. Virgil hoped he was a better Republican than his predecessor.

The brothers were still absent from Tombstone on October 11 when Milt Joyce, who in addition to his post as county supervisor had recently bought into the Oriental, bent the arm of a drunken and fevered Doc Holliday and hurled him through the batwings into Allen Street. Doc lay for a time in the dust and manure, then pulled himself up an awning post, jerked down the points of his fouled vest, and swayed back inside with a hand in the side pocket of his coat.

"Whore-liquoring son of a bitch." The pocket lining tore

and his Colt's Lightning reared up vomiting flame. Bottles burst behind the bar.

Chairs turned over. Joyce, coming around the bar at the opposite end of the oiled floor, clawed a Schofield out of his hip pocket and closed the ten feet that separated them in a lunge. Doc fired again and Parker, Joyce's partner, fell behind the bar with a curse. Joyce and Doc collided and the barrel of the Schofield opened a gash over Doc's left ear and they fell in a tangle with Joyce on top. The Colt's exploded again as they grappled, Doc clawed at Joyce's face with his free hand, Joyce sank his teeth into the web of flesh between Doc's thumb and forefinger. The Schofield flashed up again, but a hand caught Joyce's wrist and wrenched it and a second bystander clubbed Doc with his forearm and jammed the heel of his hand between the Colt's hammer and the chamber and pried the pistol loose from his grasp. By this time the room was a haze and the air stank of rotten eggs.

A ball had smashed the big toe of Parker's left foot. Another had torn through Joyce's right hand while he and Doc were grappling and pierced the embossed tin ceiling over the bar. Justice Wells Spicer heard both sides and fined Doc $20 for assault and battery and costs of $11.25. Morgan Earp, reading of the incident in the *Nugget,* remarked to his woman Lou that Doc never could hit a board fence when he was drinking.

After settling with the court clerk, Doc packed his valise and boarded the Kinnear & Company stage for Benson.

He came back with Kate.

CHAPTER 10

IKE CLANTON EMBROIDERED A wandering pattern between
tables at the Alhambra, leaning heavily on chairs and seated
patrons and occasionally pausing to take a new sight on his
objective, Wyatt Earp sitting in for Doc Holliday behind the
cue box at Doc's faro table. Ike's face was shot with broken
vessels and the knee of his black trousers glistened where he had
spat tobacco at the ground and missed. The crown of his hat
grazed a Chesterfield lamp, looping shadows up the walls, but
he made no notice. He dropped heavily into the chair opposite
Wyatt. He smelled of horse and whiskey.

"Feeling lucky today?" Wyatt restacked the chips Ike had
spilled and slid the card counters into position. He had his coat
off and red silk garters on his sleeves.

"I looked for you in the Oriental."

"That place is commencing to take on a bad reputation."

"It has one less skunk in it today."

Wyatt went on straightening the stack. "You are drunker
than you look to say that to me."

"You been braying all around about our transaction," Ike
said. "I told you if it gets back to Curly Bill and the rest I am
buzzard shit."

"I never told anyone."

"Marshall Williams knows all about it. He treed me just now."

"Is he drinking?"

"Some."

Wyatt struck a match and warmed a General Arthur end to end, turning it. "Marsh is shooting at the moon. He sent the telegram to San Francisco asking after the reward and I suppose he has seen us talking. I guess it is too much to hope you didn't blow off and give up the whole story." He lit the cigar.

"He knows anyway. You told him."

"Yes, I run around telling everyone who will listen about my schemes to make sheriff that don't pan out."

"Frank said what we would do if you peached."

"I am a dead man twice then, because he has already told Morgan he is fixing to kill us all for arresting his friends Stilwell and Spence."

"Well, you told Doc Holliday. He never sent no telegrams nor saw us talking."

"Doc and Billy Leonard were friendly. Why would I tell him I was laying for Leonard?"

"He is a talking drunk, and he has been telling everyone."

Wyatt shuffled the deck. "He has been out of town for ten days. I don't see how he could have spread much around. But he is coming in on the six o'clock stage. We will hear what he has to say."

They played until five, when Ike ran out of money. He bought a bottle on credit and sat alone at a table outside the gaming room, where a couple of Charleston acquaintances looking in to see who was in town hovered, then moved on when they saw he was drinking and not talking. After a while he laid his head down on his arms and began snoring. Wyatt shook him awake when it was time and gave him a shoulder on the way to the Wells Fargo office three doors up Allen. It was a day without wind, a breather before the parched gales of autumn; skirts and coattails hung pole-steady and dust lay flat in the street, rising reluctantly when the stagecoach swept down it, then settling like paint.

Doc had on a duster over his gray suit and an apricot-

colored shirt. When he helped Kate Fisher down in front of the
office in a bonnet and broadcloth cape, Wyatt looked straight
through her.

"Doc, did I ever let on to you that Ike Clanton and I were
in any deal together?"

Doc glanced at Ike, leaning half-aware inside the office
doorway with the front of his trousers damp. "No."

"Ike says I did."

"Ike's a liar."

"You been braying it all around." Ike's eyes moved into
focus one at a time.

"Braying what all around?"

Ike opened his mouth, became aware of the crowd
gathered on the boardwalk to meet the stage, and closed it. He
lurched out of the doorway and weaved off, bumping into
people. Doc watched him with eyes fever-bright.

"Watch out for those loud ones. They have a way of
finding people who will listen to them."

"If Curly Bill or Ringo is one of them they will quiet him
soon enough. How was Tucson?"

"Better than Globe."

Wyatt let the challenge ride. "I heard you had a difficulty in
the Oriental while I was away."

"If Joyce has not died of lead poisoning because of that
hand I don't feel like talking about it." Doc caught Kate's
carpetbag from the driver. The sudden weight staggered him.
He was thinner than Wyatt remembered and there was a pepper
of blood on his right shirtcuff. Wyatt reached to take the bag
but Kate got to it first. He asked Doc if he was all right.

"Just thirsty."

"He'll be all right when I get him to bed." Kate wasn't
looking at Wyatt. "He should not be standing out here in the
air."

"Right, I need smoke and whiskey."

"Alhambra?" Wyatt suggested.

"Oriental."

Kate said something and walked away from them carrying
her bag.

Doc looked grim. "She has commenced to go temper-
ance."

"You have Jim's salt to thank for that," Wyatt said.
"Doc—"

"What's this transaction with Ike?" Doc asked.

After a moment Wyatt picked up Doc's valise and went
with him to the Oriental and didn't bring up the subject of
Kate.

Some hours later Wyatt let himself into the house he shared
with Sadie and undressed in the dark. His nightshirt rustled as
he climbed into bed beside her. She smelled beer.

"You're awake," he said.

"I have not slept. Marietta Spence was here tonight."

"I don't want you talking with anyone connected to that
stage-robbing crowd. The *Nugget* has made enough hay of me
and Doc and that Benson thing as it stands."

"I came to Tombstone with Marietta. She is a friend." She
sat up. In the dark she smelled of lemon verbena and soap. "She
heard Pete talking with Frank McLaury. Frank and Ike are
going to call you and Virgil and Morgan out and then Pete and
the rest are going to kill you from ambush."

For a moment he breathed and said nothing.

"When is this fixed to take place?"

"She did not know." Sadie paused. "I believe her."

"It is big-hearted of Pete to take her in."

"Women hear things. You men forget we are around.
Marietta says Pete has not been fit to be with since he got out on
bond. She has a black eye."

"Ike is mostly blow."

"Frank McLaury is not."

He breathed. "Ike has been squawking to all who will sit
still for it about how he has no transaction with me. It is like
Curly Bill to crowd him and Frank into proving they are not
back-stickers by calling us out. Curly Bill will turn most any
situation to his profit."

"What has he against you and your brothers?"

"Nothing personal. You cannot help but like Curly Bill. It
is just business. Hold Tombstone, hold the county. And we
hold Tombstone."

"What are you going to do?"

He groped in the darkness and found the tie to her nightdress. "Crowd Ike into doing something stupid."

The autumn winds came, slowing the work on roofs burned away in June and hammocking brown dust in door-frames and window casings. Mornings they carried a chill off the snow mountains, frosting windows and coaxing steam like smoke from the corrals where horses huddled.

At one o'clock on the morning of October 26, 1881, a greatcoated Doc Holliday followed Ike Clanton into the lunch room off the main room of the Alhambra and stood over him at the counter grinning. Doc's ears stuck out and his skin was shrunken over bone like a comic mask of jolly Death.

"What will you have, you son of a bitch of a cattle-stealing cowboy?"

The room was anything but deserted at that late hour. At sundown the underground life of Tombstone opened its eyes and crawled out of a hundred burrows, and when the store-keepers snuffed out their lamps and candles the bartenders started the pilots burning on the gas-powered ceiling fans and the dealers broke open fresh decks for the miners coming down from the mountains on ore wagons and the cowboys riding up from the valley on roping horses and buckboards to see the elephant. The pace was as brisk as nine A.M. and the hours were the same only reversed, so that at midnight the lunch trade rivaled that of noon. Crockery rattled, and stopped rattling at Doc's high-pitched drawl.

Ike finished tucking his checked napkin inside his collar. "I am not after trouble."

"You have been using my name."

"I have not."

"You are a damned liar."

Morgan, drinking on the saloon side, set down his glass. "Give me that scattergun," he said.

The balding bartender glanced down at the sawed-off twelve-gauge in its rack under the bar and shook his head. Morgan took out his Colt's, checked the load, and swung himself over the counter that separated the saloon from the lunch room.

Ike used a corner of his napkin to wipe tobacco spittle out of his beard. He was almost sober, although his face was still puffy and the color of cardboard. Behind Doc he spotted Morgan Earp sitting on top of the lunch counter, his cravat undone and a liverish flush on his face. Ike said nothing.

"I hear you are going to kill the Earps," Doc said. "Get out your pistol and commence with me." His white hand rested between the lapels of his coat.

"I never said I would kill no one. Fetch whoever says I did and I will prove him a liar."

"Are you going to jerk your gun, you whore-walloping little lickspittle?"

"I have no gun."

"You cowboy sons of bitches go heeled wherever you go. Jerk yours and go to fighting if there is any grit in you."

Ike stood, catching his balance on the counter. Doc backed up a step. His hand was inside his coat now. Ike started past him toward the street door.

"You son of a bitch, if you are not heeled, go and heel yourself."

Morgan hopped off the counter and stood in Ike's path. The pistol was back in his pocket with its dull black gutta-percha handle eared out. "Yes, you son of a bitch, you can have all the fight you want right now."

"I don't want any of it now." Ike went around him.

Virgil Earp stood outside on the boardwalk with a mackinaw on over his deputy marshal's star. Wyatt joined him as Ike stepped out but said nothing. Morgan Earp came up behind Ike and spun him by the shoulder. "You'd best be heeled when you come back out on the street."

They were all on the boardwalk now, Doc supporting himself against the doorframe. He looked more sick than drunk, but Ike was getting lighter in the head just smelling his breath and Morgan's. Virgil said, "Take Doc home, Morg. Ike, go back to the Grand and sleep it off."

"I don't want to be shot in the back."

Morgan inhaled sharply through his nose and clothing

rustled. Wyatt strode past Ike and caught his brother's arm. "This won't do."

"I was just going to buffalo the son of a bitch."

"There will be no buffaloing done tonight unless I do it," Virgil said. "Get the hell away from here, Ike."

After a moment Ike struck off across Allen. His great shoulders were bunched so that from behind, his hat appeared to be resting on top of them. The rest of the group broke up, Doc and Morgan starting up Fourth and Virgil going into the Occidental. Wyatt headed for Fifth. Boots clonked the boards behind him and he turned, backing into the shadows. Ike stopped. His bulk carved a black hole out of the corner gaslight.

"Earp, will you walk with me a ways?"

Wyatt slackened a notch. "If it is not too far. I have a game in the Eagle Brewery to close."

They turned the corner together. Ike was looking down at the scuffed toes of the boots he had had made in Tappanier's in June.

"I was not fixed right when Holliday come up on me in the lunch room. I am now if he is still about."

"He has gone to bed."

"We will have man for man in the morning then. This fight talk has been going on for a long time and I guess it is about time we fetched it to a close."

"I'll fight no one if I can get away with it," Wyatt said. "There is no money in fighting."

They stopped in front of the door in the beveled corner of the Eagle Brewery. Liquid yellow lamplight angled out, throwing their shadows into Fifth Street. Ike's eyes were dead in his fleshed face.

"You must not think I won't be after you all in the morning."

The two separated there and Ike went to the Occidental, where he played poker until daylight with Tom McLaury, Johnny Behan, and Virgil Earp, who dealt with his big Colt's Army resting in his lap. The betting was lively and the talk was all of the game.

★ ★ ★

Harry Jones found Wyatt Earp with his coat off counting
money into stacks on his table in the Oriental gaming room.
The door to the black iron safe stood open and the room was
shafted with light, with dust motes floating around in it. The
time was just past noon. The chairs were on the tables in the
main room, and the bartender, Frank Leslie, was pushing dust
and broken glass into little heaps on the oiled floor.

"What does this mean?" Jones asked.

Wyatt hoisted his eyebrows. The lawyer's long yellow face
was more animated than usual.

"Ike Clanton is hunting you boys with a Winchester rifle
and six-shooter."

"Hunting where?"

"Haring up Fremont when I saw him last."

"He say anything?"

"He said, 'As soon as those damned Earps show their faces
on the street today the ball will open.' Should I round up the
Citizens' Committee?"

"No, I will go down and find him and see what he wants."

"I bet it is that little cock-of-the-walk Johnny Behan set
him to it."

"Johnny hasn't the balls." Wyatt snapped an India rubber
band around each of the bricks of bills and returned them to the
safe.

Jones said, "If he didn't have balls I would not have cause
to hate him."

Wyatt rose and put on his mackinaw. It covered the slick
red cedar handle of his .44 and he arranged it so he could grasp
the pistol through the slit in the side pocket. "You lost your best
chance to euchre him at Doc's stage-robbery hearing. You were
there when Harry Woods and Johnny cooked up that charge.
All you can do now is skeedaddle back to that wife of yours and
hogtie her to see she does not kick over the traces again."

"Yes, this town is full of wife-stealers."

Wyatt's blue gaze stayed on him until Jones left the room,
moving awkwardly with his cheeks striped scarlet.

At that moment, Virgil Earp, who like Wyatt had risen at
noon from a morning bed, stepped up behind Ike Clanton on
Fourth Street between Fremont and Allen and laid the barrel

of his Army along the mastoid bone behind Ike's right ear. Ike's knees buckled and Virgil caught the Winchester in his free hand while Morgan, who had accompanied his brother there, bent and tugged the Frontier Colt's out of Ike's trousers.

Virgil looked down at the man crumpled on the board-walk. "I hear you are hunting for us, Ike."

Ike hissed air through his teeth. His hat had slid over his eyes and he started to bleed behind the ear. When he raised a hand to it, Morgan kicked his elbow.

"Get up, you son of a bitch. We are taking you to Judge Wallace." The younger Earp's eyes were red and sunken and his face was gray. He had not been to bed.

The courthouse on Fremont was in the possession of the portraits of Garfield and Fremont, a dead president and a deposed governor. The front of the room milled with idle attorneys and that class of citizen that finds a legal show as good as a Toughnut Street cockfight in any age. Justice Wallace was not present. Virgil and Morgan half-carried Ike behind the railing and deposited him on the clean pine bench along the east wall. Virgil handed his brother the Winchester.

"Don't shoot him until I get back with the judge."

He had not been gone a minute when Wyatt entered and sat down on the bench nearest the railing. "Well, Ike, you found us."

"I will even up with you for this." Ike sat bent over with a dirty handkerchief doubled twice and pressed behind his ear. "If I had a six-shooter right now I would make a fight with all of you."

Morgan was standing at the end of the bench, holding Ike's Winchester with the butt resting on the floor. He stepped away from the wall and spun the pistol he had taken off Ike, offering the handle. "If you want to make a fight right bad I will give you this one."

Ike started up off the bench. Jim Campbell, one of Behan's deputies on permanent assignment to the courthouse and a sometime prizefighter, shoved him back down hard enough to split the pine. He was rawboned and wore his handlebars curled and his hair cropped close like John L. Sullivan. "No fuss in here, boys."

Wyatt stood and approached the railing. His knuckles yellowed as he gripped it.

"You cattle-thieving son of a bitch, if you are so anxious to make a fight I will go anywhere to make one with you, even if it's over to the San Pedro among your crowd."

"Fight is my racket."

"Then I will pay your fine for you and we will do it right here."

"All I want is four feet of ground."

Wyatt left the building. Crossing Fremont he bucked a current of spectators coming to see Ike Clanton fined for carrying firearms on the street. One or two of them asked Wyatt for details but got no answer. On Fourth he met Tom McLaury coming up from Allen. Tom, the dandy of the Charleston delegation, was wearing a good pearl Stetson with a silver band and a cowhide vest over a dark blue flannel shirt hanging outside his trousers, the tail lifting in the strong wind. He was taller than his brother Frank and his moustaches were trimmed as carefully as Wyatt's.

Wyatt stopped in front of him. "I just promised your friend Ike I will fight him anywhere and there is a piece of it for you too."

"I have no differences with you." Tom smiled tentatively.

"Don't weasel. You and that cow-thief brother of yours have been making fight talk against us for weeks."

"I have never said or done nothing against you. I don't know where you got that. I am a friend of yours."

"Are you heeled?"

"This has to do with Hattie, ain't it?"

Wyatt stepped closer. Their hat brims were almost touching. "I asked are you heeled."

"No, I have got nothing to do with anybody."

Wyatt slapped him left-handed, drew the American with his right, and slammed the barrel along Tom's left temple under his hat brim. The hat rolled off and Tom fell back, raising his palms. Wyatt struck him again with the pistol and he lost his balance. The American flashed down and up and down again. Tom was down on the boardwalk now with both arms crossed over his head.

The stream of pedestrians had clotted around the scene. Wyatt stood over the dazed man, breathing loudly, his pistol dangling from his hand. Then he returned it to his pocket and shouldered a path through the crowd.

"I could kill the son of a bitch."

He was out of cigars. The counter in Hafford's was deserted and he bounced a quarter on top and helped himself to a handful of Humos from a tin next to the bronze cash register. He was standing in front of the building smoking when Frank McLaury, Ike's brutish younger brother Billy, and a pale Tom McLaury passed him without a word heading up Fourth off the boardwalk. Frank was leading a strawberry roan with a saddle and bridle. Wyatt ground the butt under his heel and followed.

They were all inside Spangenberg's gun shop by the time he reached it. Frank McLaury's horse was standing on the boardwalk with its head stuck through the open doorway. It lifted its tail and dropped a load of apples on the boards.

On the other side of the shop window, Billy Clanton and Frank McLaury were busy thumbing cartridges into the empty loops on their belts from a box on the wooden counter. Wyatt passed his right hand through the slit in his coat pocket, gripped the handle of his pistol, and reached up for the roan's bit with his left. The horse blew.

Tom McLaury, standing just inside the door, turned. Billy and Frank came forward from the dim interior. Billy's hand rested on the Colt's in his hip scabbard.

"Ordinance, boys," Wyatt said. "Horses shit in the street."

"Let go of my horse!"

Frank's voice was shrill. Shorter even than Johnny Behan, he wore his trousers high so that his sack coat hung almost to his knees and his pistol rode even with his elbow. His face was feral under the flat brim of his hat.

"When he is where he belongs." Wyatt kept his hand inside his pocket and backed the roan off the boardwalk. He flipped the reins one-handed over the hitching rail, snubbing them with a yank.

Frank said, "That's the last horse of mine you will ever lay hands on."

"Bald talk for a Mississippi mule thief."

Ike Clanton joined them. Weaponless now, he wore his hat at a comic angle, allowing for a white bandage that was the cleanest thing on him.

"Who cut you loose?"

"I paid my fine." He started into the shop.

Wyatt laid a hand on his arm. "If you come out of there heeled I will bust your head clean open."

Before Ike could reply, Virgil and Morgan appeared with their coats open and their pistol handles twisted outside the flaps. Wyatt let go and Ike joined the others inside.

Virgil said, "Let's go down to Hafford's."

"Doc up yet?" asked Morgan.

He was dying faster than usual that morning, striping the sides of the dry sink with bloody sputum and shreds of shattered lung. . . .

PART THREE
SAN PEDRO

. . . You never saw such people. Those banks of beautiful ladies, shining in their barbaric splendors, would see a knight sprawl from his horse in the lists with a lance-shaft the thickness of your ankle clean through him and the blood spouting, and instead of fainting they would clap their hands and crowd each other for a better view; only sometimes one would dive into her handkerchief and look ostentatiously broken-hearted, and then you could lay two to one that there was a scandal there somewhere and she was afraid the public hadn't found it out.

—Mark Twain, *A Connecticut Yankee in King Arthur's Court,* 1889

CHAPTER 11

SHE WAS BORN MARIA Katharina Horony on November 7, 1850, in Budapest, the first child of Katharina Boldizar of Debrecen and Michael Horony; and came to the United States with her parents and four surviving brothers and sisters in 1863, arriving in Davenport, Iowa, two days before her thirteenth birthday. A brother, Imre, had died of a fever at age four, and another, Julius, grew thin and pale in the tween-decks during the ocean crossing and finally faded into a dry husk that was sewn into sailcloth and weighted down with two hand-wrought fireplace dogs that had been in her father's family for a century and slid between the waves. Michael himself, the patriarch, bought a small farm and burst his heart between the potato rows seventeen months after their arrival. In the Horony family, Death was a hideous old uncle who came Sundays to drink the strong tea in the parlor and laid his bony hand on the knees of young and old and then left with apologies for his short stay and promises to return.

Mary Katherine, as she was then known, for the entire family had by that time passed through the crucible of Americanization, matured quickly, and at fourteen was often mistaken for a grown woman when she appeared in town with her mother on errands in mourning black. In the 1860s mourning was fashionable, and thanks to the Widow of

Whitehall and the alarming chain of coffins steaming up the rails from Manassas and Sharpsburg and Antietam and the Wilderness, the shop windows and catalogues were strung with silks and broadcloth and velvet-palmed gloves becomingly cut and dyed with India ink; the stately adolescent, unaware then of the effect, cut an arresting figure on the streets of Davenport in lace-trimmed black bonnet and cape and ankle shoes with onyx buttons ordered from Montgomery Ward. Her face in those years of comparative slimness was an exotic oval, not at all the moon it would become, her forehead high and domed, her eyes like an angelic little boy's, and her lips full and bent permanently into a smile in imitation of her mother, who believed that a pleasant expression prevented a face from aging. If she had the long thick nose of her Magyar forebears, that defect only added to the overall handsome mannishness of her appearance.

With young womanhood came stays, which squeezed an early tendency toward matronliness into the hourglass beloved of a healthy young nation with an overfondness for Rubens's cherubic nudes. A fascination with prints and colors asserted itself as soon as Michael Horony's memory was respectfully put down in camphor and cedar. This coaxed a bloom not only from her cheeks but from her mother's as well, for the little income strained out of mulish earth by a widowed mother, a half-grown son, a distracted daughter, and three small children was not to be squandered on bright scarves and calico that cost as much as three bolt-ends of stout gingham. Her father's razor strap was employed almost as frequently during these years as it had been when he lived.

By then Mary Katherine had divined the meaning, if not precisely the import, of the looks she drew from men. Davenport was a major stop for steamers plying the Mississippi River, and although while in town her mother made certain that neither of them passed near the levee, Mary Katherine flushed at the appreciative expressions that came into the otherwise poker faces of silk-hatted gamblers and the rubber, professionally cheerful faces of derbied drummers when she passed them farther inland and felt her mother's gloved hand tighten around hers and hasten her on past. She detected pomade and whiskey on their persons, smells associated with her father; and her veins ran warm.

One month before her seventeenth birthday Mary Katherine dressed for town; and if Katharina Horony thought her daughter's cape too much for the balmy early-autumn climate, she made no mention of it. If she had, Mary Katherine had a cough handy by way of explanation, although not severe enough to banish her indoors, as that would have made it all for nothing. For under the cape she wore her best dress over another one more serviceable, two petticoats, and three pairs of drawers, enough clothing to fill the small portmanteau she had elected to leave behind for want of a way to smuggle it into town.

Her chance came in the mercantile while her mother was comparing cloves of garlic under the patient eye of the proprietor behind the counter. Wandering toward a stack of ladies' hats in the corner next to the dress material, Mary Katherine pretended interest in the dyed ostrich plumes, then when the merchant turned away to weigh the cloves, opened the door carefully so as not to disturb the bell looped to the handle and left the store. From there she ran the three blocks to the levee as fast as two legs bound in five layers of linen would let her. There the US *Oleander* was loading. For an anxious half-hour while she knew her mother was looking for her she stood among the passengers waiting to board, then eased onto the bottom deck while the man taking tickets was arguing with a fat woman who insisted that her son, nearly six feet tall with a blue shadow on his chin, was under twelve and so eligible to ride half-fare.

The bottom deck was an adventure in odors. For a girl reared near a port, there was nothing novel about the smells of baled jute and molasses in barrels and freshly sawn lumber; but when they came together with various fine scents emanating from parasoled women on the arms of men in striped vests and planters' hats, with water slapping the hollow hull and the boat actually shifting beneath her own tread when she crossed the deck, they assumed an enchantment befitting the oils of China. The aroma was not to be matched and had only to be encountered again to return an aging fancy-woman to a youth in which nothing was beyond reach. She was, however, dismayed to learn that even on this fine whitewashed craft with its great painted paddles floating gently astern, the stench of fish overlay everything, from the barrels of salted salmon resting in the hold. It reminded her unpleasantly of the voyage across the ocean and of her brother Julius quietly dying in his rope hammock.

But the past was no fit opponent for the present. The throated steam whistle, often heard in town but never before from directly overhead, with its vibration buzzing beneath the soles of her feet, opened the future.

A deckhand closed it. After observing her for some minutes wandering unescorted between the decks, he asked to see her ticket, and when she took too long searching for it in her tiny reticule he escorted her to the bridge. The pilot was a red-bearded man in his forties with a long brown face under a beetle-black derby, a joint of charred bulldog pipe nailed into the center of his face, and a tan leather coat with distressed elbows worn over a pinstripe shirt without a collar. He, too, had a fishy smell, like everything else aboard except the passengers. Standing at the wheel he heard the deckhand's report, interrupting him once to reach up and tug the whistle, then dismissed him.

"What's your name, lass?"

He had a thick, burring speech from which she had to sort the words before she answered.

"Kate."

"What's your surname, Kate, lass?"

The glassed-in cabin was strong with him. "Fish."

"Fish?"

"Fisher. I'm Kate Fisher."

He rotated the wheel slightly. His pipe gurgled. "Well, Kate Fisher, lass, what are we to do with ye?"

"I'll work for my passage."

"I have all the hands I require."

"You won't take me back." It wasn't a question.

"I would were that my inclination, but I've a ruddy schedule to make." His softening of the "sch" put her in mind of the English sailors among the crew during the Atlantic crossing. But he wasn't English. "I would put ye ashore in Saint Looey did I not ken ye'd be raped and your white throat slit five minutes after we put off. The war took its toll of gentlemen, ye see."

"I am twenty-one and can care for myself."

"Ye're eighteen or younger, or I'm no judge." He gave the whistle two short blasts and corrected course around a float full of fishermen. "Are ye Catholic, Kate Fisher?"

She wondered if Roman Catholics had a smell of their own, and if it was as evident to him as his was to her. "Yes."

"I've a place for ye, then. Now get below and tell that ruddy barbarian Isherwood he's to keep his sweaty paws off ye until we land. In a nice way, mind. He killed a woman in Hannibal and he has terrible bad nightmares aboot it."

She never found out if he was joshing about the deckhand. When the boat docked in St. Louis the pilot took her inland to a great stone building behind an evil-looking cathedral as large as downtown Davenport and then he passed out of her life forever. She never learned his name, but in later years, when whiskey and memory overtook her, she would smirk at his bluff innocence and despise him.

The Mother Superior of the convent was a fat French-woman of indeterminate age with a nose twice the size of hers with an angry red boil on the side of it and a moustache. She gave Kate—for from then on Mary Katherine was never known by any other name—to a very tall, very thin woman in a nun's habit, who took her to another room where she was made to strip and climb into a wooden tub full of cold water and grasp her ankles while Sister scrubbed her back with brown soap and a coarse cloth until it stung. A bucket of icy water was dumped over her head and she toweled off shivering with thin terry and put on clean drawers—not her comfortable linen ones but a pair made of gray shoddy that chafed her thighs—and a plain white cotton shift. Sitting on a wormwood bench she pulled on coarse black knee-length stockings secured with plain garters and laced on a pair of man's scuffed brown brogans that extended two inches past her toes and felt corrugated inside.

When Sister advanced on her with steel shears she tried to

run, but the thin woman was faster and much stronger and sat her on the bench with an arm wrench that made her cry out. She was still recovering from it when her wet black hair was gathered in a wiry fist and cut off at the nape of her neck with three crunching snips. No mirrors were allowed in the convent, and when that night she was locked in a ward with a dozen other shorn girls who spoke among themselves in whispers and stared at her without addressing her, she lay on her narrow cot crying, convinced she looked a horror. A few days later, however, when she was allowed to pass under Sister's escort through the courtyard into the cathedral, she admired the boyishly ethereal face framed in a scarf looking back at her from the surface of the holy water. Although she genuflected and hurried to a pew before Sister could box her ears for the sin of Vanity, on her knees she determined never to let her hair grow back out.

Big Nose Kate was born in the convent. The other girls called her that from the time they learned her name, and tailored jokes to her that were previously reserved for Mother Superior's fearsome fistulated snout. The first time a girl used the name to her face, Kate knocked her down and straddled her and clawed at her eyes until Sister separated and whipped them both across their bare buttocks until they bled. Nevertheless it quickly became popular, and even the nuns came to use it to distinguish her from the other two Kates in their charge.

So Big Nose Kate came out of that time, but more than just the name. On occasions later when the clergy got in the way of her vocation she would claim that the only difference between God's house and a whorehouse was the pointed roof, and those who heard would think she was merely trying to shock them, but what she never spoke of was the Private Instruction in Sister's cell. There among the hymnals and Latin dictionaries and votive candles she discovered that the reason nuns never squirmed like the girls under the scratching of their shoddy drawers was that they never wore them. The diet in the convent was mostly salmon from the riverboats, and Sister tasted of it, so that despite the irony of her adopted surname Kate never ate fish the rest of her life. After hours the girls practiced what they had learned from Sister with one another in their cots. Although Kate often took part, she gained far more knowledge than release from these sessions. For her the convent would be a lesson in the universal craving for physical fulfillment that she would carry to the grave.

There were only two ways to get out of the convent.

Escape was not one. The first week Kate was there, a sixteen-year-old girl whose baby had been remanded to an orphanage downriver slipped out of the cathedral while Sister was in holy rapture and was gone two days and one night. She attempted to sneak aboard a riverboat, was found out, and scrambled down the levee a hop ahead of the out-of-shape deckhand who pursued her and lost his footing and her trail at the bottom. On the second day a city policeman caught her picking through a trash barrel behind a restaurant, recognized the dirty convent shift she was wearing, and delivered her to Sister, who attended her lovingly during her long recovery from Sister's whipping. Other attempts were made while Kate was in residence, but none came even that close to success, although the punishment was the same. The St. Louis city fathers were staunchly Catholic and the police were always willing to aid in recapturing runaways.

Coming of age was the first of the sanctioned roads to freedom. Upon reaching twenty-one, the petitioner had the choice of entering the novitiate or leaving by the front door. A surprising number opted for the former, and Kate could always identify these among the novices, who spelled the nuns in the classroom and kept order in the dormitory, by their broken wills. She herself had no intention of letting that happen to her, or of spending the next four years begging carbolic off the nuns for her abraded thighs and tasting salmon in Sister's cell. The second key to liberty—of a sort—was marriage.

One of the convent's unadvertised purposes was to serve as a kind of animal shelter for pioneers looking for wives. Several times a week, men stuffed into high boots and new suits of clothes tramped through the classroom and dormitory to look at the girls and talk with some of them. Mother Superior said they were settlers inspecting the spiritual arrangements before putting down stakes in the area, but no one was taken in by it and Mother Superior herself made no great effort to be convincing. Kate talked with a few of the men, but was offended by the blunt way they studied her build under her shift and by the sour earthen smell of them, and they in turn lost interest when their questions about her people went unanswered. Their wills, moreover, were as strong as hers if not stronger, something she had had quite enough of from her mother and from Sister. If they were shopping, she was too. When Sister noted her attitude and rebuked her during Private Instruction for the sin of Pride, Kate feigned ignorance; and rather than allow herself to be backed into admitting the true purpose of the visitations, the thin woman merely clenched her long jaw and raised her habit.

Once a month the girls' teeth were inspected by a dentist named Silas Melvin. Melvin was a fussy little man with a pink face and rimless spectacles and black hair receding into a half-moon four inches above his eyebrows, although he was still in his twenties. He affected a laughable fastidiousness of dress in view of his shabby coat and turned collars that convinced the other girls, who called him Aunt Silas, that their sex held no interest for him. Kate was less sure and settled the point one day by borrowing a shift from a girl several sizes smaller and arching her back so that her nipples stood out against the taut cotton while he was leaning over to look inside her mouth, causing him to drop his little mirror and crack the glass.

She liked his clean smell. He admired her "Greek profile" and said she had fine teeth. Mostly she liked the fact that he was plainly afraid of Sister and avoided her as much as he could without offending. A man who could be intimidated represented freedom. Kate encouraged his attentions, and soon he was making his visits twice a month, blaming an outbreak of pyorrhea in the city. No one credited it. By then it was commonly accepted that Aunt Silas was smitten with Big Nose Kate.

Mother Superior blessed the match. Professional men were a sturdy influence on rebellious young women. Moreover, despite the fact that his stubborn Protestantism precluded their marrying inside the Church, Mother Superior was serene in its teachings and believed it would encompass them both in time; which made it a victory of Faith. So it was that six months after

Kate came to the convent, she was wed by the pastor of the Presbyterian church.

Dr. and Mrs. Silas Melvin booked steamboat passage on the Mississippi, she no longer a stowaway but a large handsome woman in stays and taffeta with a flat flowered hat pinned to her short hair, part of a modest trousseau presented to her by an admiring husband. At Vicksburg, a town rising slowly from mortar-smashed rubble and blasted trees, they transferred to a sleeper car and clattered over polished steel through scorched fields tangled with the rusty twisted corpses of old rails torn up by Sherman's troops on the way to Atlanta. There the couple settled.

In the late 1860s that town was still reeling from Sherman. Most of the burned blocks had been cleared, but for the rest of Kate's life the stench of char would remind her of her first marriage. Widows took in washing, and so many backyards were crisscrossed with burdened clotheslines she wondered that any men were left in Atlanta. But they were in the streets, straggle-haired and bitten-bearded in rags of Confederate shoddy with sockets for eyes and stumps on display and filthy palms outstretched. At night they grew fangs and preyed on their daytime benefactors in alleys stinking of slops. For all that, Atlanta was rebuilding. Professional men were desperately needed, but because no one could afford to pay for their services they were rare. Soon after Silas nailed up his shingle he had a full practice. Although there was no money, the Melvins dined on pork pies and venison roasts and baskets of eggs and flasks of milk brought by his patients. Kate gained weight rapidly.

Before long it became evident that the rich food was not to be blamed for this. Concerned when his wife became too ill mornings to eat breakfast, Silas brought home a doctor who had served as surgeon with General Bragg and who examined her and congratulated them both while accepting a large apple pie in lieu of his fee.

She bore him a son.

The son died.

No one knew why he died. Not Kate, who bathed and cared for him as lovingly as she tended Silas's instruments, which had to be boiled on the cookstove in the kitchen between usings, and the basin that had to be scoured of blood and iodine. Not Melvin, who wanted to send the boy to Baltimore to learn dentistry as soon as he was through with public school and looked to the day when he would be Old Doc Melvin to his son's Young Doc Melvin. Certainly not the doctor, who signed the death certificate and shook his head and said that the war was still claiming victims in Atlanta. Baptized Presbyterian, the boy could not be buried out of the Catholic Church as Kate requested, but the local priest, a patient of Silas's, agreed to preside at a secular ceremony in the couple's house, after which a Presbyterian minister officiated at graveside.

Silas died soon after. Yellow fever was sweeping the city, and as the symptoms were in keeping with the disease, Bragg's old surgeon wrote it on the certificate. Kate knew it wasn't that, or even the broken heart suggested by the doctor in private. It was Uncle Death come back to pay his respects to her family.

Industry had come to Atlanta, and with it northern money. Kate buried Silas next to their son and sold their house and his practice to a dentist from Vermont with a birdlike wife and three pale children and went west. As she watched the green southern scenery sliding past the train window she could not know that she was tracing the steps of another Atlanta exile whom Uncle Death had compelled to leave some months earlier, a dentist like Silas, although that was where the resemblance ended; as indeed it did to anyone else she would ever know.

When they met, the year was 1877 and the place was a clabber of adobe dugouts and unpainted shacks swept up against the base of Government Hill below Fort Griffin, Texas. He was a picket-thin man of twenty-five, with a phlegmy cough and a preference for colored shirts and gray suits of good material that flapped on him. She was Big Nose Kate, hefty at twenty-seven and developing a roll under her chin but a long way from fat, and working John Shanssey's saloon on a financial arrangement with the beetle-browed ex-pugilist. Dentists were an interest, and although this one had swung a board from the peak of his tent on the edge of town with JOHN HENRY HOLLIDAY, D.D.S. inexpertly painted on it, he spent most of his time playing poker and dealing faro in Shanssey's. The men with whom he played were all big and filthy and stank of guts, but they bought their chips with fist-size wads of crisp bills obtained from the Fort Griffin paymaster in return for buffalo hides. The kill was so lush that year they lost hundreds of dollars and got up from the table lurching and laughing. Sometimes they didn't, but the way Holliday played, smiling as he pulled in the chips and telling nigger jokes in his soft drawl and sipping frequently from the tumbler of whiskey that was always at his elbow, the mood around the table remained guardedly genial.

She began as his partner. Some of the buffalo runners had wives and sweethearts back in civilization for whom they held back hide money not required for food and supplies. It was her role to make their acquaintance and get them to buy her drinks and jolly them into trying to double and treble those reserves. Kate was good with the quiet ones. She charmed and bullied and shamed and groped at them—for she had learned a long time before that a man who was drunk and aroused was more likely to spend money than one who was just drunk—and Sister's Private Instruction had taught her that no oath was equal to the demands of the body. And if, after dropping the earnings of an entire season's shooting and skinning on the turn of a pasteboard, a player showed signs of becoming truculent, a trip upstairs with Kate was usually all that was required to put him back on his feed, as Doc put it. For this she received a cut of the winnings after Shanssey had sliced his off the top.

At sunup they went back to Doc's tent, where she rubbed his back with alcohol and held his head when his coughing gutted him and lay with him when he had the strength for it. He was a fitful lover, stronger than he looked, and he kept at it with the same concentration he displayed at his table until he exploded and then collapsed wheezing. When he stirred she would have a tumbler ready for him and he would drink it off in two swallows and go to sleep. Her business fell off after that. She knew it was because the other Fort Griffin men, who spent all day with their bare arms inside buffalo carcasses to the shoulders and made breastworks of them when the Comanches came looking to strip off their skins, were afraid of catching what Doc had from her. She didn't care. Doc's action supported them both, and caring for him when he was low fed something in her that had been cheated when her son and husband died so suddenly. Every afternoon that Doc climbed out of his roll to put on a fresh shirt and take his place behind the cue box in Shanssey's was ground held against the terrible Uncle.

They shared secrets insofar as their self-protective natures allowed. Once when drinking he told her of his cousin in an Atlanta convent—she recognized the name of her alma mater's old rival—to whom he still wrote letters, and beat Kate up for mentioning it when he was sober. After that she didn't bring it up again, even at times when he looked at her and she knew she was being measured against the angel of the Lord back home and felt the urge to enlighten him as to what went on in convents. It wasn't fear. If she gave any thought to such things at all, she would suppose that she loved Doc.

Kate wasn't present in the saloon when Doc and Ed Bailey fell out. Bailey was a buffalo runner and a sometime scout for the army who wore an issue Colt's in a cavalry scabbard with the strap unbuttoned. Doc caught him looking at the dead-wood—sneaking a peek at Doc's discards during poker—and admonished him quietly to "play poker," which was the gentleman's way of asking an opponent to refrain from cheating. Bailey withdrew his hand from the pile, drew two cards from the deck, then resumed his inspection of Doc's deadwood. When Doc laid his cards face down and began pulling in the pot, Bailey challenged him, his hand dropping under the table. Doc jerked a pearl-handled knife from his inside breast pocket and eviscerated him.

A marshal's deputy was present, and threw down on Doc and relieved him of the knife and two pistols while Bailey was still trying to keep his entrails from spilling over his belt. Doc was removed to a hotel while a wagon was readied to take him to the Shackleford County seat at Albany for a hearing.

The story that got told later was full of lynch mobs and vigilantes and had Kate dressing up in man's clothes and setting fire to a stable and then taking Doc away at gunpoint from the deputy left to guard him while the others were fighting the fire. The part about the man's clothes and the fire was true enough, but they were just gestures to keep the glare off the deputy, an old customer whom Kate paid a hundred dollars to watch the blaze outside the window while she and Doc walked out. At dawn John Shanssey brought two horses to the cottonwoods by Collins Creek where the fugitives were hiding. From there they rode four hundred miles to Dodge City, Kansas, where cowboys were squalling for more games to lose money on and where Doc had a friend named Earp.

That was four years ago. Kate missed Dodge; not the town itself, clapboard huts on a grass street studded with cow flop, and certainly not the profitable understanding Doc had as a gambler with Wyatt Earp, a man she distrusted, on the local police force, but rather the several weeks during which Doc practiced dentistry for real out of a walk-up office and introduced Kate to acquaintances as Mrs. Holliday. It all blew up when Doc stopped coming home nights, staying up drinking with Wyatt's kid brother Morgan and betting on whether the next man through the door of the Long Branch would be wearing a kerchief or a cravat. She and Doc fought over it. He broke her nose; she clawed his face and decamped for Ogallala. He said she'd be back. She said he'd write begging her to come back. They were both right. He would get in a bad way and write her in his fine hand—always immaculate, whether he was drunk or sober—saying he needed her, and she would respond by returning. It was a pattern they would repeat in Colorado, New Mexico, and Arizona, with Uncle following them all the way. He and Doc were old acquaintances.

The first time she left him in Tombstone, Kate had gone to the copper-mining center of Globe and spent the five hundred dollars he had given her on a down payment on a hotel, which became a whorehouse with very little alteration and an arrangement with the girls that pleased everyone. During her reunion with Doc she had left the books in care of her brightest girl. Despite detailed instructions the girl had made a mess of them, wandering outside Kate's carefully ruled lines and getting the debits mixed up with the credits or just plain neglecting to record transactions, and since her return Kate had been involved in reconstructing the past month's finances. That the girl had been robbing her blind was a certainty, but she couldn't concentrate long enough to determine by how much. Her eye was still tender where Doc had hit her this time and her bruised ribs hurt when she moved or drew a deep breath. Worse, she felt guilty for having left him with the investigation into the deaths on Fremont Street still pending. That was why, when the mail came bearing a letter in the familiar flowing hand, she got up so quickly to accept it the pain doubled her.

November 5, 1881

Dear Kate,
    Well, they have got me in jail again. . . .

CHAPTER 12

JOHN CHARLES FREMONT, ARITHMETIC teacher-*cum*-Northwest explorer-*cum*-soldier-*cum*-senator-*cum*-gouty and doting governor of Arizona Territory, stepped down, spurs clanking, from that position on October 15, 1881, under relentless encouragement by President Arthur to do so. John J. Gosper was appointed to fill the gap until a permanent successor could be chosen, but as no portrait of Gosper was forthcoming, the framed likeness of a bilious Fremont clutching a sword and a rolled map remained on the wall behind the justice's bench in the Cochise County courthouse on the street named for its model. As in life the old eagle's eyes were directed beyond that room and its contents, out past the Whetstones to where glory lay, and with it something more fitting than the custodianship of a rocky desert inhabited by roadrunners and wild Indians.

Beneath the portrait, looking like an unworthy heir, Justice Wells Spicer scratched his head and left the hair standing. His small eyes followed the scribbled lines on the sheet before him and his voice ground on, inflectionless and soporific, an aural projection of his putty-faced dowdiness in gray collar and lopsided cravat and baggy coat with stains on the lapels. In appearance and manner he gave no indication of the jurist who since June 1880 had stood like an iron post between the grasping Townlot Company and the disputed property fronting on

Tombstone's three principal streets. Paintings lie; so too do personal impressions.

"Witnesses of credibility testify that each of the deceased, or at least two of them, yielded to a demand to surrender," droned Spicer, turning to a fresh sheet. "Other witnesses of equal credibility testify that William Clanton and Frank McLaury met the demand for surrender by drawing their pistols, and that the discharge of firearms from both sides was almost simultaneous."

Outside, the wind was blowing, rattling hard early snow-flakes like dried peas against the windows and fluting around the panes through spaces where the chinking had dropped out, causing the hanging lamps to sway and glow fiercely with each gust. Nevertheless the room was warm, even hot. Deputy Jim Campbell kept the parlor stove charged with mesquite and cottonwood, and spectators jammed the benches, exuding body heat. Rank with wool and sweat, it hung like an invisible cloud over the proceedings.

"There is a dispute as to whether Thomas McLaury was armed at all, except with a Winchester rifle that was on the horse beside him. I will not consider this question, because it is not of controlling importance. . . ."

Behind the railing, on the same bench occupied by Ike Clanton on the day of the fight, Wyatt Earp sat plank straight with a high collar supporting his round chin and his hands resting on his thighs, cuffs showing. Doc Holliday slouched on his spine next to him, wearing a pale yellow shirt under dark gray flannel, hands in pockets, boots crossed, the indolent younger prince with no hope of ascending. His eyes were moving, counting the house. On Wyatt's other side, Tom Fitch, the pair's attorney, sat with his chin on his chest and his feet flat on the floor, staring at the boards between them. His graying handlebars had a sober curve. Underneath them he was smiling ever so faintly.

"Witnesses for the prosecution state unequivocally that William Clanton fell or was shot at the first fire, and Claiborne says he was shot when the pistol was only about a foot from his belly. Yet it is clear that there were no powder burns nor marks on his clothes. . . ."

Virgil Earp had commandeered the end of a bench in the gallery to enable him to straighten his healing leg in the aisle. He wore his deputy U.S. marshal's star on his vest—his city position, not his federal appointment, had been taken away—and had a cane hooked over the back of the bench in front of him. James Earp, dour and in evident pain from his war-smashed shoulder in the cold weather, sided him. Morgan and Warren were absent, the former still recovering at home from his back wound, the latter off adventuring somewhere in the territory since before the fight. The women were home awaiting news.

"Considering all the testimony together, I am of the opinion that the weight of evidence sustains and corroborates the testimony of Wyatt Earp, that their demand for surrender was met by William Clanton and Frank McLaury drawing or making motions to draw their pistols. . . ."

Ike and Phin Clanton sat on the far end of the same bench with half a dozen people between them and James Earp, Ike chewing rapidly and looking around with head sunk between his shoulders, Phin smooth-faced, eyes wondering. He was regarded in some company as the idiot of the family. Other San Pedro residents were present, and some of the vigilantes, including John Clum, taking notes for his newspaper; but for the most part the gallery contained Tombstonians who had been following the hearing in the columns of the *Epitaph* and *Nugget* for a month and had come there out of a dim sort of herd-consciousness that some kind of history was going on, and the shops could stay closed and the gate hinges could await replacement until it got through, provided it wasn't too long about it.

"The testimony of Isaac Clanton, that this tragedy was the result of a scheme on the part of the Earps to assassinate him and thereby bury in oblivion the confessions the Earps had made to him about 'piping away' the shipment of coin by Wells Fargo and Company, falls short of being a sound theory, on account of the great fact, most prominent in this matter, to wit: that Isaac Clanton was not injured at all, and could have been killed first and easiest, if it was the object of the attack to kill him. . . ."

The front bench was in the possession of the prosecution team, a dull brown presence with Johnny Behan brightening one end in his morning coat and immaculate collar and a spare man in a black clawhammer and silk vest shoring up the other. Silver gleamed softly in the spare man's longish brown hair and glittered in his semicircle of dark beard. It mitigated somewhat the fierceness of thatched brows nearly as mobile as Tom Fitch's, beneath which a pair of brown and, to the Earps and Holliday at least, familiar eyes smoldered. His name was William R. McLaury—Will to his dead brothers, and a Fort Worth attorney of no little note who had swept in on the fifth day of the hearing to galvanize the prosecution. He had begun by harrying the quiet Spicer into jailing Wyatt and Doc for a time, and since then had cut and slashed at the defense's witnesses with a minimum of oratory and a keen nose for warm blood. In that, he was much like his late younger brother Frank. The killer strain had thus taken separate routes to the same destination. As he listened to Spicer's decision, his profile might have been punched out of sheet metal for all anyone could read of his reactions; and many tried.

For the first time the justice's voice rose. Spectators lulled into a doze by its unchanging tone lifted their heads.

"In view of the past history of the county and the generally believed existence at this time of desperate, reckless and lawless men in our midst, banded together for mutual support and living by felonious and predatory pursuits, regarding neither life nor property in their career, and at the same time for men to parade the streets armed with repeating rifles and six-shooters and demand that the chief of police and his assistants should be disarmed is a proposition both monstrous and startling!"

He was not reading now, but looking directly at Ike Clanton, and a sheet of color had slid down behind the gray of his features. Here at last was the man who had denounced the Townlot conspiracy to the Land Office Commission as "a fraud run by a lot of hoodlums." The gallery leaned forward. But at that point Spicer returned to his papers and his tone subsided to its normal flat line.

"The evidence taken before me in this case would not, in

my judgment, warrant a conviction of the defendants by trial jury of any offense whatever. I do not believe that any trial jury that could be got together in this territory would, on all the evidence taken before me, with the rule of law applicable thereto given them by the court, find the defendants guilty of any offense.

"It may be that my judgment is erroneous, and my view of the law incorrect; yet it is my own judgment and my own understanding of the law as I find it laid down, and upon this I must act and decide, and not upon those of any other persons. I have given over four weeks of patient attention to the hearing of evidence in this case, and at least four-fifths of my waking hours have been devoted, at this time, to an earnest study of the evidence before me, and such is the conclusion to which I am forced to arrive."

Ike spat, dinging the edge of the cuspidor at the foot of his bench and splattering the floor beyond it. The noise broke a tension in the room, which seemed to resume breathing afterward.

Spicer laid aside the last sheet and picked up his gavel. "I conclude the performance of this duty imposed upon me by saying in the language of the statute: There being no sufficient cause to believe the within named Wyatt S. Earp and John H. Holliday guilty of the offense mentioned within, I order them to be released." The gavel cracked.

A barrier crumbled then and the room, with exceptions, lunged forward to swing open the gate and reach over the railing and shake the defendants' hands and pound their backs. Doc, who would not be so manhandled, feigned a coughing jag that turned the well-wishers away from him and toward Wyatt. Wells Spicer, his sun set, got up from behind the table and took himself quietly through the side door into his chambers, carrying his notes and gavel. Souvenir hounds were a plague on the frontier.

Johnny Behan went over to talk with Jim Campbell. Will McLaury hoisted his scuffed brown leather briefcase under his arm and started down the aisle, clear now that most of the crowd had clotted around Earp and Holliday. He encountered Ike Clanton in front of the door.

"What's next?" Ike asked.

"You heard Spicer."

"Not all of it. Man talks like he's got him a mouth full of shit."

McLaury regarded him for a space. Wedging the briefcase between his elbow and ribs, he stripped the foil off a cigar. Phin Clanton, hovering by the benches, watched the maneuver, his eyes like a dog's fascinated by movement. In the heat of the room it was evident that neither of the brothers had bathed in a week.

"The grand jury is in session," McLaury said. "With proper witnesses and depositions they will hand down an indictment over Spicer. It is for us to provide that evidence. If I had been in charge of the prosecution from the outset we would have had it before this and Earp and Holliday would be bound for Yuma in chains."

"Supposing they don't hand one down; what?"

McLaury lit the cigar without ritual. They had been joined by a horsey-smelling group from Charleston in flannel shirts and striped pants, most of them cowboys the attorney didn't know. But he recognized John Ringo's jug ears and swooping moustaches under the sombrero he never took off. Despite the fact that Ringo stank as highly as the others, there was about him a personal neatness that put McLaury in mind of Doc Holliday. It was not their only similarity.

Before McLaury could answer the question, John Clum asked his pardon and slid between him and the group on his way out the door. Ringo's eyes followed Clum, then returned to McLaury. They were as dull and flat as two pennies on a counter.

The attorney looked away. "Let's not board that train until it stops."

He excused himself. But Ringo at least had caught him looking after the mayor and *Epitaph* publisher.

Ringo and the straggle of less luminous cowboys present for Spicer's decision were the advance for an army, if not a particularly uniform or disciplined one. After the hearing, ending as it did in the loose time between the fall drives and spring round-up (and in a season when the vaqueros who rode for the grandees below the border were paid eight pesos apiece for the heads of American rustlers), they trickled in from Galeyville and Charleston on town horses and buckboards and pitched camp outside town or checked into the Grand Hotel, whose owners always welcomed them because they paid for their rooms in advance with silver and settled all damages on the spot. The checkroom filled with pistols and rifles with penciled tags attached to the trigger guards identifying their owners, leaving no room for coats or luggage. Which was all right, because the guests carried most of their belongings in blanket rolls stashed in their rooms. Even Curly Bill Brocius, whose square grin and head of coiled locks were more discussed than actually seen since charges against him for the murder of Marshal Fred White had been dropped, was observed standing a roomful of cowboys to drinks in the Occidental one night. It was widely repeated that Curly Bill and Ringo had led a party into Huachita after their friends Leonard and Head were killed there and cut down the Haslett brothers in front of their own store. But killings without witnesses out there and in that time were spectral things, and Ike Haslett had been reported seen ordering a whiskey and branch in a Benson saloon a week after he was supposed to have been shot full of holes and left for the coyotes. Speculation ran heavy that his brother Bill would be discovered operating a tram in San Francisco before the end of the year; and in this way the two were declared soundly dead.

Fights broke out, and one bloodless shooting over a dancer's rosette garter in the Bird Cage. Behan deputized two new men and put them on rotating shifts with Breakenridge and the others. It was a time in which even he had cause to ream out the city council for removing Virgil Earp as chief of police. Wyatt meanwhile dealt faro in the Oriental and collected from his concession in the Eagle Brewery, and Virgil helped their brother James tend bar in the Sampling Room. They had moved Morgan, recovering now, and their women from Fremont Street to a suite in the Cosmopolitan Hotel after a scare involving a man dressed as a woman who knocked on Virgil's door, then when James answered, mumbled an excuse and clomped off into the darkness. Wyatt believed that if any of the Earps who had participated in the fight on Fremont Street had come to the door he would have been murdered, and arranged to settle Sadie into Mrs. Young's boardinghouse. Allie and Lou had insisted upon inviting Mattie to come with them to the hotel.

Doc's customers at his table in the Alhambra tended to be Tombstone newcomers—eager, win or lose, to boast of having crossed cards with the man who had killed two of the three slain at the O.K. Corral (for so the location of the fight was coming to be misidentified, from the several references made to the place during the hearing)—or that brand of local stalwart who had grown up accepting all bets and taking all dares. The rest stayed away, avoiding a target. When challengers sat down Doc would ask them how it felt to play against a marked man, and enjoyed watching them jump whenever he reached into a pocket, only to produce a cigar or his handkerchief. Everything he did during this period—drink, gamble, cough, or excuse himself to step out the alley door and take a piss—was for the benefit of recording eyes. He would write Kate that he was getting to be as famous as Eddy Foy and work out schemes to turn his celebrity into profit. He did manage to sell an A.T. & S.F. fireman a few gold bricks left over from Leadville, but he felt mean about it afterward. Fleecing came too easily to a legend.

But for the most part he was idle, dealing himself patience inside a ring of empty tables while John Mellgren and Joe Meagher, the saloon's owners and Doc's silent partners in the gambling concession, divided their dwindling split and argued over which of them would ask Doc to take his game elsewhere. Doc drank more when there was less to do. He had increased his intake to three quarts daily, and without Kate around to bully him into eating he made only infrequent appearances at Mrs. Fly's table and the Can Can. He grew alarmingly skeletal; his trousers bagged on him and when he stood beneath a gas lamp to light a cigar the ghastly glow made empty sockets of his eyes and seemed to shine right through him. But he was never seen to lurch or stagger.

Johnny Ringo, whose own drinking habits were becoming folklore, encountered him in this condition on Allen Street late

one afternoon in December when they were each crossing to
the opposite side. Both men had on greatcoats and their breath
curled in the frosty air.

"I hear your whore is taking them on in Globe these days,"
Ringo said.

Doc grinned, stretching the skin tighter over his skull.
"Yes, she got out when she heard you were spreading crabs all
over town."

"Well, what's a few more to a hatchery?"

"How are we going to do this?" Doc threw away his cigar.

Ringo's posture changed. Slowly, with his left hand, he
unbuttoned his ulster and tugged loose the blue bandanna
knotted around his neck. He twirled it between both hands and
stuck one end between his teeth. Coming down, his right hand
slid the flap of the coat behind the yellow ivory handle of a
Colt's in an oil-stained scabbard.

Doc opened his gray coat and came forward to take the
bandanna's dangling end. Just then Billy Breakenridge stepped
off the boardwalk behind Ringo and threw his arms around
him, pinning his arms to his sides.

"You little cunt." Ringo struggled, but the deputy was
wiry and held his grip with laced knuckles gone pale. His hat
tumbled off.

Doc was still grinning. "John, I never guessed it about you
and Billy."

Wyatt Earp joined them, hatless in his Albert with no
overcoat. He had been watching from inside the Cosmopolitan.
"Let it go, Doc."

"I can take him."

"Him maybe. There's an open window upstairs in the
Grand I don't like."

Ringo stopped struggling to get his breath. Moving
quickly, Breakenridge released him, jerked Ringo's pistol, and
stepped back pointing it. "I am arresting you for carrying
weapons on the street."

Doc said, "John, I guess anybody can throw down on you.
I almost hurt my good name."

"It is like you Earps to hunker behind Billy's skirts." Ringo
was panting. The air was ripe with half-digested whiskey.

"I'm not an Earp."

"I think of you as a bastard brother and part nigger."

"You are a first-class horse thief, John. Bushwhacking is away under you."

They had collected a small crowd of merchants and miners, through which Jim Campbell pried a path with his pistol. He and Breakenridge flanked Ringo and took him toward Fremont. At six feet two he towered over both deputies.

"Behan will just turn him back out, six-shooter and all," Wyatt said.

Doc looked up at the open window on the second floor of the Grand Hotel. "I guess it is too cold to say they are just letting in air."

"I'd bet the house it's to let buckshot out."

"I never featured Ringo for a play of that nature. He's an honest killer."

"Will McLaury has a long purse."

Wyatt accompanied Doc through the door of the Maison Doree. A wreath woven from green-and-orange sage flapped against it. The gas lamps burned blue in the winter gloom. They took a corner table, where Wyatt ordered steak and eggs for both of them. Doc changed his order to just eggs. He poured a slug from his pocket flask into his coffee. "How about that Billy? You never know what's in a body until it comes out."

"Girls fight too." Wyatt watched him drink. "I cannot go around bailing you, Doc. Hiring Tom Fitch cost me the best of my mineral rights and I am the only customer I've had at my table in two days. I lost," he added.

Doc produced a thick fold of currency from an inside pocket and counted three hundred in fifties onto the table. "That's the rest of what I owe you for Kate." He put away the remaining notes.

Wyatt didn't pick them up right away. "You must have pulled every sore tooth in Tombstone."

"I sold some carpetbaggers the pistol I used to kill Tom McLaury."

"You used a scattergun on Tom."

"They wouldn't hear that."

"How many did you sell?"

"Two old Colt's and a derringer with a busted firing pin. Spangenberg gouged me twenty for the lot. I got two hundred each."

"You notch them?"

"I did after the first one. They take to pouting when you don't."

"What happens when they meet?"

"Probably nothing. Carpetbaggers cannot shoot for shit."

"It sounds like something Bat would do." Wyatt put the notes in his wallet.

"I surely hope not. I don't like Bat."

Doc's eggs arrived. He pricked the yolks with his fork and watched the yellow run out but didn't lift it. He leveled off his cup from the flask. Wyatt said, "That bandanna trick is plain crazy. If you are not gutshot you'll burn to death from the powder flare."

"Better that than the cough."

"We all agreed not to go anywhere alone until this business finishes blowing off."

"*You* agreed. I sat out that hand."

"You dealt yourself in quick enough that day."

"The game then was different."

"At least move into the hotel," said Wyatt. "We are holding the room across the hall for you."

"I can do that. Fremont is too quiet since you Earps pulled out."

"We could do with some quiet." The waiter brought Wyatt's steak and he ladled ketchup on it from a china boat. "You heard they tried gunning John Clum aboard the Benson stage Thursday."

"If it says it in the *Epitaph* I guess it is so." Doc made a face and pushed away his plate with the eggs uneaten.

"Ringo would be my guess, or more likely Frank Stilwell. If it was Ringo, Clum would not have just got off and strolled away like Sunday in Saint Louis. McLaury has us all marked up like a butcher's chart."

"Cowboys and horse thieves, the lot of them."

"There still is no percentage in it. I came to this place looking to make money, not widows. It has all gone to shit, Doc. I'm off to California as soon as I find a buyer for my water and timber rights."

"See to yourself."

Wyatt chewed. "You know I am moving my game to the Alhambra. The Oriental is an unfriendly place since you tried to shoot off Milt Joyce's hand."

"I wasn't shooting at his hand."

"That rotgut is no good for your aim."

Doc poured some more into the cup. There was no longer any coffee in it.

"I will ride the tiger here for a spell and then see what is doing in Colorado," he said. "I hear Gunnison is busting loose."

"I hear it is good country for bad lungs."

"Six to five a ball takes me first," Doc said.

CHAPTER 13

MORGAN WAS THE FIRST of the Earps whom Josephine Sarah Marcus had met on her way to Tombstone with the Pauline Markham troupe; and to her he remained the handsomest of the brothers by far.

She got her first glimpse of him at the Benson station when her stage was about to leave and he strode out to mount to the messenger's seat, all lanky grace in a buckskin coat and dungarees, carrying a shotgun. His hat was tipped as far back as it would go and his hair and whiskers were burned yellow against the red of his face. In bright sunlight his eyes were porcelain blue. By then she had met and become enamored of Johnny Behan, and when the time came to make a change from him, there was Wyatt with the same eyes and fair coloring and better prospects. But Morgan's more casual, less aware good looks continued to please her.

Unlike his brothers he had no investments in Cochise County. The wages he drew from Wells Fargo went into food and rent and gambling and whiskey and an occasional visit to the Bird Cage, where (it was said) he was a favorite of the motherly Mexican whores and the hourglass dancers alike. Around respectable women he exhibited a shy politeness only dimly related to Wyatt's courtly polish, but in male company he was known to tie clotheslines around dozers' ankles and introduce mustard seed into unattended tobacco pouches and, when the eruptions occurred, smile in his handlebars while others roared. When his poke grew flat he spelled Wyatt at his cue box in the Alhambra or shoveled slag at the Vizina hoisting works on Toughnut, quitting when he had enough money to renew his credit around town. His financial irresponsibility and general—some thought studied—carelessness of appearance drove the ambitious and meticulous Wyatt into rages, but although no mention was ever made of it, it was no secret that Morgan was his favorite brother. James had been a man grown when the rest of them were boys, and Virgil's war service had absented him from the Earp household before Wyatt had established any kind of relationship with him. Warren, an infant when Wyatt began his travels, was a stranger. Morgan had been Wyatt's charge since boyhood, and if in later years he rebelled against his older brother's outward puritanism, his own refusal to take himself seriously mitigated a family drift toward pomposity. Arguments between the two quickly grew tense with sarcasm (the Earps were nothing if not acerbic) and invariably ended with Wyatt tousling Morgan's unruly blond hair.

For all his closely nurtured lack of direction, Morgan was devoted to Lou, the dark, quiet young woman with whom he lived as man and wife. The two behaved as honeymooners in public and were never overheard shouting at each other in private, as were Virgil and the tiny but formidable Allie—and Wyatt and Sadie's neighbors had also felt the heat of two powerful wills in friction. Sadie, who had run away from a happy home to join the theater and deserted Johnny Behan for Wyatt, revered fidelity; it was to her an awesome attribute. Although she knew with all the complacency of a child of the Industrial Revolution that Wyatt's single-tracked determination to acquire property and standing assured him a sounder future, she was jealous of Lou and felt that Morgan's theatrical good looks were wasted on her. That Lou and Allie had closed ranks around Mattie Earp to freeze Sadie out only fueled this conviction. She did not know Lou, and so decided that Morgan deserved better.

Life behind the footlights had palled early on Sadie. The

theater, which had offered escape from a middle-class Jewish
adolescence in San Francisco, soon proved itself a mobile trap.
Her identity apart from the eternal chain of rainy-eyed ingenues
and cabin boys she played onstage was packed away with a few
personal belongings in a single battered portmanteau, and given
the thievery on the circuit she was always in danger of losing it.
Coupled with a mediocre talent and a broken romance with a
choral member of the *Pinafore* troupe, the life was no more
substantial than the painted canvas flats that got to ride in the
company's only spring wagon while the cast jounced over
broken roads on ironwood axles. This was spare comfort for a
girl drilled since the age of comprehension in the importance of
material goods. When brown-eyed Johnny Behan entered her
little sphere spinning visions of political advancement and
senators' wives in ball gowns, she had deserted the proscenium
without turning her head. Now she only thought of it when the
sun went down.

Backstage, the hour of dusk was the busiest, a frantic
scramble for scattered bits of wardrobe and voices rehearsing
lines from different scenes all at once and spilled greasepaint
making the footing treacherous and locally recruited grips
fumbling with the rigging and scenery. She would peep
through the curtains at the audience waiting out front and her
stomach would flutter. Without all that it was a quiet time and
lonely—too dark to read, too bright to light a lamp, and all the
husbands were on their way home to wives preparing supper.
The quitting whistles at the mines, drawn and deadened by
wind and distance, sounded excruciatingly mournful, like
widowed geese pining for their lost mates. Sadie dreaded being
alone at twilight.

Morgan therefore was a doubly welcome visitor this day.
At his knock she opened the door on him standing on the porch
with his hat in front of him, looking sprucer than usual despite
an improperly buttoned vest and smelling of Genuine Yankee
soap.

"I never meant to disturb you," he said, almost mumbling.
"I'll leave."

She'd forgotten she was wearing a kerchief around her

head. She reached up and tugged it off, releasing a fall of dark hair to her waist. "Don't, I was just packing some things. Wyatt wants me out of here and in Mrs. Young's by tomorrow. Where is he?"

"Out showing some rich limey a timber stand he has up for sale in the Dragoons. He won't be back before morning and asked me to look in on you."

She invited him in for supper and served him something that passed for veal in Bauer's with biscuits and gravy. They spoke of mutual friends, including Harry and Kitty Jones, who had thawed to each other after the Behan episode and were behaving as newlyweds. Morgan's table manners like Wyatt's were impeccable. He buttered his biscuits with scalpellike precision and used the napkin tucked inside the V of his vest to wipe the corners of his moustaches. His conversation was somewhat less facile, and when he remarked for the third time upon her uncommon skill with an oven she asked him what was on his mind.

He drained his water glass, offered to refill hers from the pitcher, and topped off his own. He moved carefully; his shoulder wounds were freshly healed.

"When Wyatt leaves, will you be coming with him?"

"If he asks."

He nodded and drank.

"Are you worried about Mattie?" she asked.

"We have got used to her. The women especially."

"I guessed that."

"Will you be marrying him?"

She shook out her own napkin and refolded it. "He has not asked."

"That is an answer." He rose.

"Is that why you are here?"

He got his hat and coat. "I'd better get out now so people won't talk, but if you would not mind I'd admire to sit on your porch awhile."

She said she wouldn't mind at all, and thanked him for the compliment. It was a custom on the frontier for cowboys to ride many miles just to sit on the porches of respectable women. She was still considering their conversation and wondered with a disloyal little surge if Morgan and Lou were having trouble. She tried flirting. "It will help my reputation to have a comely man camped out in front of my house."

"I am armed."

It seemed a strange thing to declare.

Much later, when she was in bed, a porch board creaked. She pulled on a dressing gown, took from her vanity table an Allen sidehammer that Wyatt had given her for a muff pistol, and pulled aside the window curtain in the gaudy parlor. Morgan was huddled on her porch swing with a heap of snow on his greatcoat shoulders and the crown of his hat.

"Morgan, you sweet simpleton, get in here this instant."

He started awake at her voice coming from the open doorway and stood up quickly, cascading snow. When he saw who it was he made a little movement and she saw his hand coming away from a pistol in his belt just before he buttoned his coat over it.

"I went to sleep there," he said. "I did not start out to."

"You will freeze."

"Well, if you are going to prod me in that way I guess I had better come."

She glanced down at the little revolver still in her hand and put it in the pocket of her dressing gown. When he stepped inside she closed the door and set the latch and fixed a bed for him on the davenport in the parlor with sheets and a quilt. "Am I to know what this is about?" She took his hat and coat.

"Tombstone is no fit place for a woman alone."

In the morning, while Morgan was still sleeping, Johnny Behan passed the kitchen window heading toward the front of the house. Sadie was dressed and walked through the parlor and stepped out onto the porch before he could knock on the door. He had on his sombrero and a black chesterfield that caught him below the knees and made him appear tall, although he was just Sadie's height. The whites of his eyes were pink and she smelled Sen-Sen, always a sign that he had been drinking.

"You are as pretty in the morning as you are at night," he said. "I always said that."

"What do you want?"

"Can't a man visit his wife of a morning?"

"I am not your wife."

"You were quick enough to use my name at the Papago Cash Store when we were together."

"I asked you what you wanted."

"You are squatting on a lot belonging to me," he said. "I have come to dispossess you."

"This house is mine."

"The lot is in my name."

"I put it in your name," she said.

He showed straight white teeth behind his moustaches. "That was short sight. I'll not have you rolling with that murderer on my property. You can move your house or move out."

"You are drunk."

"You used to prefer me this way. You said it slowed me down so you could catch up."

"You are no gentleman."

"At least I am not a whore. I have the papers to serve if you care to see them." He unbuttoned his coat.

He was reaching inside it when Morgan came through the door and struck him in the face. Behan fell backward off the porch, arms windmilling, and sat on the ground. He put fingers to his mouth and brought them away to look at the blood. When he started to rise, Morgan stepped off the porch, bent his knee up under Behan's chin, and struck him low in the stomach. He jackknifed, throwing up. Morgan had him by the collar when Sadie inserted herself between them and pushed at Morgan's chest. "You will kill him!"

"That was the plan." But he lowered his fist, bleeding at the knuckles. Behan tore himself loose from Morgan's other hand and picked up his sombrero.

"You are a particular woman," he said to Sadie. His eyes had glassed over and the lower half of his face was a smear of blood and vomit. "You will only roll with an Earp."

Morgan started toward him. He turned hurriedly and crossed Fremont, tripping over his boots.

"He has been drunk and boasting of his intentions since yesterday," Morgan said.

Sadie fingered the brooch at her throat. She wondered how much Morgan had heard of her conversation with Johnny. "If he had waited one more day he could have walked in and taken the house and lot without conversation."

"It wasn't them he was after."

"Just like a morality play." She kissed him. The gesture surprised Morgan, who hadn't meant that at all.

CHAPTER 14

"THERE IS LITTLE JOHNNY Behan, the great house thief of Arizona Territory."

Behan, puffy-lipped and swaying, passed Doc's table in the Oriental without comment and ordered a whiskey at the bar. Doc called out to Buckskin Frank Leslie behind the bar to give the sheriff plenty of extra ice for his eye in case Morgan Earp stopped in. "Or was it Sadie done that?"

Glaring back, Leslie said something in a low voice to Behan. The bartender was all fierce handlebars and pale gray eyes and wore a Peacemaker on a special belt rig that left the pistol exposed. Parker, Joyce's partner, sat on a high stool under Custer's Last Fight with his bandaged left foot elevated and resting next to the beer pulls. His big toe was still suppurating where Doc had shot the top off the first joint in October.

"Quit riding him," Virgil said.

He was sitting across from Doc, sharing his bottle. Although his calf had healed to the extent that he could venture out without his cane, he had fallen into the practice of extending the leg between tables. Passersby had to walk around it or trip.

"What good is a balky little ass if he is not for riding?" Doc's voice carried.

Virgil leaned across the table, cursing when his leg

twinged. "Don't borrow trouble. A shooting scrape now will put us all in front of the grand jury."

Doc said loudly, "Johnny wouldn't know a trigger from his little cock."

"I will shoot you myself, you one-lung bastard." Virgil spat the words.

Doc paused with his mouth full of whiskey, then swallowed, his Adam's apple working up and down visibly like a slow bobbin. His eyes dulled.

Wyatt came in during the silence and sat down, exuding cold fresh air from his horsehair trail coat with the hair side in. He helped himself to a swallow from his brother's glass and pulled a face. "I looked for you both in the Alhambra. I thought we were through sending Joyce and Parker our business."

"It is like Ritter's embalming parlor over there," Doc said, still watching Virgil. "Things picked up as soon as we came here."

"I saw. If McLaury waits long enough we will wind up gunning each other and save him coin."

The moment ebbed. Virgil sat back and belched into a meaty fist. He had taken on flesh during his recuperation, puffing his jowly Earp face and pushing white shirt out under his vest all around. His star lay flat on a roll of material. "If he is like his brothers he will be a year getting anything done with it."

"If he is only just six months we will be away from here."

"Sell that timber?"

Wyatt shook his head. "The English son of a bitch was never going to pay me until he took a profit off his first load. That is like buying a bed and never paying for it until you get around to sleeping in it."

"He smelled how bad you want to sell."

"I will bust the smeller of the next man that offers me such a transaction."

Doc said, "I told you to salt the place with silver nuggets."

"I am in trouble enough now."

"That variety girl has made a padre of you."

Doc produced a deck and dealt three-handed poker until they were joined by Sherman McMasters and Turkey Creek

Jack Johnson, a friend of Wyatt's from Deadwood. They brought their luck with them and Virgil ran out of chips after eleven o'clock. He got up to go home.

"If you'll wait out a few hands I'll go with you," said Wyatt, who had thrown down most of the winning cards.

"I would be here until sunup waiting for you to climb down off that tiger."

The air outside was cold and sweet after the smoke trapped under the Oriental ceiling. The stars were hidden and there was a raw-iron taste of snow on the wind blowing in off the Whetstones. Yellow light from the saloons scalloped Allen and fanned out the corner front of the Eagle Brewery on the other side of Fifth. Opposite the Oriental on Allen, the two-story adobe under construction by the Huachuca Water Company was dark and jagged, its paneless windows like eye sockets in an ivory skull. Virgil pulled down his vest, stuck his hands inside the pockets of his ulster, and started across Fifth. His leg ached, but not unpleasantly.

He didn't hear the crashes, only their echoes throbbing in the mountains. Light flashed and a rockslide struck him from the left, staggering him. Out of the corner of his eye he saw one of the Eagle windows belly in and fall apart and then he was aware of a warm wet sheet sliding down his left side under his clothes. He took his left hand out of his pocket. Something that was black under the corner gas lamp forked down the back of the hand and ran between the fingers and pattered in the dust at his feet.

Five men erupted out the doorless opening of the Huachuca Water Company building and broke in two directions, three running down Fifth toward Toughnut, two loping east along Allen. Long bronze barrels caught the light as they ran.

For a moment Virgil stood on the spot, uncertain. He had been headed toward the Eagle Brewery. That thought eroded more slowly than his strength. Finally he turned and recrossed the street to the Oriental, where Wyatt and Doc and others were just coming out on the bound with their pistols out. It was a funny thing, but Virgil was most concerned with the thought that his leg had stopped hurting.

"Wyatt," he said, "I'm hit." And then someone was saying, "Catch him!" and darkness lapped him.

This time Allie Earp was there ahead of the doctors. In a dress that Virgil had given her for Christmas, and which she had put on to greet him in when he came home, she hurried ahead of the men who were carrying her husband and held doors for them while they swept through the lobby of the Cosmopolitan and laid him on his stomach on a table in the dining room. She had an eerie sensation of having lived through it before; it came and went and came again, so that certain thoughts and motions seemed trod on many times, but only at the moment of occurrence. She couldn't predict it. Dr. Goodfellow arrived soon afterward, followed by Dr. Matthews, the latter winking uncontrollably, and they cut away Virgil's ulster and frock coat and vest and shirt and underwear like butchers flaying a carcass, exposing torn meat and polished spine, the bone unbearably clean and white against the blood and the dingy gray of his long johns. Allie gasped when she saw it, and gasped again when his sleeve came away along with a handful of buckshot and splinters of shattered bone.

Virgil was conscious. "Never mind, Allie. I've got one arm left to hug you with." His voice was thin and distorted, the right side of his face flattened on the table.

Goodfellow and Matthews turned him over. The tabletop was slick with blood and so were the doctors' arms and shirtfronts before they were done. Both had their sleeves rolled almost to the shoulders. Allie, her world narrowed to details, saw that while Matthews's wrists were pink and hairless, Goodfellow's showed a healthy black matting to the elbows; the arms of a pipe-cutter rather than a surgeon. They bulged when he tore a tablecloth into strips and tied one around Virgil's upper arm and knotted it so that the flesh showed white above and below it. When that was done, the bleeding from the other terrible wounds seemed to increase. The air in the room was musty with the odor of it.

Wyatt came in then, his eyes blue nailheads in a face nearly as pale as his brother's.

"He was hit more than once." Matthews rummaged in his pebbled bag and handed Goodfellow an amber bottle of ether.

Wyatt said, "There were five blasts."

"Amazing," said Goodfellow, drawing the cork. "If he were standing a couple of feet closer you might as well have just called Harry here. He's the coroner."

"He never fell. He walked back across the street to tell me he was hit."

"He is like a bull. That's a help." Goodfellow leaned toward Virgil with the bottle. Virgil pushed it away with his good hand.

"Wyatt, when they get me under don't let them take my arm off. If I have to be buried I want both arms on me."

"No one is burying you today, Virge."

"I need your word."

"All right."

Goodfellow held the mouth of the bottle under Virgil's nostrils and told him to breathe normally. He obeyed, and soon his lids were flickering. The surgeon tamped the cork back in.

"Amputation may be necessary. I have never seen worse damage to a limb."

Wyatt said, "You heard him."

"You must understand that the elbow is gone." Matthews winked. "Even if we can save the arm it will be a useless appendage for the rest of his days. He may wish we took it off just to have it out of the way. That is, if he lives."

"Jim gets on all right, and he has not been able to use his since the war. If Virge dies it won't matter."

Goodfellow looked at Allie, who nodded. "Please yourself," he said. "Tell the hotel staff we need clean towels, as many as they can supply. If they are short, have them boil more or borrow them. Then stay out. There is a deal of bone that must be removed and we must stop the bleeding." Blood was tapping the floor now like drips from a leaky roof.

Wyatt and Allie went out and Wyatt talked to the clerk at the desk. Morgan and Jim were in the lobby with Lou and Mattie, Wyatt's woman, who had been with Allie when the news came about Virgil. After some conversation with Morgan, Lou stayed to wait with Mattie and Allie. The men left. Wyatt had not spoken to Mattie once.

The shotgun blasts that had shredded the biceps and ligaments in Virgil Walter Earp's left arm and obliterated the complex structure of the elbow had also flayed open the lateral and lumbar region of the trunk, increasing blood loss and the risk of infection. Stray pellets had lodged subcutaneously down the left thigh and created an epidermal lividity like a strawberry mark as far as the knee. While Matthews regulated pressure on the tourniquet to prevent gangrene, Goodfellow plucked out the pellets with forceps and flushed the cavities with alcohol and dressed the side and removed four inches of bone from the arm, using tweezers for the smaller spurs. By the time he had the arm swathed in gauze and towels, the bandage on the patient's side had bled through and had to be changed. Matthews kept hotel employees busy boiling and fetching towels that wound up in gory ruined heaps on the floor. Several times the patient showed signs of awakening and had to be put under again. Because of the volatile nature of ether, the doctors had ordered the fire in the hearth extinguished, and as Goodfellow bent over his labor his breath curled and steam rose from the wounds. From time to time he warmed his stiffening fingers in the vapor. Both men were sweating in spite of the cold. Rivulets snailed down Goodfellow's nose, quivered big as marbles on the end, then dropped into the bloody orifices with audible splats. Matthews merely stank. The coroner gave off a sweetish stale smell of corrupting corpses; or so it seemed to his companion, a relentless saver of lives who considered death an intolerable affront to his profession. The floor grew tacky under the soles of their shoes.

At length Goodfellow straightened, his bones cracking. Matthews seized the moment to uncork another bottle from his bag and handed it to his colleague, who sniffed at it.

"Grain alcohol?"

"I get it in samples from San Francisco. Patent medicine." A schoolyard smile flaked years off the coroner's high-domed face.

"Filthy stuff." Goodfellow tipped it up, swallowed, waited for the heat to start spreading, and returned the bottle to Matthews, who swigged at it and winked.

That confounded tic, Goodfellow thought.

They summoned the clerk and two waiters to help them move the patient to a bed in a room on the ground floor. Allie and Lou followed from the lobby. They had sent Mattie upstairs when she couldn't stay awake. Mattie spent most of her time sleeping these days.

"We could not stop the bleeding, only slow it down," Goodfellow told Allie. He had washed up and put on his old shabby coat over his incarnadined shirt, but he had neglected a crusty brown smear on the side of his large nose. He was not old but looked it, with coarse oily pores, a pendulous lower lip, and scales in his beard. Matthews, no great hand at diplomacy, had left. "If he survives these next twenty-four hours his chances are fair. He's a big man, and strong. The heavy coat spared him the worst of it."

"He bought it in Dodge City just before we left. We had an argument about whether he would have need for it in Arizona." She was looking at Virgil's face in repose. He was pale and looked very young.

"It seems we are always fighting," she said. "One time I sent him to buy a calico bonnet and he came back with a lace one because he didn't know what calico was. We had an awful fight over it. I guess people listening to us would think we don't get on." She scraped the heel of a hand up one cheek.

Goodfellow looked away. "We will worry about infection later. I will be back at sunup to change the dressing. Someone should stay with him meanwhile."

Lou volunteered to sit up with her, but Allie told her to go back to her room and sleep. "You have a husband of your own to stay awake for." Allie placed a chair beside the bed where Virgil lay snoring quietly now and held his right hand. Twice as big as hers, it felt soft despite the calluses and slightly clammy, looking knuckleless like a baby's in the glow of the lamp. She heard dripping throughout the night. When the sun came red through the window its rays reflected off a puddle beneath the bed.

She was sure then that he would die, but she felt neither fear nor sorrow, only a numbness, and beneath it the sensation of having lived through it before.

★ ★ ★

A midnight search by Wyatt and Morgan and Doc
Holliday of the unoccupied Huachuca Water Company building had yielded a harvest of paper shotgun shells and a trail-
polished sombrero with J. I. CLANTON burned in big moronic
capitals into the leather sweatband. While John Clum was busy
counting pellet holes by matchlight in the awning posts outside
the Eagle Brewery in the interest of editorial accuracy, an Irish
watchman in an ice house on Toughnut Street reported seeing a
party running past with shotguns shortly after the blasts. He
identified Frank Stilwell and Hank Swilling, a San Pedro
cowboy, and recalled that they had been in the company of a
third man who may or may not have been Ike Clanton—
depending upon how much credit one assigned to testimony
delivered with Doc's Colt's Lightning thrust under the chin. At
the Vizina hoisting works farther up Toughnut, a miner
wearing a mask of caked dust said he saw the same three
scrambling down into the gulch south of Toughnut, but he
didn't think the third man looked anything like Ike Clanton.
Several people had seen two men with shotguns running along
Allen, but only a railroad man boarding at the Palace lodging
house was able to describe one of them as a tall man in an ulster.

"That snakeshit Ringo," Doc said. "You should have let
me take him before."

"I was remiss," said Wyatt.

From there the two Earps and Doc reported to Behan's
office, where the sheriff refused to gather a posse.

"With a city election coming up next week I am disinclined
to commit county funds to any personal quarrels you Earps
may have," he said.

Morgan cursed, and Wyatt stepped in front of Doc.
Deputies Breakenridge and Flynn were both present and
armed. But Doc was steady. He said, "A rich sheriff that cannot
hold a woman in a town like Tombstone may as well hitch his
outfit to Billy there."

Breakenridge colored. Behan, small behind his big yellow
desk with a bottle and glass on the blotter, kept his eyes on
Wyatt. "You are not an officer now. If I hear of you Earps

cutting out after honest citizens I will swear out that posse, and you will be the men we track down."

"Be sure and bring Frank Stilwell," Wyatt said.

At the Wells Fargo office the three woke up the night man and Wyatt sent a wire to United States Marshal Crawley P. Dake in Prescott. Hours later Dake wired Wyatt back an appointment as deputy U.S. marshal to replace Virgil.

John Clum was not running for reelection as mayor of Tombstone. In his place, the Citizens' Safety Committee put up John Carr and endorsed Dave Neagle, a former deputy sheriff who had fallen out with Behan and who had ridden with the September posse that had captured Frank Stilwell and Pete Spence, for chief of police. The candidates bellowed about law and order through megaphones from platforms strung with torches and bunting to crowds pounding their shoulders and stamping their feet in the cold. On election day—Tuesday, January 3, 1882—Behan deputized cowboys from the lower San Pedro Valley to maintain the polls, and throughout the day they patrolled between Fremont and Toughnut streets carrying Winchesters and Henrys with pistols stuck in their pockets. The committee in answer dispatched two armed men to walk behind each of the cowboys. Clum, a man of rare humor who struggled with great success to keep it out of his columns, remarked privately that it was like paying a reporter to edit his own editor. Carr and Neagle were elected and Behan billed the county two thousand dollars to pay his temporary deputies.

Three days later, five men in bandanna masks stopped the Bisbee stage in the Mules and rode off with eighty-five hundred dollars earmarked for laborers at the Copper Queen Mine. During the robbery Frank Stilwell's mask slipped, after which Curly Bill and Pony Deal, the Galeyville half-breed, obligingly lowered theirs. The shotgun messenger identified the remaining two robbers as Ike Clanton and Pete Spence.

District Court Judge William H. Stilwell—no relation to Frank Stilwell—was a long narrow tobacco-smelling man with a graying pompadour, fat sidewhiskers that his political enemies accused him of touching up with lampblack, and that general air of judgeship that jurists were required to have in the territories if they had nothing else. Wyatt stood in front of the judge's carved desk alternately pushing out and denting the crown of his hat while Stillwell signed his name to a stack of closely typewritten sheets, rocked a blotter over each signature, and looked at them again.

"I am not convinced about this Clanton sighting," he said. "The man kept his mask and Clanton has no history of holding up stagecoaches."

"One is all it takes."

"I am of the opinion that Clanton's former friends from Charleston left that hat in the Huachuca building. They would not be likely to bring him along on a robbery with his reputation for duplicity."

Wyatt creased the crown of his hat. "I know Bartholomew, the messenger. He has a good eye."

"It would have to be exceptional to see through a bandanna at night."

"Make it a John Doe if you are doubtful."

"I dislike authorizing them. Some men take them as open hunting licenses." He reread the language. "How is your brother?"

"Goodfellow says he should make it."

"A sighting is a sighting." Stillwell shuffled the warrants and thrust them out. Wyatt reached for them, but the judge held on. His eyes were like brown marbles. "If I were serving these warrants I might be tempted to leave my prisoners in the mesquite where alibis count for nothing."

Wyatt made no response.

"That is not advice, mind."

"I don't take it to be."

Stillwell released the warrants. Wyatt put on his hat and folded the sheaf lengthwise and put it inside his horsehair trail coat. His spurs clanked and rattled on his way out.

PROCLAMATION

To the Citizens of the City of Tombstone:

I am informed by his Honor, William H. Stillwell, Judge of the District Court of the First Judicial District, that Wyatt Earp, who left this city yesterday

with a posse, was intrusted with warrants for the
arrest of divers persons charged with criminal of-
fenses. I request the public to abstain from any
interference with the execution of said warrants.

John Carr, Mayor

Copies of the handbill, printed in the *Epitaph* office in black
serifs on ivory stock, were nailed up on vertical surfaces
throughout Tombstone on January 24; and by noon most of
them had disappeared, to resurface again years later, yellowed
and cracking apart between the pages of family Bibles and in
stacks of letters bound with faded ribbon.

Wyatt's posse consisted of Morgan and Warren Earp, the
latter newly returned after a long absence; Doc Holliday,
Sherman McMasters, and Turkey Creek Jack Johnson, as
efficient a man with a horse and a pistol as Wyatt had known.
At the West End Corral they selected big chesty mounts built to
carry a lot of iron and rode south with Winchesters and
shotguns and saddle pistols in scabbards and revolvers under
their coats—six grim men with moustaches in wide hats and big
coats, who looked like pallbearers.

While they were gone, Ike Clanton, Frank Stilwell, and
Hank Swilling walked into Johnny Behan's office and surrendered their weapons. The charge of attempted murder was
dropped for lack of positive witnesses. Clanton and Stilwell
posted bail on the robbery charge and were released.

The news reached the Earp party a week later when they
stopped at Lewis Springs to water their horses and fill their
canteens, but they didn't turn back. Curly Bill and Pony Deal
had been named among the men who had robbed another stage
at Contention a few days after the Bisbee holdup and they were
laying down a hot trail to old Mexico without pausing to cover
their tracks.

"Curly Bill is the nigger in the woodbox." Wyatt wriggled
thawed fingers back into his glove and used a stick from the
campfire to light his pipe.

"Bill has no truck with you," Doc said.

"He has been moving in my direction ever since he and Ringo adjusted the Hasletts's case in Huachita."

"That is just guesswork."

"It is no less fact for that."

They were camped on the western face of the Mules and the snow was piled in neat heaps against rocks and snarled bushes; everywhere else the ground was bare. Doc's high cheeks were windburned and a week's growth of sand-colored beard had filled out the hollows. He was loath to own to it, but the clear cold air agreed with him. Warren and Morgan were asleep in their rolls, or pretending to be, and Sherman McMasters had his Centennial Winchester knocked down and laid out in flickering pieces on his spread blanket while he wiped oil off the barrel with an old blue bandanna. McMasters, a Wells Fargo shotgun messenger like Morgan and Wyatt before him, preferred the carbine to the Stevens ten-gauge issued by the company. Doc suspected that if the ruddy, chin-whiskered man could find a hole in the gun big enough he would fuck it. Turkey Creek Jack was standing watch farther up the grade.

Doc said, "I thought Ike was our man."

Wyatt shook his head, sucking life into the pipe. "Ringo and the others have got him licking their boots over that Leonardhead and Crane transaction. They planted that hat to get us on him so they would not have to waste the powder. The business has Curly Bill all over it. The *Nugget* has us and Ike down as stage robbers falling out, and if we kill Ike or he kills us we will prove it right."

"It is too various for me."

"Curly Bill is a devil. He got Fred White to shoot himself with the border roll and this is the same thing only it is our finger on the trigger."

"What about the rest?"

"If Swilling was in that adobe he was paid. Stilwell and Ringo need killing."

"I have said that right along. I hope you remember where you heard it." Doc unstopped a canteen half-full of whiskey and tilted it. "McLaury?"

Wyatt ground his teeth on his pipestem. "Curly Bill first."

But the signs grew scarce near the border, as they always

did in that rocky country, and with Bat Masterson gone marshaling in Colorado they hadn't a tracker with the skill to pick them out and returned lathered and blowing to Tombstone. There they read in the *Epitaph* that Johnny Behan and Ike Clanton had sworn out warrants in Contention charging Wyatt, Virgil, and Morgan Earp and Doc Holliday once again with the murders of William Clanton and Frank and Tom McLaury on Fremont Street on October 26, 1881.

CHAPTER 15

THAT NIGHT IN MARCH he dreamed of Urilla.

He hadn't thought about her in months, or dreamed of her in years; and on those most recent occasions when he had thought of her, she was like someone else's memory, something belonging to the tall yellow-haired boy who had graded track for the U.P. with his older brother in Wyoming and barked his knuckles on stubbled chins behind the saloon tents in Cheyenne and Laramie and fled a horse-stealing charge in the Nations. Those times he saw a girl with a round face and straight hair that smelled of brown soap, plain really, in a loose print dress tied under her bosom to disguise her condition. It was always day in the memory and dusty sunlight leaned in through the windows.

But in his dream it was night. A lamp shed a greasy globe of light that barely reached the walls in a tight room thick with Missouri in October, with crickets stitching outside the open window and not enough fresh air coming in to jiggle the flame in the glass chimney. Urilla's face was bloated and glistening, white against the ticking. She was shrieking—silently in the dream, her mouth a twisted hole with nothing coming out of it, but Wyatt's ears rang and the midwife barked at him to hold the lamp still—and her nightgown was rucked to her waist and plastered transparent to her swollen breasts and her legs were spread obscenely and the blood—dear Lord, it was black—was dumping out between them, over the midwife's raw hands trying to stop it with kerosene-soaked rags. The midwife in the dream was Mattie. That made no sense, because he hadn't met her until weeks later.

The boy had emerged feet first. Urilla was small down there and when Mattie had summoned Wyatt into the room he had seen the tiny naked body flailing for freedom like a toad being devoured slowly by a massasauga and he heard the crackling of bones. His first thought was that they were the boy's and he tore Mattie away, shouting that she was murdering his son. She slapped him hard (in the dream, but observing it too, he saw the bloody handprint appear on his cheek even as he felt the sting) and spat at him that the boy was murdering his mother. After that Wyatt did as she told him. She strangled the infant pulling him out, had to; but by then the blood had a good start, thick and black and stinking of heated iron. Urilla shrieked silently.

Wyatt knew when it was over. Mattie's hands slowed, she stopped bunching and pressing the rags and started using them gently, as sponges to control the mess. Urilla's mouth slackened and she lay panting. At length her breathing grew more even. She smiled weakly. The pain had ended. She was looking at him, and he saw in her eyes that she knew he was there. He smiled back and held her hand. It was warm and sticky. He was still holding it when the bleeding stopped—stopped because the heart was no longer pumping—and Mattie and someone else pried his hand loose and led him from the room. In the dream the someone else looked like Wyatt's half-brother Newton. But Newton and his family had been living outside Missouri and were nowhere near that shack at the time.

The room the pair led Wyatt into was the same one they had just left. A lamp shed a greasy globe of light that barely reached the walls and Urilla was shrieking silently. . . .

He jolted awake with a tongueless shout. He gaped around, and for a moment the bed was stained with Urilla's blood. Then it faded and the cool air in the hotel room chilled the slippery flesh under his soaked nightshirt. It was March 1882, not October 1870; and he was in Tombstone, Arizona Territory, not Lamar, Missouri.

A bar of moonlight lay across the clock on the mantel. Twenty past ten. He had been asleep for less than ten minutes, although it seemed much longer. He had turned in early after a long day spent quartering the town with Morgan in search of Frank Stilwell, Hank Swilling, Pete Spence, and Johnny Ringo, all of whom had been seen earlier. All but Swilling, who had been found not guilty of the murder attempt on Virgil, were still wanted on Judge Stillwell's warrants. But there was no sign of them, and in the evening Wyatt and Morgan and their women had gone to Schieffelin Hall to watch the Lingard Opera Company performing *Stolen Kisses*. They had bought the tickets to celebrate their release after the court in Contention had remanded the Clanton-McLaury murder case back to Tombstone. Wyatt hadn't liked the opera; the music was forgettable and the actors trumpeted their lines, and anyway he preferred Shakespeare. Sadie and Lou had enjoyed themselves, however. Lou had even unbent so far as to wish Sadie good night when they dropped her at Mrs. Young's boardinghouse. Wyatt had wanted to invite Sadie back to the Cosmopolitan, but Mattie was staying with Virge and Allie and the day had been frustrating enough without a scene in the hallway. Morgan had then kissed Lou and went off to Bob Hatch's billiard hall for a game with the owner.

The dream was too real. Rather than pick it up where he left it, Wyatt swung his feet to the floor and dressed in the same white shirt and black suit he had worn to Schieffelin Hall. He checked the load in the big American and pocketed it with the handle turned out.

The cherrywood bar in Hatch's saloon separated the billiard parlor from the rest of the establishment. Wyatt paid for a beer and carried the glass around the end of the bar and took a chair against the wall. Morgan, bent over a rear table in his vest, glanced across the felt at his brother. The chesterfield lamp suspended over the table caverned his eyes under a carapace of white brow.

"It's too early to go to bed," Wyatt said.

Morgan nodded and shot. The six ball glanced off a cushion and came to rest against the four ball with an apologetic click. He grunted.

Hatch, all wrists and Adam's apple without collar or cuffs and only the lower half of his ecclesiastical face visible inside the cone of light, stepped away from his spot in front of the alley door to take his turn. He had on his hat with the brim turned up all around. Morgan circled behind him and chalked his cue. He winked gravely at Sherman McMasters, watching with a drummer named Berry by the stove next to the bar.

The room was stark, sawdust-floored and all naked yellow plaster above the wainscoting with an embossed tin ceiling and a pronghorn head staring agate-eyed from the east wall, Morgan's hat hung on one antler. An iron cuspidor stood under it on a stained rubber mat. The upper half of the door to the alley was paneled in glass, the only window in the room. The two lower panes were painted over.

Icicles of glass tipped out of the upper frames, shivering down as silently as Urilla's nightmare screams under the bang. The butt of Morgan's cue skidded on the floor and he fell forward. Berry shouted and glass tinkled in a pause, and then a second report swelled the room. Plaster pounded out of the wall above Wyatt's head, powdering his hat and shoulders.

Blue smoke turned in the air. Morgan lay on his face in the sawdust and glass splinters. Berry sprawled on his side next to the stove, the ball that had passed through Morgan lodged in one thigh and his weak heart stopped by the shock. He had come west in search of his health. Wyatt, moving the instant the second ball slapped the wall above him, hurled himself behind a table and tore his pocket freeing the American. He cocked, shattered a door panel, cocked, misfired, cocked, collapsed one of the painted panes—triangles of milk-glass tumbling—cocked, misfired, cocked, misfired, said, "Shit!" and crab-ran to his brother while McMasters and Hatch and another man who had come in from the saloon clawed at the bolted door and swung out into the alley. They returned after a moment dragging their pistols and put them away to help lift the wounded man.

"Don't, I can't stand it."

"His back's broken," Wyatt said.

Goodfellow and Matthews arrived minutes later. The surgeon pulled back Berry's lids and felt his neck and turned away toward Morgan as they tried lifting him again. This time they got him up—Morgan cursed—and Hatch held open the door to the card room, which contained a davenport. They set Morgan down on it. The mohair quickly turned dark.

"Put my legs straight."

"They are straight, Morg," said Wyatt.

"They're my legs, damn it."

Wyatt adjusted them.

"Is Bob here?"

Hatch spoke up.

Morgan smiled. "This is the last game of pool I'll ever play in here."

"Damn it, Morg," said Wyatt.

"Tell Ma and Pa. I don't want them getting it in the papers."

"They won't."

Matthews was unbuttoning Morgan's shirt. He motioned him away with a feeble gesture. "Wyatt."

Wyatt bent over him.

"You were right, Wyatt," he said. "I can't see a thing."

The latch split on the second blow and the door whacked the wall on the other side, throwing crooked a framed Stephensgraph of the Blessed Mother and sucking dust balls out of corners in the current. The nickel-plated Colt's Lightning hurtled into the room towing Doc behind it. He towered there in his tall-crowned hat, the tails of his greatcoat spreading behind him like buzzard's wings.

"Where is he?"

The woman was looking, not at the weapon, but at the skull face of the gringo who was holding it, his eyes molten in

their sockets. She thought it was *Señor Muerte* come to claim her
children and she pulled them closer. They wriggled, unable to
breathe. She was reciting the Rosary in rapid Spanish, staring
up at the skull face and not aware that she was saying anything.
He was taller than the doorway; from the floor where she
crouched with her dusty skirt drawn down over her knees and
her arms around the boy and girl, he seemed to stretch to the
sky, big in the boots and shiny pistol bending his wrist under its
weight and narrowing up to the terrible skull. His teeth were
bared in a rictus.

There was another man standing behind him. An ordinary
one this, not as tall, and of the flesh; but of course *Señor Muerte*
always had a mortal helper to ferry the soul into the Afterlife.
This was the reason one weighted down the eyelids of the dead
with new centavos, to give to the ferryman for the ride so he
did not push off and leave the soul standing on the shore
between worlds. She would have crossed herself, but she was
afraid to let go of the *muchachas*.

Turkey Creek Jack Johnson looked past Doc at the plump
young Mexican woman cowering on the plank floor with her
arms encircling a barefooted boy and girl in dirty cutdown
clothes. The girl was light-haired, probably half American. He
lowered his shotgun.

"Squatters," he said. "I tell you, McLaury's hauled freight
out of here."

"Donde esta Señor McLaury?"

The woman went on reciting. Doc rolled back the hammer
and repeated the question.

She stopped. *"No sabe."*

He pointed the pistol at the light-haired girl. *"Donde?"*

"Por favor, señor!" And then her Spanish got too fast for
Turkey Creek Jack to follow. Some kind of heathen chant.

"She don't savvy Will McLaury from a buck nigger. Let's
go, Doc."

"No, she knows."

"She's just a dumb *puta*." He was studying the woman's
face and was satisfied when there was no reaction that he had
calculated her right.

"Maybe if I shoot the girl."

"Shoot the boy if you have to shoot one of them," Turkey Creek Jack said. "He is all Mex."

"Does the girl look a little like Ringo to you?"

"He has not been in the territory long enough."

"Quién es el padre de la muchacha?"

The woman went on chanting. She was rocking on her heels now with her eyes shut tight. The children stared with black-olive eyes at the two strange Americans with fine clothes and shiny guns.

"No, I guess she doesn't." Doc seated the hammer.

They withdrew, leaving the door standing open. Turkey Creek Jack could hear the rhythmic Spanish all the way down the block. All of these greasers were half Indian.

Doc kicked open several more doors on Fremont, terrifying Pete Spence's wife Marietta, who said she hadn't seen her husband in days, finding several houses empty, and interrupting Harry Jones—whose wife Kitty was in Tucson—with a girl from the Bird Cage. When Doc came out of one of the vacant houses trailing Turkey Creek Jack, Wyatt Earp was standing out front. Wyatt hadn't changed clothes and his brother's blood had dried in a brown crust on his white shirt. The sky was bleeding out behind him.

"Stand away," Doc said.

Wyatt said, "Haring off like this is a sound way to get yourself killed."

"I have been looking for just such a way for years."

"I need you alive."

"You place too much store in keeping folks alive. You let Ike run and he ran straight to Johnny Behan. You let Ringo go off with Billy Blab and he shot Virge and killed Morg. Your high morals come too dear for me."

"Stilwell killed Morg. He was seen running with Pete Spence and some others."

"Ringo was in it."

"Virge and Jim are taking Morg's body home to California on tomorrow's train," Wyatt said. "I am seeing them as far as Tucson. Warren is coming and so is Sherm McMasters. I want you along if you will come. You too, Jack."

"To carry the coffin?"

"To fill some others."

The sun broke behind Wyatt, an open wound on the flats south of the Whetstones with their shadows clawing the valley. Doc scabbarded his pistol and stepped down off the porch.

PART FOUR
THE
PALLBEARERS

It is often said that every nation has the government it deserves. What is much more certain is that every nation has the newspapers it deserves.

—Matthew Arnold, *Civilization in the United States,* 1883

CHAPTER 16

"STILWELL AND IKE CLANTON are here."

Sherman McMasters wiped coffee from his red whiskers. He had managed to sleep aboard the train and his thoughts were always slow to turn over when he had slept during the day. "Well, hell, they are standing trial for that Bisbee stage holdup. Are we fixing to blast our way into the Tucson courthouse?"

Wyatt rested a hand on the table and leaned closer. His breath smelled of stale tobacco. "I mean here at the station. Warren saw them."

Morgan Earp had boarded the westbound train at Contention in an unlined white pine box with the lid nailed shut and *Colton, Calif.* scribbled on the foot in thick carpenter's pencil in the head porter's round hand. The others had left the buckboard and buggy and horses at the livery and ridden in a coach to Tucson, where there was a supper stop. Lou wore a black dress and veil and the men had on black armbands and guns under ankle-length dusters. Mattie and Allie wore capes and broad hats tied with scarves under their chins to protect them from cinders. James and Nellie and her daughter Hattie had taken an earlier train.

"How do you want to handle it?" McMasters asked.

"First let's get Virge and Allie back on board."

The couple were eating alone at a table in the dining room

of Porter's Hotel near the depot. McMasters occupied a corner table with a view of both entrances and his Winchester leaning against it. Wyatt carried a sawed-off Stevens ten-gauge shotgun mounted on a brass frame. When Virgil and Allie were finished they walked ahead across the platform with Wyatt and McMasters following. They were not hiding their weapons under their dusters now, but carrying them in both hands out in the open. Virgil leaned a little on his wife as they walked. His left arm hung in a black sling.

Warren, getting rawboned now like his brothers, no longer just lanky, and sporting proper moustaches, was standing by the passenger coaches with a Winchester. Wyatt caught his eye and Warren pointed across the track with his chin. It was dark out and steam from the oily black boiler curled white in the lights of the station.

Doc climbed down from another car as Allie was helping Virgil up the steps. Doc had his coat wrapped around his right arm with a shotgun inside it. "Stilwell's on the other side," he told Wyatt. "He's heeled."

"Rifle or pistol?"

"Pistol."

"What about Clanton?"

"I never saw him."

Wyatt reached up and touched his brother's good arm. "Turkey Creek Jack is to stay with you and Allie until the train starts moving. Remind him."

"I guess I am not so crippled I cannot protect my own wife."

"Morg was not crippled at all."

Virgil nodded. His face had grown fat, pigging his eyes, which had lost some of their blue directness.

"So long, Virge. I'll be seeing you soon." Wyatt stuck out his free hand.

Virgil took it. "Take care of yourself, Wyatt."

"I intend to."

The whistle brayed, summoning passengers. Wyatt and the others started up the track toward the engine. They spread out as far as the platform would let them. McMasters's shortness spoiled the formation a little. Steam churned around their legs.

"There!" Doc raised his shotgun.

The acetylene lamp mounted on the front of the towering engine made a stick-figure of the man running through it, throwing his shadow thirty yards. The shadows received him on their side of the tracks.

Wyatt gestured with his shotgun and the men turned left toward a line of coaches standing on a siding. The westbound was pulling out now, its wheels scraping for traction on the greasy rails. A jet of steam reflected light off a face in the shadow of the stationary cars. McMasters and Warren Earp fired their Winchesters. The reports rattled with the levers working between them. Doc's shotgun boomed.

The train was picking up speed, shaking the ground and fluttering yellow light from its chain of windows into the narrow alley between the platform and the siding. Frank Stilwell, hatless in a store suit, lay on the cinderbed supporting himself on his right elbow. His left leg was sprawled at an unnatural angle and he had a hand on his right thigh, darkening between the fingers. His left sleeve and both trousers legs glistened. His pistol was in his right trousers pocket, trapped under his own weight.

Wyatt's shadow crossed his face. Without the trademark cigar it was a boy's face, white and contorted. "Morg!" Trying to rise, he grasped at the only lever that presented itself, the barrels of Wyatt's shotgun. "Morg!"

The whistle brayed.

Special to the *Epitaph*

Tucson, March 21—This morning at daylight the track man from the Southern Pacific Railroad found the body of Frank Stilwell, about one hundred yards north of Porter's Hotel at the side of the track, riddled with bullets. . . . Just as the train was leaving six shots were heard in the locality of the assassination, but attracted no particular attention and nothing was known of the tragedy until this morning when the body was discovered. Six shots went into his body— four rifle balls and two loads of buckshot. Both legs were shot through and a charge of buckshot in his left thigh and a charge through his breast, which must have been delivered close, as the coat was powder-burnt, and six buckshot holes within a radius of three inches.

Turkey Creek Jack Johnson—sometimes called Mysterious Jack after his hero, Mysterious Dave Mather, but only by himself—was six feet of backward-leaning male panther with a set of pointed whiskers like Louis Napoleon's and a slight limp from a twisted ankle suffered when he leaped off the westbound train. He caught up with the Earps and McMasters and Doc on their way across the railyard after the shooting and spent the next two hours with them pumping frightened desk clerks for descriptions of their guests and searching faces in saloons. But the town was fresh out of Ike Clanton, and the group returned to the station and shared an empty boxcar on the eastbound freight. It was steel cold inside and hoboes had urinated in the corners. Warren slept. McMasters tried to, gave up and lit a cigar. The pungent smoke deadened the ammonia stench from the corners. Turkey Creek Jack and Doc played blackjack with Doc's deck, Holliday doing most of the winning, until the moon moved behind a cloud and stayed there. Wyatt rode in silence near the open door with his knees up and his arms folded on top of them supporting his chin. His strong jowls were last to fade into shadow.

At Contention they claimed their horses and the buckboard and buggy and rode back to Tombstone, five men scratchy-bearded and nodding in clothes they had been wearing for thirty-six hours. The *Epitaph* had carried the wire story of Stilwell's killing; a crowd clotted around the entrance to the West End Corral while they were inside and followed them on foot up Allen to the Cosmopolitan. The five formed a flying wedge on the boardwalk with weapons exposed, ignoring questions and jerking their buttstocks at anyone who came close. When they entered the hotel the crowd remained outside.

McMasters and Turkey Creek Jack shared Virgil and Allie's old room. Doc took his, and Wyatt and Warren bunked together. At three o'clock in the afternoon Tom Fitch tapped on Wyatt's door and when Wyatt answered with his shotgun at belt-buckle level the attorney told him that Johnny Behan and City Marshal Dave Neagle were waiting in the lobby to arrest him.

He lowered the gun. "How many others?"

"Six or eight out front," Fitch said. "They are all armed."

"I never featured them to come any other way." Wyatt let him in.

Doc Holliday entered close behind him in outdoor gear and cradling a shotgun, and Fitch knew then that he had been watching from the room across the hall. He looked fitter than Fitch had seen him in months. Warren, barefooted and in long johns patched at the knees, was sitting on the edge of the bed with his hair in snarls and a .44 American like Wyatt's in his right hand. When he saw Fitch he let down the hammer gently and laid the pistol atop the walnut bureau. He reached for his trousers slung over the back of a chair.

"Tom, maybe you'd better wait up here until this blows off." Wyatt shrugged into his horsehair coat and duster and put on his hat.

"Not for a dollar. I will see this."

"It's your hide." He picked up his shotgun. "I'll take point. Warren, you're behind me. Sherm and Jack will back you and Doc will slam the back door."

"I am always riding drag," Doc said.

"You just spray the room if we go down. Be sure and get Johnny."

"If I get only one, Johnny will be the one I get."

The door to the others' room sprang open as soon as Doc rapped on it. McMasters and Turkey Creek Jack were dressed and carrying their Winchesters. They filed into the hole waiting for them and the group started down.

"I'm fond of parades," said Jack.

Neagle, a square brown man in a felt hat and canvas coat with a star pinned to it, was standing with Behan on the floral carpet in the lobby. The sheriff's face was shadowed under his broad flat brim and he had a Cooper pistol in glistening leather on his hip. They watched the party descend the narrow staircase

behind rifles and shotguns. Doc stopped as soon as he cleared
the arch and stood with one foot on a higher step and his ten-
gauge in both hands at hip height. Fitch watched from the
landing.

Wyatt paused on the lowest step. His shotgun rested in the
crook of his right arm. The grandfather clock next to the
staircase chimed late with a grinding of gears thirsty for oil.
Behan jumped a little on the first gong.

When it was finished, Neagle said, "This is none of my
affair. Johnny thinks if I talk with you we can save some
trouble."

The newel post on the staircase banister supported a brass
knob the size of a croquet ball. Wyatt shifted the shotgun to his
left arm and rested his right hand on top of the knob, spreading
the fingers.

"Dave, you tell that chickenshit sheriff that I will let him
cut off any finger on that hand if he will only try to arrest me."
He was looking at Behan, who had raised his face out of
shadow.

"I will see you alone," Behan said.

Wyatt came down off the step and brought his open right
palm up swiftly. The sheriff's hat spun off, exposing his balding
pate. He started and touched the handle of his Cooper. Doc
palmed back both hammers on his shotgun with a double click.
Behan dropped his hand.

Wyatt said, "Johnny, if you're not careful you will see me
once too often."

Behan looked small without the hat. He picked it up,
swept dust off the crown, squared it over his eyebrows, and
went out. Warren laughed shortly.

Wyatt told him to shut up. "Dave?"

Neagle turned his palms out at his sides. "My jurisdiction
does not include shootings in Tucson."

The others came down into the small lobby. Fitch descended last. "Johnny will find his balls out there in the street
with the others," he told Wyatt.

"He hasn't warrants or he'd have served them. If he
admires to open fire on a deputy U.S. marshal and his sworn
posse he will answer to Prescott."

"He will do his explaining in hell," Doc said.

Wyatt shook hands with Fitch and went out, trailing the others in the same formation they had assumed on the stairs. Allen Street was busy and Behan and his deputies stood next to the boardwalk out of traffic, their shotgun muzzles resting on the edge of the walk. As the Earp party turned west, Warren blew a kiss to Billy Breakenridge, who flushed to his hat. They stopped at the Papago Cash Store for supplies, McMasters and Turkey Creek Jack standing watch outside, then saddled fresh mounts in the corral. Wyatt threw his pouches over Dick Naylor, a round-muscled black he had brought with him to Tombstone from Dodge City. They rode single file out Fremont Street with their linen dusters eared back behind the handles of their pistols and their long guns across their saddle throats and cartridge belts slung from the horns. They passed the narrow empty lot next to Fly's boardinghouse where the fight had started and the house on the corner of Third where Billy Clanton died and where the McLaurys were laid out and didn't look at them.

At the top of a bayonet-studded rise overlooking the sprawl of frame and adobe buildings that made up Tombstone, Wyatt dragged the last out of a cigar and snapped the stub at a horned toad, which darted into a mescal clump an instant before it struck. Then he swung Dick Naylor's head northeast. The others followed.

They never went back.

The Dragoons reared straight up out of a flatiron plain littered with chaparral and mesquite, a broken wall ocean-blue against a bright metal sky and fluted like a hornpipe. Cochise had hidden there and then Geronimo, burying their naked braves face down in the sand for a mile around the foothills, to come erupting up out of the ground like the Colchian dead and fall upon small parties of whites with clubs and Springfields, yelping like coyotes. Sudden country.

"That's Pete Spence's timber stand there to the south," said Turkey Creek Jack. He had dismounted to let his piebald nuzzle water out of his cupped palm. The animal lipped the last of it off his fingers and he swigged from his canteen.

Doc spat, got some pink on the toe of his boot in the stirrup, and rubbed it against his gray's barrel side. "How do we know he's there?"

Wyatt said, "He was not in Tucson and he is wanted in Tombstone. Charleston will not have him and I do not covet riding into Galeyville without Wyatt Berry Stapp and the federal cavalry."

The timber was scrub and cottonwoods and a number of the tall straight pines the Indians called lodgepole, standing around a spring-fed watering hole on the western slope of the Dragoons, blue-green and cool, a cathedral of shade in a desert cracking under a summering sun. As the party drew within earshot a hammering noise like gunshots reverberated in the mountains. It was followed by an agonized crackling and a rush of falling foliage, a tree surrendering to the blows of an axe.

The riders circled east to come in from high ground. Long before they would have been seen, the horses smelled water and a high whinny escaped Doc's bay before he could clamp a hand over its nostrils. They broke into gallop then, and Sherman McMasters lifted his rifle when a small brown man standing near the water hurled down his axe and ran away up the rocky incline.

"Slow him down!" Wyatt shouted. "Don't kill him."

McMasters swung off at the base of the slope and dropped to one knee on the marshy ground with his cheek against the buttstock and his elbow braced on his raised thigh. He drew a bead on the half-naked figure spread-eagled on the rocks above and stroked the trigger. The man shouted and slapped his leg. The echo of the report wobbled among the broken peaks and died rustling.

McMasters levered another cartridge into the chamber. "Come down."

The man was crouched holding his left thigh with both hands. He stood up awkwardly and picked his way down the steep grade, dangling the leg. At the base he raised both hands and stood with most of his weight on his right foot. He was a narrow Mexican, shirtless, with clumps of muscle in his upper

arms and an incipient pot with a knob for a navel. He had long
black hair, slick like his body, and triangles of black stubble on a
long upper lip like a monkey's. He wore broken boots laced to
his knees and dirty white cotton trousers belted with a rope and
stained red down the left leg. McMasters lowered his Winchester and got up.

"Hardly drew blood." He sounded disgusted.

"Wind was against you," said Doc, dismounting. He
coughed and spat.

Wyatt stepped down in front of the Mexican. "Who are
you?"

The Mexican said nothing. He was breathing heavily from
his climb but his face was a plank with knotholes for eyes.

Wyatt backhanded him. The Mexican caught his balance
on the injured leg and took in his breath. "I said who are you."

Turkey Creek Jack was watching from the saddle. "I don't
think he savvies American."

"Doc."

"If it hasn't to do with raising stakes or pulling teeth my
Spanish is no good."

"*Que es su nombre?*" McMasters asked.

The Mexican's face became animated: light came into the
knothole eyes and the monkey lip lifted away from amber teeth
and black gums. "*Me llamo* Florentino."

"Is that his first name or his last?" asked Wyatt.

"*Que es su nombre otro?*"

"*Tengo no otro, señor.*"

Wyatt slapped him again. "Only a bastard hasn't a second
name. Ask him is he a bastard."

McMasters didn't know the word for *bastard*. He asked him
if he had a father.

"*Sí, naturalmente.*" He looked puzzled.

"Tell him he's a liar."

The Mexican shook his head hard, spraying sweat. "*No,
por la vera cruz.*"

"What did he say?"

"I think he said it's Cruz."

"That is progress. Ask Florentino Cruz why he ran."

"*Por qué corra usted?*"

The Mexican answered in a torrent of Spanish and Yaqui.

"He says it's his practice to run when gringos with guns are chasing him."

Warren was watering his blaze-face at the spring. "He looks like a half-breed to me. What's the name of that breed was seen with Stilwell the night Morg got it?"

"Indian Charlie," Wyatt said. "This one's no breed."

"Around the eyes, a little," said Doc.

Turkey Creek Jack said, "You can go either way with a greaser."

"*Se llama* Indian Charlie?" McMasters asked.

"Forget that. Ask him where's Spence."

"Tombstone, *señor.*"

Wyatt slapped him, putting his weight behind it. The Mexican sat down on the ground.

"Tell him to get up."

McMasters kicked him in the ribs. "*Arriba.*"

The Mexican rose with difficulty. All the flatness was gone from his expression now.

"Ask him again."

"*Donde esta Señor Spence?*"

"Tombstone."

Wyatt slapped him.

"*Donde?*"

"Tombstone."

Wyatt slapped him.

"*Donde?*"

"Tombstone, *señor!*"

Wyatt tugged his American from his pocket and thumbed back the hammer. The Mexican backed up a step, putting his weight on the wounded leg now, not noticing. "*Es verdad, señor! Por dios!*"

"Tell him I believe him."

McMasters translated. The Mexican relaxed a notch, shifting his weight back onto his good leg.

"Ask him how much Spence pays him to do killing."

McMasters couldn't remember if *matar* or *meter* meant "to kill." He shortened it. "*Cuanto dinero paga Señor Spence a usted?*"

The Mexican glanced around at the trees marked with red paint for cutting. *"Veinticinco dolares."*

"He said—"

"Twenty-five dollars." Wyatt fired. A blue hole appeared under the Mexican's left nipple. He jerked, looked at Wyatt, looked down at himself, let out a loud fart, knelt, and lay over on his right side.

"Jesus." Turkey Creek Jack took off his hat to fan away the stink.

McMasters said, "I don't think he was talking about the same thing we were."

CHAPTER 17

JOHN CLUM RODE INTO their camp that night outside Charleston. The former Indian agent had on a duster and a stained felt hat, which he removed slowly so that Warren would recognize his bald head in the moonlight. Warren took his Winchester off cock and Clum stepped down and handed him his reins and went over to where the others had their blankets spread. They were keeping a cold camp. Wyatt put down his sardine tin and fork and walked off with him a few yards, where the two stood silhouetted against the kerosene glow from town. A warm dry wind lifted their dusters and swept sand into little ridges against their boots.

"I sent for Fred Dodge," Wyatt said.

"He is down again with the mountain fever. He asked me to come in his place."

"Who else knows we're here?"

"Just the man you sent."

"What have you heard?"

"Curly Bill is somewhere up on the Babocomari," Clum said. "You know Johnny has deputized him, also Ike and Phin Clanton and half of Galeyville to look for you."

"I didn't know. But Johnny knows no one else to swear. Curly Bill at least will find me."

"They are saying you murdered a Mexican at Pete Spence's wood ranch today."

"I killed Indian Charlie in a fair fight when he owned to helping kill Morgan for twenty-five dollars. I gave him to three to jerk his pistol. He lost count."

"Johnny has Spence in custody. He turned himself in yesterday."

Wyatt stroked the stubble on his neck. "The breed said he was in town. I never credited it."

"You never gave a man to three to do anything when you were holding all the cards. You're talking to me, not the *Epitaph*."

"I stopped answering to both when they killed Morg and crippled Virge."

"People are weary of this killing stuff," Clum said. "Riding up to waterholes and gunning anyone who looks like he might know Curly Bill or Spence or Ike Clanton does nothing for your case."

"If it isn't Geronimo it is Curly Bill, and if it isn't Curly Bill it is me. They are quick to fix blame in Tombstone. I am their scalded dog this season."

"Your old friend Bob Paul is sheriff in Pima County now. He has put in for warrants to arrest you and Doc Holliday for Frank Stilwell's murder. Johnny will serve them."

"I truly hope he tries. Where does the Citizens' Safety Committee stand on this transaction?"

"Our concern is Tombstone. What goes on outside its limits is between you and Johnny and Curly Bill."

"Cunts, the bunch of you."

Clum said nothing. His head was a marble carving in the pale light.

"What do you know of Ringo?" Wyatt asked.

"Quit the territory, they say."

"Ringo is not one to tuck his tail in that way."

"I am only telling you what's being said." Clum realized he was still holding his hat and put it back on. "Governor Gosper has asked President Arthur for authority to organize a territorial police force like the Texans have, to deal with the situation in

Cochise County. If he gets it he will shut down Tombstone like the smallpox."

"By then I will be square with Curly Bill or dead. Have Marsh Williams send someone to meet me at Iron Springs with a thousand dollars. Crawley Dake in Prescott will see Wells Fargo gets it back."

"Williams is no longer with Wells Fargo."

"What happened?"

"I heard he was stealing from the company and informing on money shipments."

"Old Marsh."

"There are some who think this proves Ike Clanton's charge that you and Holliday participated in the Benson stage robbery last March. You and Williams were in it together, they say."

"Poor coin for protecting them from Johnny and his friends. I don't guess the committee has been doing much talking in our favor."

Clum's hat shadowed his eyes and made crow's-wings of his moustaches. "This was your game from the start, yours and the cowboys'. We backed your play because Fred White was killed and Ben Sippy jumped town and it was either your brother Virgil or one of Johnny's crowd. You gun men come haring in and shooting each other up and then charge off leaving those of us who were here ahead of you to put out your fires. What value have you? If God reached down and plucked your whole tribe out of this territory tomorrow you would not be mourned nor missed. You create your own need."

Wyatt fished out his pipe.

"I'm obliged to you for coming in, John. Don't come back."

"Am I to take that as a threat?"

"Take it how you will. From now on out we are shooting at anything that draws inside range."

An eagle hung wings down on a brass sky with a white-coin sun nailed to it and mountains crawling at its base. On a patch of webbed earth surrounded by brown grass a gila squatted with one foot raised, cooling it. For miles around only the small tattered column of men on horseback was moving, beetling across a scabrous plain tufted with mesquite and calcined with chaparral, with lather foaming around their legs and their own sweat beading under their hat brims and burning where leather and coarse cloth met flesh. The backs of their necks stung and their gunmetal was scorching to the touch.

Sherman McMasters suffered more than any of his companions. He had been wearing two cartridge belts crossed around his middle, and although he had finally unbuckled and hung them from his saddle horn, the sores they had worn into his hip-hollows made him suck in his breath every time his chestnut put its foot wrong. He had not known until that day what a tanglefooted mount he had drawn. The flesh inside his thighs had broken out as well and it was no help that even with his stirrups adjusted as high as they would go he was forced to stand in his borrowed saddle like one of these iron-assed cavalry kicks out of Fort Huachuca. Some souvenir-hunting son of a bitch had stolen his good butt-broken McClellan from the West End Corral while they were all resting in the hotel.

He was irritated further by Doc's constant coughing—the thick air was a strain on his lungs and he left a little trail of pink spots beside his bay's hoofprints—and by Turkey Creek Jack's toneless and apparently unconscious humming as he slouched along with his piebald's reins looped around one wrist. McMasters had barked at him twice to stop it; he had obeyed, only to start up again before they had gone a mile. Warren irritated him by sleeping in his saddle, a trick the older and more trailwise McMasters had yet to acquire, and anyway the sprout slept too easily and deeply to suit him. Wyatt alone rode in silence and without eccentricity, steering Dick Naylor with his knees and arching his back only occasionally to work the knots out from between his shoulders. McMasters found it irritating.

The horses blew out quickly in the heat and they dismounted frequently to lead them until their sides stopped heaving. They whickered hopelessly and whisked their tails without much conviction at the flies glittering around their rumps. Wyatt loosened his cartridge belt as he rode. Ahead of

the party, always the same distance away, a patch of green lay
like the felt on a billiard table between the low broken-edged
Whetstones and the less distinct, more occluded Mustang
Mountains in the pool of heat on the horizon to the northwest.
It was this patch they were heading toward, called Mescal
Springs on some maps but referred to by anyone who had ever
tasted its metal-edged water as Iron Springs.

The Babocomari River scratched the desert miles to the
west and there was no water between them and the springs.
They watered the animals sparingly from their canteens,
rubbed them down with handfuls of dead buffalo grass, wet
their own tongues, and continued. The green patch was
moving closer at last. By late afternoon, with the sun turning
copper over the Mustangs, they drew within sight of the wash
that separated the springs from the basin created by the
Babocomari and the San Pedro River. Willows grew thick as
corduroy on the other side. The riders dismounted to lead their
horses.

Puffs of gray blossomed in the willows, followed closely
by a crackling, as of green sticks bursting in a fire. The air
around the five men splintered and something chugged into the
earth in front of Wyatt's right foot, throwing clumps of dirt as
high as his knees. By then he was unleathering his shotgun,
closest to him in the boot on Dick Naylor's left side. Lowing
gently to calm the horse, which was trying to rear, he turned it
in front of him and laid the barrels across the belly of his saddle.

The others had remounted in the fusillade and fallen back,
and now men in hats and dusters emerged from the willows,
firing and levering rifles and carbines as they advanced through
the smoke of their own fire. Wyatt centered the Stevens on the
man nearest him and emptied both barrels. The man pitched
forward with his middle gone and fell on his face on the mossy
ground cover. He hunched his back once as if trying to rise,
then subsided.

Wyatt scabbarded the shotgun and reached across the black
for the Winchester on the other side. But Dick Naylor was
rearing and plunging now and instead he lunged for the saddle
horn and started to mount. His loosened cartridge belt slid
down his thighs and he released the horn to reach down and

pull it up. He was leaning with his face close to the cherry-colored pommel when someone struck a match off the end of his nose and his nostrils filled with the stench of rotten egg.

The horse wheeled. Wyatt had one foot in the stirrup and went with it, the belt pinning his legs together. The air was cracking around him. Every gun in the willows was firing at this easy target. He yanked up the belt finally and got a leg over and made the spurs bite. By this time Doc, Warren, McMasters, and Turkey Creek Jack had reached cover behind a ridge shaggy with mesquite and returned fire. The others fell back, levering and shooting.

"You yellow sons of bitches left me out there twisting." Wyatt swung down behind the ridge.

Doc said, "Yes, you looked a fair hero out there with your breeches down around your ankles. Where are you hit?"

Wyatt showed white teeth in a face blackened with spent powder and handed him his saddle horn. It had come off in his hand when he dismounted. A ball had shorn through the stem.

Doc examined it gravely. "Next time I will shoot you myself to determine if you bleed."

"Jesus, Wyatt." Warren had a corner of his brother's duster in his hand. The linen looked moth-chewed.

"Johnny never could hit a buffalo if he was inside it," Doc said.

"Johnny is back in Tombstone where he belongs," said Wyatt. "That was Curly Bill I just killed."

"It wasn't Curly Bill."

Wyatt sealed one letter with a drop of wax from a white candle stub he carried in his saddlebags, squashed the wax with his thumb, and addressed the letter to John J. Valentine at Wells Fargo headquarters in San Francisco. "Sure it was," he told Doc. "I saw the mark on his face where the ball came out when he got it in the neck in Galeyville last spring." He unfolded a fresh sheet from the oilskin pouch.

They were camped four miles north of Tombstone and Wyatt was using his cantle for a writing desk by the light of the first fire they had kindled in days. Doc, wick-thin and feverish and still spitting blood, lay on his back on a bed of mesquite with his blanket up to his chin. He had a dread of pneumonia on chill desert nights and experienced nightmares in which he lay drowning in his own sputum.

"It just seems lucksome that the first and only man killed in that transaction should turn out to be Curly Bill." He hawked and splatted the ground.

"I don't know about the only. It looked to me like one or two others was hit when you and the rest got around to figuring out what your guns are for."

"We took cover like any man would that has brains in his skull instead of a straight load of panther guts. No one invited you to go out and play Custer." They had been arguing about the retreat all day.

"You were the one had a hard-on to charge in and flush them up afterwards when they were all hunkered in tight as a nun's—tight as a drum." He'd forgotten that Doc still wrote letters to a cousin in a convent in Atlanta.

"I say it was Johnny and he'd have turned tail like the rabbit he is until he ran out of desert."

"It was Curly Bill."

Sherman McMasters came in from watch, leaned his Winchester against a palo verde, and filled a cup from the coffee pot boiling on a flat rock next to the fire. He grunted when he sat down.

Wyatt said, "You put some axle grease on those fistulas of yours like I advised?"

"I never thought to bring any, there being no axles to grease for forty mile." He blew steam off the cup and sipped.

"Bottom mud's better," said Doc.

"Arizona is a mud patch, all right."

Wyatt used a bowie knife to whittle a point on his gnawed yellow pencil stub. "Wild Bill told me he cauterized a Cheyenne lance wound once by pouring black powder into it and setting it afire."

"Just once I hope to meet an Indian fighter who never did that," McMasters said. "To hear them there was more powder spent on closing wounds than opening them."

Doc said, "Wild Bill was a lying Yankee. I heard he was

going blind from the clap when that swamper capped him in
Deadwood."

Wyatt and Doc had been baiting each other all evening. It
was no new game with them, and it never failed to stand
McMasters's scalp on end. He changed subjects. "Who you
writing to, Sadie?"

"Her next. This one is for Clum and the *Epitaph*. Turkey
Creek Jack will carry them in when I spell him."

"You're telling it you killed Curly Bill?"

"It was Curly Bill, goddamn it."

"I'm not questioning that, only that he was killed."

"He fell down in two pieces. If he was not killed it was a
fair imitation." He signed his name with an extra flourish and
folded the sheet in thirds.

McMasters fed a branch to the fire. The dead leaves burned
off with a rush, firing sparks straight up the column of heat.
"Who do you feature was with him?"

"I never saw him, but Pony Deal and Curly Bill are joined
at the hip. And Johnny Barnes has a twin if that wasn't him I
saw drop his rifle when the rest of you took it into your heads
to swap fire finally."

"The rest of us don't turn away bullets as easy as you,"
McMasters said. "I am starting a rumor that you had on a vest
made of stove lids, to ride bang into Curly Bill like that and
come away straight up."

Doc said, "It wasn't Curly Bill."

Wyatt started the letter to Sadie. "I would place Ike
Clanton in that party too, but Clum says he and Phin are in this
posse of Johnny Behan's that no one ever sees."

"We saw them today," Doc said.

Warren sat up, shaking himself free of his blanket. "I never
tried sleeping at a ladies' jabbering bee before."

"It must be the only place you haven't," said McMasters.

"Who's next, Pete Spence?" In the wobbly orange light the
youngest Earp looked a little like Morgan, the same high cheeks
and loose lock on his forehead.

"If we pried him out of jail," Wyatt said, "and if Johnny
has not already hung a star on him."

"That never stopped you with Stilwell."

"Stilwell came around asking for it."

McMasters emptied his cup. The dregs tasted of lead from the lining. "I have pushed my luck in this place so far it has commenced to balk. I think I'll head south and stomp on Mexico."

"Hot as hell down there this time of year," Wyatt said.

"I admit it will require some getting used to after a cherry orchard like Arizona."

Doc sat up, spat into the fire, and swigged whiskey from his canteen to cut the bloody phlegm. "The placer dirt in Colorado looks promising, I hear."

Wyatt said, "I'll send Sadie to San Francisco and pick her up there and then maybe I'll see you in Gunnison. I and Warren have not seen our parents since before Dodge City and I want to find out how Virge is getting on."

"You mean after we finish here," said Warren.

"We're finished here. There is too much paper out with our names on it to suit me."

"What about Clanton and Spence and Will McLaury?"

"McLaury is smoke and the others soon will be if they have the brains God gave a tapeworm. I am a businessman. I can't live on killing."

"Well, I can't live knowing them three are above ground."

"It's my bet you can. You're coming with me to California. I told Ma and Pa I'd look out for you."

"Like you looked out for Morg?"

Wyatt stopped writing. The firelight made a Greek mask of his face.

"Don't start comparing yourself to Morg. You aren't Morg and will never be half of him if you go to whining like a poked bitch every time you hear something you don't like. Getting yourself killed in Arizona won't make you Morg."

"Wish to hell we never came to this place," Warren said. "Wish we never heard of it."

"I don't. Except for Morg and Virge's arm I wouldn't trade a square inch of it for a hundred acres in Missouri. A man can make something of himself out here if he has the sand for it. Back home we would all be farmers and poor ones at that."

"Morg would be alive back home."

"He wouldn't want to be."

Doc said, "No one has brought up Ringo."

Wyatt resumed writing. "Ringo has quit the territory."

"You don't credit that."

McMasters said, "I never saw a man as dead as Ringo still up and walking."

"I have," said Doc.

They started turning in after that. Wyatt finished the letter and relit the candle stub from his pipe and sealed it and put it with the others in the oilskin to give to Turkey Creek Jack. Then he knocked out the pipe and set it on the ground to cool and pulled his blanket around him. Miles away a coyote called to the moon, a joyful sound carried and warped by the wind into a dirge. It was hard to tell when it stopped and became the wind itself.

"It was Curly Bill," Wyatt said.

Doc lay on his back with his eyes gleaming under a spray of stars. "What makes it Curly Bill?"

"It was just him." Wyatt turned over.

CHAPTER 18

I NEVER SAW A man as dead as Ringo still up and walking.

He was christened John Peter Ringgold in Missouri, and the inevitable shortening was done by classmates when he attended William Jewell College in Liberty, studying Homer and Euclid while others his age were burning in the Wilderness and learning to get along with the stumps of limbs piled up for burial behind the church at Shiloh. In the late summer of 1864 he rode home from classes on one of his father's mules to find three badly used quarterhorses in the stable and his cousin Jim Younger guarding them with a Spencer rifle. Jim had a new black beard and his officer's gray greatcoat was ragged at the hem and showing two mismatched bone buttons among the brass. His hat was Union issue without band or insignia, and some attempt had been made to block it so that the brim swept up on one side like Jeb Stuart's.

He took some time recognizing John, for they had not seen each other in four years, and even then he braced him and patted him down for weapons before taking him inside to the kitchen, where a braided length of jug-eared farmer with big hands and a turkey neck and a smear of chestnut beard around his mouth was eating a slice of John's mother's cherry pie with his fingers. He was in dirty underwear, no shirt, and shoddy trousers held up with pink braces like a dandy's and stuffed into

new cavalry boots that must have been too small for him by the
way he stood pigeon-toed. When the door opened he grasped
the amber handle of a Navy Colt's stuck in the front of his
trousers, but he let his hand fall when Jim came in behind John
carrying the Spencer.

Jim introduced the farmer as Buck James and the farmer
wiped his fingers on his underwear top and took John's hand in
a crusty grip and told him his father was in the parlor and that
his mother had left to bring back the doctor. John asked if his
father was hurt. The farmer got a look from Jim that said he
hadn't told John anything and the farmer said to take him on in.

His father was standing in the parlor smoking his pipe, a
thing he never did in that room, at the request of John's mother.
On the davenport, his thin shoulders propped up on pillows,
lay a boy not older than seventeen, narrow-faced with a great
dome of smooth forehead like a baby's. He was naked to the
waist with a patchwork quilt drawn up over his chest and a
yellow-stained bandage slanting over his left shoulder toga-
fashion. When the three entered he followed their progress
without turning his head. He had a habit of blinking both eyes
rapidly like an owl.

"Jess, this here is Jim and Cole's cousin Johnny Ringgold,"
said Buck James. To John: "He taken a ball at Crooked Crick.
Soon's he can ride we are fixing to throw them Yanks a shivaree
they will talk about in Washington City."

John would remember little worth telling a historian of
that first and only meeting with Frank James and his baby
brother Jesse, which ended abruptly when John's mother came
back alone to report that the doctor had refused to aid a
guerrilla. Fearing betrayal to the Federals, Jim and Buck
bundled the boy into a litter lashed together from willow
branches and dragged him into Carroll County where the
Jameses knew a doctor with Confederate sympathies. John
never heard from any of them again, but learned of Jesse's
complete recovery when he was identified among the nightriders who stopped a Union train in Centralia a month later and
lined up and shot down the disarmed soldiers in cold blood.

That, and a subsequent engagement in which that same
band under Bloody Bill Anderson wheeled and ran down the

pursuing regulars, finished John at college. Concentrating on
Thermopylae and the conquest of Gaul became increasingly
difficult when the roll of cannons to the south was making
ripples in his inkwell. But the war ended before he could enlist,
and a young man drilled in the hopelessness of history's lost
causes from Ilium to Waterloo was poor clay for the bands of
border raiders who traded skirmishes in the woods for bank
assaults and train robberies after Appomattox. Like hundreds of
others whose roots had been blasted by mortars and grapeshot
and a victory-bloated Union's tyrannical Order No. 11, Johnny
Ringo went to Texas.

It was the place to be when you were young and strong and
had few skills not drawn from a book. The cattle industry was
in the process of being invented, and any man who could keep a
horse under him and hold his water in the face of angry fire was
welcome to join the raiding parties dipping across the Rio
Grande for Mexican beef and a cut of the market yield in
Chicago. Like any good Missouri boy, John had hunted his
share of meat on the hoof, but the rangy, hook-horned
descendants of Cortez's cattle were the test of a man; after a few
hundred spills and a dozen near-tramplings he grew hard as
jerky and developed a leather hide stretched over six feet and
two inches of wolf muscle. During drives north he traded fire
with vaqueros and rurales and bandits, sometimes all three in
one mounted bunch, and his natural abilities with rifle and
pistol preceded him. He worked with and for more ex-
Confederate senators and colonels than he figured the South
could have held on its best day. If his fellow hands were
concerned by his soft-spoken good manners and occasional
absences from dugout poker matches to burrow in a corner
with one of the books he carried in his blanket roll, they
extinguished their doubts in the prodigious quantities of alcohol
he consumed when he had cash in his poke. Once he pulled a
cork out of a bottle he threw it away. At such times his
company was avoided, for the man who when sober would
ignore a deadly insult would lash out with his long arms when
drinking and beat a man half to death for smiling wrong. In this
way he drifted from camp to camp, his welcome lasting only as
long as the time between bottles.

Cattle work, once the trade was established and confrontations with the grandees became unnecessary, was not for him. He was too big for the normal cow pony to carry over a long drive and few men trusted him when nothing was happening to keep his mind off drinking. He did some rustling for the small outfits, and when range disagreements like the Mason County Hoodoo War broke out he hired on with the bigger ranches as a regulator. How many men he might have killed during this period, if he killed any, would probably never be known, for no witnesses ever came forward to connect him to any of the deaths.

Legends grew up around him, as they did around quiet men with euphonious names and no apparent past, like vines climbing a condemned corral. It was said that he had ridden with Quantrill in Missouri and Kansas; that he had studied for the seminary in Virginia and learned six languages before he fled to escape a murder charge; that he was born in Texas and had given up a promising career in law with his family firm when his intended bride left him standing at the altar. It was a time of women's novels and campfire ballads that would not let a man choose life on the scout without some evil romantic quirk of fate to trigger the choice. Somehow the story started circulating, and it would outlast most of the others, that from time to time he received letters addressed to him in a feminine hand that would leave him morose and dangerous to be around for days. Since no one claimed ever to have actually seen the letters, it followed him everywhere and would not die.

He never talked about his people or his past, nor told lies about them that someone could track down and prove false and in the proving uncover a truth. His very silence was taken as evidence that one or the other or both were dark, for in the long and frequent stillnesses west of St. Louis, asking questions and providing entertaining answers came second only to theater and funerals. It would not occur to any of them that the reality might not be worth mentioning. In truth he had loved no woman since his teacher in third grade, although he had bedded several and picked up a dose of clap in El Paso; and he could never kill as many men as had been charged to him.

Gun work was not steady. Ranchers couldn't stand paying a hand to do nothing when no shooting was going on. Between jobs he robbed an occasional stage. They were easy. But money meant whiskey, and the gangs were continually breaking up to re-form somewhere else without Ringo to have to walk around on eggshells. Texas itself began to get too various for him when the Comanches surrendered after Adobe Walls and the Rangers turned their attention to the outlaw element beginning with his friend Wes Hardin. They followed Hardin to Florida, took him off the train in Pensacola, and sent him back to Huntsville for twenty-five years and Ringo rolled his books and Winchester into his blanket and struck out for Arizona Territory.

Ed Schieffelin had gone looking for his own tombstone among the diamondbacks and Apaches in the Dragoons, found a vein of silver as thick as his wrist, and almost before he got back to the San Pedro the city of Tombstone had begun to blister up out of the flats. Johnny Ringo was one of dozens of predatory animals who smelled blood and money and began drifting in that direction in 1879. On the way he stopped in the adobe hamlet of Safford to cut the dust. In a saloon with a plank bar and an earthen floor he sat in on a few hands of poker, couldn't find his luck, and threw in to drink at the bar. He was joined moments later by a cowboy named Lou Hancock, whose own luck had gone sour after Ringo left. Ringo signaled the bartender to slide another shot glass down the plank. Hancock thanked him but said he was drinking beer. Ringo had two more drinks, began to stew over the answer, then produced one of his ivory-handled Colt's and shot Hancock. The cowboy's luck had turned, for Ringo's aim drunk wasn't good. Hancock lost a piece off his neck and his assailant finished his bottle and rode out. No one pursued him. There had been no deaths, and on the frontier when one man invited another to drink with him and the other man refused, the matter was out of the law's hands.

Tombstone was mostly adobe when he got to it, but some frames were going up on Fremont and Allen streets. Lumber was packed in from the Huachucas and was as valuable as silver in an area where a man made his own shade. No prospector or woodcutter, Ringo got in quickly with the local cattlemen who drank tanglefoot in the saloons, and laid bets on how soon the silver would play out or Geronimo would tire of white men crawling like ants over his mountains and burn the place to the ground. He took an instant liking to a fellow named Curly Bill Brocius, a big, buffalo-headed cowboy with a square grin and the endearing habit of turning his poke wrongside out on the bar and calling for everyone to drink until the last coin was gone; but he was more drawn toward a surly half-breed called Pony Deal, who wore a couple of hideout pistols under his canvas coat and a bowie knife that had sliced through the stitches in the leather scabbard on his hip. He could match Ringo swallow for swallow, and unlike Ringo he was as dangerous sober as he was drunk. A couple of ugly incidents took place in Ringo's presence between Deal and others that would have come back on them all had Tombstone been the county seat at the time and under public scrutiny. Ringo, who apologized to women for keeping his hat on at poker for luck, had no use at all for Pete Spence, whom he had once seen beating a Mexican whore with his fists in a corner for biting him.

Most of them deferred to a bandy-legged old crank with a brown bald head and a broom-thatch of white whiskers fanned out and cut square across his cravat, or where his cravat would have been had he worn one and not a preacher's black coat buttoned to the throat even in the hottest weather. His name was Clanton. If he had a Christian name Ringo never learned it, because everyone called him Old Man Clanton to separate him from his three sons: Ike, the eldest, bearish and goat-whiskered with a tobacco lump taken root under his right ear; Phin, cow-eyed, with his father's Quaker brow and not enough sense to move his foot when he was pissing on it; and Billy, the youngest, a bull-shouldered oaf of eighteen or nineteen and a schoolyard bully. It was months before Ringo saw their sister Mary, a colorless young woman who hardly ever left the house where she cooked and cleaned for her father and brothers. Ringo enjoyed Ike in spite of his big mouth but didn't trust him, didn't think about Phin at all, and was irritated by Billy, although he didn't show it. For all his swagger Billy was no bluff like Ike, and he always had a pistol on him. Ringo had lived too long to pick fights with men who might be as ready to defend themselves as he.

The first time Ringo addressed the old man, he demanded to know if Ringo was from Missouri. When he answered that he was, the old man snapped, "Reb or Yank?"

Ringo, adept at turning aside questions about his past, replied that Cole and Jim Younger were his cousins. It was the right thing to say to another man from Missouri. Before the week was out he was riding with the Clantons and Curly Bill below the border after grandee beef, a new vocation there. This was home stuff to him, and he showed them some things about boxing strays in gullies under a rustler's moon and used his Winchester to send three vaqueros galloping home to light a candle to the Holy Virgin. The drive north was uneventful.

Tombstone was no man's land, a place to rest and drink and gamble and gather news. The cowboys' headquarters were in Charleston to the west and, in summer heat, Galeyville, forty-five miles east in the Chiricahua foothills. There he made the acquaintance of the McLaurys: Tom, a man nearly as courtly as himself and a range banker who advanced loans out of a money belt and depended upon his brother to collect them, and Frank, a few years older but much shorter, with a short man's short fuse and an image of himself as big as Billy Clanton. He had a reputation as a gun man, although he had never killed anyone so far as rumor knew, and Ringo himself, who changed horses occasionally with the others at the McLaury ranch in Sulphur Springs Valley near the border, had seen what looked like an acre of brass cartridge shells catching fire in the sun where Frank stood to practice. Ringo was polite with both of them.

He enjoyed the company of Frank Stilwell, a fixture in Charleston who liked to show off his collection of stolen Wells Fargo weapons, with which he was building himself a fair name as a highwayman. In his middle twenties and beardless, he strode around in store clothes sucking on a big cigar like a newspaper cartoon of a boy imitating Pierpont Morgan—a double caricature. His stories of youthful daring entertained Ringo without convincing him, and Ringo was relieved to see when they held up their first stage together that when Stilwell drew a bandanna up over his face the bravado stopped. He was as professional a thief as Ringo had known.

After Cochise County was formed and Tombstone made the seat, the cowboys gathered often in the house Johnny Behan shared with his common-law wife Josephine Sarah Marcus in Tombstone. Behan was part owner of the Dexter Livery & Feed and had been appointed sheriff by Governor Fremont. As the county's tax administrator, he often depended on Curly Bill and others to help his deputies convince area ranchers of the importance of public revenue. Ringo played poker at his house often but stood back from his political glad-handing and amplified Irish charm; it was the sort of welcome that blew away with the first change of wind. Ringo was far more impressed with the sheriff's trim, dark-eyed woman, who walked through every room as if she were crossing a stage, and whose waist-length hair smelled of fresh herbs when she bent over the table to empty ashtrays. But he never jumped another man's claim and so remained only polite.

With Mexico a short jump away and the nearest law with teeth in it as far off as Prescott, Tombstone was a bandits' gift from God. They owned the sheriff and the local Wells Fargo agent and made their beds between fat Mexican cattle and stagecoaches so heavy with bullion their wheels cut ruts in rockface. In the days when they were riding highest Ringo's cousins, rotting now in prison, and their friends Frank and Jesse, hiding out somewhere in Missouri, never knew times like these. Ringo alone of all his partners knew that they were running out.

Others had come into the region, among them the Earp brothers, blond giants who operated together like parts of the same animal to knock an apple off every tree in the county from prostitution and gambling to timber stands and mineral rights, and had got themselves badges to license their weapons to protect the harvest. Close behind them came Doc Holliday. In Holliday Ringo saw something familiar, a man of some culture and learning whom drink made dangerous, and who drank a great deal to stun the thing that was eating out his insides. He was everything in Ringo that Ringo avoided or else made his peace with and so stayed alive. Yet he did neither, and in fact sought Holliday's company for a drink or a few hands of faro every time the two were in town—drawn to him as a man who fears heights is drawn to a steep cliff to look down dizzy at the treetops far below. And like that man he wrestled with the almost overpowering urge to step off. The sheer heady rush of it made him drink more in Holliday's presence, and the more he drank the greater grew the danger and the headier the rush. The stepping-off would have to come. Meanwhile he bet more than he could afford and smiled in his moustaches when Doc told about the Cornish Jack who got drunk and lopped off his own phizzle with a shovel because he thought it was a bald-headed mouse.

The Earps posed a more insidious threat to the good thing the cowboys had in Cochise County. Ringo recognized in them the same single-tracked ruthlessness that ran beneath Curly Bill's outward good humor, the same need to seize and wring the last ounce of silver from the region without swinging a pick. It was rich, but not rich enough to support two rival bands of like determination, and from the outset Ringo knew that they could not work together, although they might try.

That must have become apparent to Curly Bill as early as the summer of 1880, when a tinhorn who called himself Johnny-behind-the-Deuce killed a smelting engineer named Schneider in Charleston. Curly Bill and Ringo were in Tombstone when he was brought in, found that they both owed Johnny-behind-the-Deuce money, decided after knocking back a few that the dead man was a dear friend, and elected to square all their debts with one rope. But before they could organize a mob, the prisoner was on his way to trial in Tucson in the company of Wyatt Earp, then serving as deputy sheriff, his brothers Virgil and Morgan, and temporary officers Doc Holliday, Sherman McMasters, Turkey Creek Jack Johnson, Shotgun Collins, Jack Salmon, and Fred Dodge. When he learned of it, Curly Bill stood in the middle of Allen looking like a man who had soiled himself waiting his turn in a whorehouse. No one laughed.

In November of that year Curly Bill got drunk and shot City Marshal Fred White in the belly, so close the powder-flash set White's trousers afire. Curly Bill was arrested, then released on White's deathbed testimony that he had shot himself accidentally with Curly Bill's pistol while attempting to disarm him. Back in Charleston, Curly Bill boasted that he had tricked White with the border roll, and Ringo, who knew the hazards of exaggeration, grew sad, because he knew too that if there had ever been a chance of striking up a relationship with the Earps it was gone now, because they had been close to the dead man and the claim was bound to get back to them. Curly Bill knew it too, and avoided Tombstone for a long time after that.

Sometime Charlestonians Billy Leonard, Harry Head, and Jim Crane mucked up an assault on the Benson stage the following March, killing driver Bud Philpot and a passenger named Roerig but failing to secure the bullion. Thanks to Marshall Williams, who sent a revealing telegram to San Francisco for Wyatt, Ringo and most of the cowboys on the San Pedro knew of the transaction involving Ike Clanton, Frank McLaury, Joe Hill, and Wyatt Earp as soon as they made it, to deliver the three robbers to Earp in return for the reward. Curly Bill was at this time recovering from an altercation in Galeyville in which a friend had fired a ball into his neck that came out his face, and Old Man Clanton had himself wound up to drag through the cactus any man who accused his son of treachery, so it fell to Ringo and Pete Spence to devise a fitting punishment.

It waited for other business. In June, a party made up of Pete Spence, Pony Deal, Frank Stilwell, Ike, Phin, and Billy Clanton, and led by Ringo, crouched sweating in the broken shale atop Skeleton Canyon in the Guadalupes and waited for a column of Mexicans in sombreros and bandoliers to lead their mules out of the shadows into the sunlight below. When they were all clear, Pony Deal screeched like a hawk and the men above emptied their Winchesters and Henrys into the column. The reports clattered off the canyon walls and lead twanged against stone and the mules brayed and plunged and the Mexicans tried to jerk their rifles from the packs and gave up and ran or drew pistols and sent hopeless balls toward unseen targets well out of range and shot the mules to make breastworks and spun and staggered and doubled over and fell and clawed at the cliffs and died or lay whistling through punctured lungs with their jaws shot away waiting for the gringos to come down and walk through and put balls in their heads. Nineteen Mexicans perished there for seventy-five thousand dollars in silver bullion smuggled from the gringo mines up north. Some of those who found the black and bloated bodies days later blamed the attack on Apaches. Others wondered loudly what use Indians had for silver.

Among the latter were the vaqueros who trailed Old Man Clanton and five others driving a herd of stolen cattle through Guadalupe Canyon in July. Imitating the Skeleton raid, the Mexicans poured lead into them from the rocks above, killing all but one, including the old man and Jim Crane, one of the men who had tried to hold up the Benson stage. Curly Bill and Ringo were engaged in treeing Sonora with the McLaurys and the younger Clantons to celebrate Curly Bill's recovery and got the story from a Yaqui mescal peddler. About that time, Crane's partners Leonard and Head tried to stick up the Haslett brothers' store in Huachita and the brothers shot them to pieces. When that news reached Curly Bill, busy with the others burying the putrefying corpses in the canyon, he cut out a bunch of hard riders including Ringo and Pony Deal and galloped to Huachita to clean the Hasletts's plow. After the party rode out of town shooting out windows and riddling signs, locals counted seventeen bulletholes in Ike Haslett's broken body and twenty-two in his brother Bill's.

If Ike Clanton and Frank McLaury were more aggrieved than the others by the deaths of the stagecoach raiders, they didn't show it, possibly because they'd been questioning the wisdom of their understanding with Wyatt Earp and were relieved. Phin blubbered over the loss of the old man, but Ike seemed glad enough to be free of his querulous ways, and although Billy had to be restrained from going after the bushwhackers and slaughtering any odd Mexican that crossed his trail, he had always been embarrassed by his father and made no show of sorrow. Curly Bill naturally assumed leadership of the San Pedro cowboys after that.

Pete Spence surprised everyone with his imagination when he suggested Ike and Frank's proper accounting for having conspired to betray Leonard, Head, and Crane. Cornering the pair, Spence and Ringo and Curly Bill encouraged them to draw the Earps into a face-off in Tombstone, at which time the rest of the cowboys would back them up and clear out the only opposition worth mentioning in Tombstone. Ike and Frank demurred at first, but they had already begun to suspect that their transaction was known, and eventually agreed in the face of some heavy hints on Curly Bill's part. Joe Hill was in Mexico and so was left out of the arrangement. When the face-off came, of course, the two would find themselves alone against the Earps, and either way it went was bound to show profit for the rest. Johnny Behan, whose woman Josephine had been stolen from him by Wyatt, now a deputy marshal working under his brother Virgil, could be counted on not to interfere with any genuine conviction.

Nobody expected things to go as smoothly as that. When the smoke cleared and Ike was still running, the cowboys celebrated having rid themselves of both McLaurys and Billy Clanton and figured Behan and the county would see to the Earps and Holliday. They didn't, but when Frank and Tom's moneybags brother Will came out of the wainscoting waving a bounty for the Earps and their friends, Ringo got drunk and challenged Holliday to a Texas bandanna fight, only Billy Breakenridge and Jim Campbell broke it up and Wyatt tumbled to the rifles at Ringo's back and called Holliday off. Ringo paid a ten-dollar fine for carrying firearms in town.

Some of it was just plain hoorawing, like sticking up the Benson stage with John Clum aboard and punching a few holes in the clouds and Frank Stilwell laughing fit to fall down when the bald-headed little mayor ran off flapping his arms like a rooster with pepper up its ass. That sort of play drew off steam and kept the Earps teetering and inclined to take chances to show their steel.

After Christmas, Ringo crouched inside the damp adobe of the Huachuca Water Company building with Stilwell and Hank Swilling and a couple of others and waited until Virgil Earp had crossed Fifth Street and stood silhouetted against the lighted windows of the Eagle Brewery before cutting loose with five ten-gauge shotguns. But the distance was too great and they only crippled him. They just had time to leave behind a hat tying Ike Clanton to the attack before fleeing the building. Ike had become a running joke, the man everyone stuck with the bill after a big meal because he was in no position to object.

Ringo hid out in Mexico for a time after that, drinking tequila and mescal on Will McLaury's money and spreading clap among the señoritas there, and so did not take part in the killing of Morgan Earp in Hatch's billiard hall. He suspected Pete Spence, and when he finally made his way back among the cowboys he learned that a breed named Indian Charlie had had an oar in, but couldn't feature him among the Mexicans and digger Indians who drifted around the cowboys' spurs like blown leaves.

By then Stilwell had been killed in the Tucson railyard, and someone who may or may not have been Indian Charlie at Spence's wood ranch in the Dragoons. When word came in that Wyatt and Holliday were claiming Curly Bill in the Whet-stones, Ringo volunteered to ride in Behan's posse along with Ike and Phin Clanton and Pony Deal and others, but the only satisfaction he got from that was watching that candy-ass Billy Breakenridge slink off to sulk in his tent because the sheriff gave Ringo Billy's favorite horse. A couple of times they drew within looking range of the Earp party, but Behan was reluctant to start things and Ringo suspected the posse was just barking at their heels until they quit the territory, which they did, crossing the Chiricahuas into New Mexico at the end of a week. Behan turned back after that.

Tombstone was as dead as Frank Stilwell. Pete Spence was in custody, Curly Bill was dead or in hiding, Ike and Phin were keeping their profiles flat on their ranch, and a lot of the others had lit out when Wyatt and his friends started burning the brush for Curly Bill. A second big fire had swept down Allen, following the same course as the June 1881 blaze. In a tent pitched on the ruins of the Oriental, Ringo and Pony Deal played poker with Billy Claiborne and Frank Leslie, but those two didn't get along and when Ringo filled his glass a third time they threw in. He had acquired a bad reputation after a Charleston game in which he had gotten drunk and stuck up his fellow players for what was on the table. Although he had returned the money when he sobered up, the story had made it hard for him to find a game.

Pony Deal won the last few hands and they split up. Ringo rode to Charleston, found none of the old faces there, and struck east toward Galeyville. It was July, back-of-the-neck hot but with the first iron smell of rain coming down from the mountains.

His luck was souring in Arizona. John J. Gosper had finished out his temporary term as governor and given ground to F. A. Tritle, a hard-line supporter of President Arthur, who had granted permission to establish a territorial police force to suppress outlawry. The good times were done in Cochise County, as they had been in Texas when the Rangers stopped fighting Indians and started rounding up bandits. Ringo thought that after Galeyville he would head on up to Colorado and see how the grass grew in gold country. He made camp in Turkey Creek Canyon and went to sleep in a green oak grove with his Colt's in his right hand and his Winchester leaning against a scrub close by, Colorado his last thought.

He never had another.

CHAPTER 19

———————

GLOBE WAS GOING BLUENOSE on Kate, as all towns did
eventually.

The city council started by drafting ordinances regulating
advertising and signs belonging to establishments such as hers,
then prohibited her girls from appearing on the town's north
side during the hours of daylight under penalty of fines, and
finally went to nickel-and-diming her to death with health
codes requiring monthly physical examinations for the girls by
a city-accredited physician. Kate had no objections to the
checkups, for she had seen too many young women knocked
down to drooling idiots by filth carried by swaggering cowboys and buffalo runners who thought it the measure of a man,
and indeed the precautions she took to protect the hygiene of
her girls had become a legend on the circuit during the brief
time she had been in management; but when it came to not
being allowed to choose her own doctor, and to having to kick
in to the city treasury for the services of the prig they sent, she
saw the fine white hands of the councilmen's wives in the
transaction. Time alone separated Globe from a direct ban on
pleasure houses inside the city limits. It had happened in just
about every place she had been in since Atlanta except
Tombstone, and if rumors could be counted and the bottom
was getting set to drop out from under the price of silver, it was

coming there too. People got mean about where other people's money was going when there wasn't much of it around.

When it happened here, she could go on as before, but paying the local law to keep from closing her down beyond the customary election-day raid, or she could pull up stakes and set them down outside the limits. The first plan was at least as expensive as reimbursing the council for letting its man poke instruments up the girls' business ends, and there was no guarantee that the law wouldn't just take the money the first time she offered it and bust up the place anyway, or keep hiking. the price, or cut themselves into a full partnership the way James Earp had done in Dodge when his brother Wyatt was a police officer there and their friends Ed and Bat Masterson ran the county. The second alternative meant giving up the building in Globe and going back to a mildewed tent like in Fort Griffin.

Neither choice appealed to her, so she turned the place into a boardinghouse. People had to eat and sleep, basic human needs she understood at least as well as her specialty. It had been a good year. She had enough cash on hand to stake some of the girls out of town—not including the one who had helped herself to the profits while she was away; that one had married one of Kate's best customers, a miner, and the two were currently working a claim up in the Apaches—and to pay two of the older women to stay on as cook and housekeeper. She recommended old customers to former rivals, who in turn talked up her place to satiated clients looking for a roof and a hot meal. Clean sheets and simple good food did the rest. Had she run the business like a real boardinghouse she might have made almost as much money as before, without the overhead of having to keep her girls in clothes, paint, and medical attention. But she didn't.

In the early days, when Kate employed a big Negro to keep order in the house, she would have had him throw out anyone who accused her of keeping a soft heart. Whores with that kind of baggage were strictly for dime novels, expected to oblige the reader's civilized instincts by taking a fatal bullet meant for the hero in the last chapter. On the circuit, such angels had that horseshit tromped out of them by some smelly wolfer who wore his spurs to bed, or else had it let out along with their guts by some half-breed Mexican whore with a bowie knife; and indeed the odd cowhand who came to Kate with an empty poke and a sad story got nothing free but her broad back. But for other women who had found the West something less than the Eldorado they had had described to them back East she had a weak spot as wide as a dry wash.

Women on the frontier fell into three piles. Some were hollow-eyed farm wives who skinned and cooked jackrabbits and swept the bugs out of soddies in the middle of three hundred miles of flat gray prairie. Others wore ruffled pastel dresses stained coppery under the arms and unbuttoned the flies of horsey strangers for money in cribs and hotel bedrooms. Still others were imitation men, swearing and spitting and striping mules' rumps with whips for men's wages and not being recognized as women until they got shot or died of frostbite or bad whiskey and the coroner stripped them. Actresses didn't count because they were transients theater-hopping between New York City and San Francisco, and anyway they were the same as whores. All of these women were used up at thirty and few would live to see fifty. Most of those who made their way eventually to Kate's door had been in one of the three piles, and a fair lot had been in all three. The distinctions were not sharp in a region where a man raised his hat as quickly for a whore as for a wife, and where the term *wife* referred to a woman who was keeping company with one man under his roof, with or without the blessing of clergy. They came to Kate, widowed or deserted and thousands of miles from home, offering to help around the house in return for bed and board. And she took them in, even after all the jobs worth having done were taken and nonpaying guests outnumbered her legitimate boarders. When a woman was used up for whoring Kate would not turn her away toward what was left.

Kate was no Nellie Cashman, content to minister to her guests' suffering and walk around town with her chin high enough to hang a hat on. She balanced the books and argued with the butcher and fed the chickens she kept behind the house and chopped off their heads when they quit laying and weren't too scrawny to eat and read about Doc's case in the Arizona

Star. He had been arrested in Denver in May and was being held pending extradition back to Tombstone to stand trial for the murder of Frank Stilwell. But Bat Masterson, lately marshal of Trinidad, Colorado, had persuaded the city marshal of Pueblo, where Doc had parted company with the Earps after leaving Arizona, to file a charge against Doc for operating a confidence game in that city. The *Star,* a longtime gleeful observer of the troubles in Cochise County, explained to its readers that the claim would forestall extradition and certain lynching in Tombstone and applauded it as a brilliant maneuver on the part of Doc's lawyer. Kate, however, sensed the light touch of another con man and wondered where Wyatt Earp—whose father had wanted him to study law—was keeping himself.

When Doc was finally remanded over to the custody of the Pueblo authorities in late June, Kate knew he would be headed for gold-rich Gunnison as soon as he was cut loose from the nonexistent charge, and thought of joining him. The prospect of a vacation from the cloying broken women living in her house of charity was a temptation. But she was afraid that the local wives, who took the presence of so many slatterns as evidence that she was still whoring, would burn her out in her absence, leaving her free boarders to addle in the summer heat without shade; and she feared Doc's mood. From his description in the newspaper he appeared to be experiencing a bout of stable health, and those times he was most dangerous. She hated to admit even to herself that he attracted her most when he was sick and required care.

So she stayed where she was, inventing work for the women to do so they would not feel useless and suicidal, fighting with the council, and following in the Tucson press the battle between the *Nugget* and the *Epitaph* over who belonged to the body buried at Iron Springs, Curly Bill Brocius or some nameless drifter; but most of the other names that were beginning to appear in connection with Tombstone were unfamiliar to her, and even the *Epitaph* had changed hands in May and was no longer the mouthpiece of John Clum and the Citizens' Safety Committee. The departures of Frank and Tom McLaury, their brother Will, Billy Clanton, Bill Leonard, Harry Head, Jim Crane, Old Man Clanton, Pete Spence, Joe

Hill, Hank Swilling, Frank Stilwell, Curly Bill, all five Earps and their women, and Doc left gaping holes in the place she remembered. She had the feeling that if she went back now she would know nobody. The town itself had gone up in flames again in late May, when a fire destroyed most of the buildings put back up after the 1881 disaster, as well as the O.K. Corral, a landmark now that everyone was talking about the fight that didn't take place there, and Fly's boardinghouse, where it really had taken place and where Kate had lived with Doc. That saddened her, not because she had enjoyed anything about the place—she had been miserable almost her whole time there—but because it made her feel old at thirty-one.

One at least of the old faces was in Globe. Billy the Kid Claiborne, without his guns and wearing the striped overalls of the men who worked in the local smelter, came to her door one night looking for companionship, unaware that she was no longer in that business. She directed him to a place and he thanked her and left, touching his hat. He had a good set of whiskers now and his jaw was squaring off like a man's, but his lanky slouch still suggested the young tough who had swaggered into that alley on Fremont Street and beaten leather back out. A week or so after their meeting she saw him on the street, dressed up in a town suit this time with a cartridge belt showing under the coat, and then she didn't see him again and decided that he had moved on. This hardly surprised her. Smelting was too much like work for that San Pedro crowd.

In July, before Claiborne's visit, she read of the mysterious death of Johnny Ringo, who had been found sitting on the ground in Turkey Creek Canyon with his back propped up against a young oak, a pistol in his hand and a bullethole in his temple. The ball had entered in front of his right ear and come out the top of his head on the left side without disturbing his hat. A coroner's jury had studied the evidence and ruled in favor of suicide.

Kate had a good long laugh over that one. Ringo's cartridge belt had been buckled on upside-down and there were no empty casings in the pistol's cylinder. His rifle had a cartridge in the chamber, which meant that if he had shot himself with it he'd have had to lever in the fresh round afterward. Nor did she waste much time, as many others would do in the years to come, stewing over who had done for him. A man like Ringo had enemies stacked as high as his hat and bought his own chances when he chose to sleep off an all-day drunk within sight of the Galeyville road.

She wasn't drinking these days. Unlike Doc, who seldom appeared drunk despite a daily intake that would kill a healthy man because it burned itself out fighting the thing that was consuming him, Kate had never had a capacity and was no good for anything after two drinks. The transaction in Tombstone with Johnny Behan and Milt Joyce had disgusted her, and she saw in some of the women who lived under her roof the broken thing she would become if she went back to whiskey, and so when the thirst was upon her she drank gallons of tea strong enough to stand a poker in and read novels late at night about women back East who lived in shelflike structures called apartment houses and rode bicycles in the park and fell in love with engineers. Sometimes, just before going to sleep, she thought of Sister and Mother Superior, would catch herself crossing her torso, and would be very hard to get along with all the next day. Every night without fail she prayed for the soul of her dead child, who had been baptized out of the Faith. Silas could see to himself.

The territorial papers were starting to lose interest in Tombstone. Editors who had filled pages calling for federal intervention to end the lawlessness in Cochise County saw little worth reporting there now that most of the colorfuls had quit the place feet first or on horseback. Days went by with no mention of the city, and when the odd shooting scrape did occur, whole columns gloated over the details. Kate decided that journalists were like sick old women who were only happy when they had some new complaint to chew on. The November election, in which Johnny Behan chose not to run to succeed himself as sheriff, was largely ignored. The subsequent shooting of Billy Claiborne provided fodder for days.

Being the only gun man worth mentioning still in the area, Buckskin Frank Leslie was widely credited with having killed Ringo, a rumor he did nothing to confirm or deny. Claiborne, who was still smarting from remarks directed at his decision to flee the empty lot next to Fly's when Virgil Earp ordered the cowboys to throw up their hands, had been in Globe at the time the story broke and took a job in the smelter to get enough money to return to Tombstone and kill Leslie. Once there— being Billy Claiborne and so not in possession of enough sense to lower his trousers in an outhouse—he got drunk and started an argument in the rebuilt Oriental, only to be spun and fired out the door by the more powerful Leslie, who was tending bar there. Later Claiborne appeared swaying at the corner of Fifth and Allen with a Winchester in his hands and his eyes on the saloon's front entrance, calling Leslie a son of a bitch who ought to try killing a man who was wide awake for a change. He was still shouting when Leslie stepped out the side door wearing his apron and shot him through the heart with his Peacemaker.

A hearing absolved Leslie of blame on the grounds of self-defense and Claiborne was buried not far from his friends Billy Clanton and Frank and Tom McLaury. Reading of the incident, Kate wondered if Claiborne had had a woman and if there were a Kate Fisher in Tombstone now to see to her needs. Men imagined that facing death made them men, leaving the women behind to face life.

For that matter she might be there in Globe, left to wait while her man tended to business in Tombstone; and because Kate was thinking of that when someone tapped on her front door she half-expected to find Billy Claiborne's woman there when she opened it.

She didn't. It was Mattie Blaylock, Wyatt Earp's woman before Sadie, come back from helping bury Morgan in California to take a room in Kate's house with the others.

CHAPTER 20

GIVE THE WORLD A flat spin. Grease the axis and start it turning faster, blur the days and nights and the green and umber and gray seasons into a white wipe. Deal out the years like new cards. Our clock is running, there are many players left to throw in, and the only winner is the man who clears the table after everyone has gone.

Johnny Ringo's killer, whoever he was, never came to justice, and the circumstances of the notorious gun man's death remains as much a mystery as his life, settling upon him a posthumous legend greatly out of proportion to the events that can be documented. Buckskin Frank Leslie, a shadowy figure in his own right, never discounted the tales linking him to Ringo's killing, nor did he own to any of them, and when he was sentenced to imprisonment in the territorial penitentiary at Yuma in 1890 for the murder of Molly Bradshaw, a singer at the Bird Cage, many newspapers included Ringo among the notches on Leslie's custom-designed Peacemaker. Where he went after his release in 1897 is largely conjecture, although Wyatt Earp and others claimed to have encountered him, a pathetic old man, working as a saloon swamper in Oakland, California, in the early years of the twentieth century. Wyatt Earp took Ringo for himself, telling a dramatic story of a clandestine return to Arizona Territory in spite of his wanted status there and a face-to-face duel in the sylvan setting of Turkey Creek Canyon; but the clannish Wyatt was no loner and the details run counter to his partner system of hunting and retribution. Fred Dodge, a well-known gambler around Tombstone, came out from under cover as an investigator for Wells Fargo in later years to name Johnny-behind-the-Deuce as Ringo's killer, citing Ringo's attempt to lynch him for the killing of engineer Henry Schneider as a motive. By that time, however, Ringo's fate was too popularly entrenched as a Mystery that Cannot Be Solved, and so Dodge's account is generally dismissed as an attempt to protect his friend Wyatt—although why Wyatt should require such protection after having publicly claimed Ringo remains a puzzle.

Ringo's friend Pony Deal seems to have entertained similar suspicions, for he is believed responsible for the death of Johnny-behind-the-Deuce, right name John O'Rourke, whose bullet-clobbered body was found in the vicinity some days later. Pony Deal himself was killed by persons unknown in either Greenlee County, Arizona, or Sonora, Mexico, depending upon who is telling the story.

Pete Spence, born Peter M. Spencer, considered by many to have been Morgan Earp's killer, never stood trial for that crime. In 1893 he was convicted of an assault charge knocked down from murder in the death of a Mexican and was sentenced to serve five years in the Yuma penitentiary. He was pardoned unconditionally by Governor L. C. Hughes after three years. Nothing is known of his movements after his release.

In the fight at Iron Springs, outlaw Johnny Barnes received a wound that was improperly cared for and eventually died in Charleston, reeking of gangrene and jabbering in delirium. One of his listeners was J. B. Ayers, a Charleston saloonkeeper and yet another of Wells Fargo's ubiquitous undercover men, who reported to Fred Dodge that Barnes had confirmed the death of Curly Bill Brocius at Wyatt Earp's hands. Barnes, Ayers said, went on to admit his part in the midnight attack on Virgil Earp and in the infamous attempt on the Benson stage led by Bill Leonard, Harry Head, and Jim Crane in March 1881. He also implicated Doc Holliday in that botched robbery and accused him of the slaying of driver Bud Philpot. Dodge, who like Bat Masterson held little love for the dying and bitter dentist, pronounced this "sure enough evidence" of Doc's complicity.

Joseph Isaac Clanton and his dull-witted younger brother Phineas shifted their rustling operations north to escape the increasing efficiency of law enforcement in Cochise County after John Behan's retirement from office. In 1887, during the so-called Pleasant Valley War, deputies of the famous Sheriff Commodore Perry Owens of Navajo County shot Ike out from under his hat on the Blue River as he was fleeing an indictment. He was killed instantly, but his brother Phin surrendered and served ten years in Yuma. There he, Pete Spence, and Buckskin Frank Leslie found themselves in the charge of deputy superintendent John Harris Behan. The former sheriff had been appointed by the territorial government for meritorious service to the Democratic Party. Freed in 1897, Phin took up stock raising in legal fashion near Globe, proved adept at a pursuit that involved little guile and less risk, and in 1902 was honored by the Lodge of Free and Accepted Masons for a five-year record of perfect attendance.

Following his deputy superintendency at Yuma, John Behan served as a United States Customs officer at El Paso, then became a commissary officer for the army with good-conduct citations in the Spanish-American War and Boxer Rebellion. He died of natural causes at the age of sixty-six in Tucson on June 7, 1912, while his application for the superintendent's post at the soldiers' home in Prescott was under favorable consideration.

William Milton Breakenridge left the sheriff's office at the end of Behan's term in early 1883 and was later elected Cochise County surveyor, a position he left to become special officer for the Southern Pacific Railroad between Yuma and El Paso. In that capacity he investigated train robberies by such noted desperadoes as Grant Wheeler, Jack Dunlap, and Black Jack Ketchum. He retired from the S.P.R.R. as claim agent at the age of seventy and wrote a rip-roaring book, *Helldorado,* that established his reputation as the only honest law in Tombstone and environs. He died in Tucson at the end of January 1931, a fixture at the Old Pueblo Club and the Arizona Pioneers Historical Society. He never married.

Warren Baxter Earp, the youngest of the five full Earp brothers, drifted with Wyatt and Sadie from one boom camp to another after the three left Arizona, returning there alone in 1891 to work as a hand on Colonel Hooker's Sierra Bonita ranch. Later he tended bar in nearby Wilcox, where at one o'clock on the morning of July 6, 1900, John N. Boyett shot him to death in Brown's Saloon after an argument in which Warren accused Boyett of accepting money to kill him. No warrants were issued for Boyett's arrest, despite testimony at the coroner's inquest that Warren was unarmed at the time of the shooting. Virgil and Wyatt investigated, but no evidence has surfaced to confirm Sadie Earp's dark implication in her autobiography, *I Married Wyatt Earp,* that Boyett was made to answer for his act.

Wyatt and Virgil saw each other one more time before death separated them as well, in Goldfield, Arizona, in 1905.

Virgil Walter Earp never regained full use of his shattered left arm, and although he could chop wood with his right hand and eat with both he had to support the bad arm with his right hand during the latter operation because there was no bone at the elbow, only gristle and sinew holding the arm together. The handicap did not prevent him from opening a detective agency near his parents' home in Colton, California, or from securing election later as Colton's first city marshal. By this time his involvement in the troubles in Tombstone in 1881 was a matter of some legend, outshining that of Wyatt, whose fame would take root in the new century with the publication of a number of popular fictionalized histories and the spread of flickering pictures on bedsheet screens across the country. From there Virgil and his common-law wife Allie went back to Arizona to prospect for gold, and in one of those tent cities a letter caught up with Virgil from a grown daughter he didn't know he had, from an early annulled marriage in Iowa. Later she came to visit him from her home in Oregon. During the rich strikes in Goldfield, Wyatt and Sadie and Virgil and Allie worked neighboring claims. What the brothers talked about during that last time together is not recorded. When Virgil died of pneumonia that same year Allie shipped his body back for burial in his daughter's family plot in Portland, Oregon.

Alvira Sullivan Earp outlived all of the other principals connected with the early days in Tombstone, dying in Los Angeles in 1947, three weeks short of her one hundredth birthday. Before her death she entrusted her recollections to a nephew, Frank Waters, who used them to write a revisionist history of the events surrounding the so-called "Gunfight at the O.K. Corral," which she read, pronounced a pack of lies, and threatened to kill him if he published. Whether or not Waters took the threat seriously, it is a matter of record that *The Earp Brothers of Tombstone* did not see print until thirteen years after her death.

James Cooksey Earp, eldest of the fraternal clan, buried his wife Nellie in San Bernardino, California, in 1887, and died in Los Angeles in 1926, aged eighty-four. Although he turned up as a saloonkeeper, gambler, and whoremaster in most of the towns visited by Wyatt and the other Earps during the peak days of the circuit, the wound he had sustained in his left shoulder fighting in Fredericktown in 1861 prevented him from taking an active part in the violent episodes.

For a little over a year after her return to Arizona, Celia Ann Blaylock, known during her time in Tombstone and from then on as Mattie Earp, lived in Kate Fisher's boardinghouse in Globe, then moved on to Pinal, a town that owed its existence to the Silver King Mine eight miles to the north. There she lived as a prostitute, complaining in the saloons by day of her husband's desertion, and mixing laudanum with her whiskey in her shack at night so she could sleep. She spent the night of July 2, 1888, with a miner, discovered some cheap jewelry missing the next day, and drank an entire bottle of laudanum. On the Fourth of July she was buried in the desert north of town and a trunk containing her effects was sent to relatives in Iowa. Among these were some Earp family tintypes and a Bible that had been presented to Wyatt by a law firm in Dodge City when he was a deacon.

When the extradition threat against Doc Holliday was

lifted, Wyatt Berry Stapp Earp and Warren traveled by train from Colorado to Colton, California, to visit their parents and Virgil, collected Sadie from her parents in San Francisco, and returned to Denver, where Wyatt and Doc gathered crowds in the gambling halls in the wake of the Tombstone legend. In Gunnison Wyatt's prospecting turned up only dirt and he and the clan left Doc riding a tiger in town to seek their elusive fortune on a dwindling frontier. Wyatt and Doc never saw each other again. In June 1883 Wyatt responded to a summons from Luke Short in Dodge City and founded the Dodge City Peace Commission with Short, Bat Masterson, and five other gun men to help establish Short's right to run a saloon there. The spectacle of so many determined-looking dandies with pistols on under their coats won the point without bloodshed and the commission was dissolved amicably.

In Idaho, Wyatt and brother James were reunited, running a saloon in Eagle City in the Coeur d'Alene District and working a few claims, including two that were not their own, for which they paid heavy fines that forced them to close the saloon in 1884. After that the three Earps and their families wandered through Texas, gambling, pimping, and working confidence games in cowtowns and mining camps from Fort Worth to old Mexico. But the circuit was drying up. Money was no longer quickly come by and slower spent, the law was everywhere, and Cochise County had spoiled Wyatt's appetite for politics. They returned to California.

In San Diego, Wyatt invested funds borrowed from Sadie's parents in real estate and horses, buying interests in racing stock. Wyatt often raced them in person, and his lanky figure in cap and goggles with linen duster flying behind his sulky became a familiar sight on the California dirt tracks. One of his horses, Lottie Mills, took the seven-furlong running away at the World's Columbian Exposition in Chicago in 1893, where Wyatt introduced his common-law wife to red-faced, white-whiskered Will Cody, an acquaintance from his Kansas buffalo-hunting days. As Buffalo Bill the flamboyant old frontiersman was hosting his Wild West exhibition across the street from the fair entrance.

At the end of 1896, Wyatt reluctantly agreed to referee the

Sharkey-Fitzsimmons World Heavyweight Championship fight at Mechanics Pavilion in San Francisco. Amid shrill claims that the match was fixed, he awarded it to Tom Sharkey on a foul. The tempo was set before the opening bell, when Wyatt stripped off his coat in the ring and forgot that he was wearing a pistol underneath. He was fined fifty dollars for carrying a concealed weapon and the charge of corruption would follow him the rest of his life.

The new century found Wyatt and Sadie in Alaska, lured there by the scent of gold. He established the opulent Dexter Saloon in Nome—entertaining, among others, middle-aging John Clum, come to make sense out of the Alaskan postal system—and operated it, with time out to meet Virgil in Arizona and look into Warren's killing, until the fall of 1901, when he sold it for eighty-five thousand dollars and shipped home. Their next stop was Tonapah, Nevada, another in the string of mining boomtowns that came to an end finally in Goldfield in 1905.

Bad investments brought Wyatt to a charge of vagrancy in Los Angeles and an arrest for bunco-steering in 1911. He was sixty-three years old.

In Los Angeles, picture people came to Wyatt and Sadie's rented bungalow to pump him for information on his frontier past. At first he told it straight, or at least as straight as he had told the reporter from the San Francisco paper before the Sharkey fight, but then he got tired of repeating himself and started making things up. He stretched one for a fellow named Ford about sidewinding his way into the O.K. Corral inside a cloud of dust from a passing stagecoach and told William S. Hart a howler about Frank McLaury putting a ball through a wedding ring at sixty paces that animated the actor's horse face like his western fans never saw on the screen. When things he said started showing up in theaters he grinned at Sadie and said it was too bad the *Nugget* wasn't publishing anymore, with so many potential subscribers around.

John H. Flood, a family friend and willing pair of hands and legs whenever the aging couple required a service, collaborated with Wyatt at this time on his autobiography, producing by the 1920s a melodramatic and overwritten account that even the endorsement of Hart at the height of his screen fame could not force into print. Because the manuscript was still circulating, Wyatt declined to help Walter Noble Burns with a similar project, published in 1927 under the title *Tombstone,* which emphasized Wyatt's skills as a gun man—transmuted into the modern term *gunfighter*—at the expense of the truth. That, together with rumors of the forthcoming publication of Billy Breakenridge's hostile *Helldorado,* persuaded Wyatt and Sadie to cooperate with a man named Stuart Lake in the construction of a fact-based biography. Wyatt and Lake corresponded frequently throughout 1928 with that end in mind.

Wyatt Earp died at eighty of prostate cancer early on the morning of January 13, 1929, in the rented bungalow he shared with his wife. Sadie had his remains cremated and buried near her parents' plot in San Francisco. Pallbearers at his funeral included William S. Hart and John Clum.

As the widow of Wyatt Earp, Josephine Sarah Marcus spent the rest of her life as custodian of his memory. This included backing up Allie's threats against Frank Waters and *The Earp Brothers of Tombstone* as well as denouncing the implausible icon erected in *Tombstone* and Lake's florid *Wyatt Earp, Frontier Marshal,* published in 1931. She did succeed in creating a climate sufficiently hostile to persuade Houghton Mifflin to change the subtitle from *Gunfighter* and in 1934 bullied Twentieth Century Fox into removing her husband's name from the film version. On two occasions she dictated her memoirs in hopes of publishing a book that would debunk the myth, but they did not see print until 1976, when Earp historian Glenn Boyer edited and consolidated the two manuscripts into *I Married Wyatt Earp*. She died in Los Angeles on December 19, 1944.

Kate Fisher, sometimes referred to by her other alias of Kate Elder, christened Maria Katharina Horony, sold the boardinghouse in Globe to be with Doc Holliday when he died in Colorado in 1887. In 1888 she married a blacksmith there, George Cummings, and moved back to Arizona, living with him in Bisbee and other cities struggling to make the transition from boom camp to permanent settlement. But Cummings was nearly as heavy a drinker as Doc, with none of Doc's superhuman capacity, and she left him to preserve her own sobriety. He expired by his own hand in Courtland, Arizona, in 1915. She worked in a hotel in Cochise until 1900, when she quit to move in with mining executive John J. Howard near Doz Cabezas, where she stayed until his death in January 1930, inheriting the bulk of his estate and administrating the remainder. Later, claiming poverty, she entered the Pioneers' Home in Prescott and died there at the age of ninety in 1940. Before her death she wrote a long autobiographical letter to a niece that remains the most reliable of the many chronicles of her life. The niece and all the surviving members of the Horony family called her Aunt Mary.

John Henry Holliday went to Deadwood, Dakota Territory, in the summer of 1883, got in an argument with a bartender there, and put a ball through the man's wrist as he was reaching in a drawer for a pistol. Returning to Colorado, Doc found celebrity in the aftermath of the business in Tombstone and the extradition battle and was often seen strolling the streets of Silverton and Leadville towing a crowd of boys and would-be gun men who listened to his stories of fast-shooting prowess and fought one another over his cast-off cigar butts. In Leadville he ran three faro games and shot the city marshal, Bill Allen, over five dollars he owed Allen. The man survived, but when a deputy named Kelly braced him over the incident in a saloon sometime later, Doc shot him twice, mortally wounding him, and was preparing to finish him off when another deputy disarmed him and placed him under arrest. At his hearing the killing was judged justifiable and he was discharged. He had more trouble with the earlier shooting, which went to full trial before he was acquitted on March 30, 1885.

Of all his scrapes with the law, it was the first to get past the preliminary hearing stage. The circuit was dying, and with it public tolerance of the actions of gun men. The strike towns were drying up and blowing away or else had grown too big to tree. They were connected by the railroad and telegraph and a man had to run farther and faster if he wanted to keep buckshot

out of his coattails. Doc sold his horse for a stake and
commuted between games by day coach.

He drank much, ate little, and his sleep was so close to
waking that he gave up trying. He was a scarecrow in the
smoke-clogged tents and adobe huts where games of chance
were played, a marble face with coal eyes and protruding ears,
broken-straw wrists in cuffs that flapped as he shuffled cards
and clacked faro counters with a noise of old bones rattling. The
cough was constant; he was no longer aware of it, and indeed in
his more feverish moments considered that he had beaten it. His
conversation rambled, he lost track of bets. His business fell off.

In May 1887 he went to Glenwood Springs, and he had to
be helped down from the train. Sulfur was the universal
curative, but it only gagged him and brought up the rest of his
lungs and he was carried to a bed in a ward where on good days
he sat up and played patience or wrote letters addressed to a
convent in Atlanta, and on bad days he vomited his meals into
the bedpan. He got up for the last time late in October. After
that he lay tossing, accusing Wyatt of having panther guts for
brains and telling Mexican whores in Spanish to rinse and spit.
Kate came to visit. Sometimes he recognized her and spoke of
Fort Griffin and Dodge. His smile had become ghastly, full of
long teeth like a horse's. Mostly he raised bets and asked
Morgan if he had time for another snort before heading over to
the Bird Cage.

Coming on ten o'clock on the morning of November 8 he
opened clear gray eyes for the first time in twelve hours and
asked the sanitarium attendant for a tumbler of whiskey. When
it was brought, he drank it off in two slow draughts, returned
the empty vessel, looked around at the people gathered at his
bedside, and smiled.

"This is funny."

He was thirty-five.

The drastic drop in the price of silver after 1883 and the
flooding by underground springs of the richest of the mines
around Tombstone in succeeding years reduced the city's
population from its peak-production high of fifteen thousand to

a tenth of that number by the turn of the century. For a time after that the city subsisted on its distinction as county seat, and when that was taken away, rather than going the way of neighboring Charleston and Galeyville and other frontier metropolises that are now only foundations overgrown by grass, it assumed its new legend as "the town too tough to die." Somehow it survived long enough to enter its present incarnation; the reasons are likely more social than historical and are not for discussion here.

Today Tombstone is a detour off U.S. Highway 80 between Tucson and Bisbee, three rows of brick and frame buildings on broken pavement, the latter earmarked for destruction in the pursuit of the settlement's authentic past. Mexican crafts and turquoise jewelry are sold in the Oriental Saloon and James Earp's Sampling Room, the Bird Cage still stands in shabby grandeur on the east end of Allen Street, and the Crystal Palace, originally the Eagle Brewery Saloon, has had its late-Victorian furnishings restored, with the addition of a large oil painting of Wyatt Earp on the wall next to the restrooms. The *Epitaph,* shrewdly transformed by its owners from a newspaper to a historical journal, boasts an international circulation many times greater than John Clum's. Books and pamphlets on the violent days may be purchased in the gift shop at Boot Hill Cemetery, where the markers on the graves of Billy Clanton and the McLaurys are kept up, including the legend: MURDERED IN THE STREETS OF TOMBSTONE. Every year around the anniversary of the gun battle on Fremont Street the city celebrates Helldorado Days, welcoming thousands of tourists who come to see dramatic re-creations of the more famous killings and to have their tintypes taken in rented costumes. The city that cried out for law and order now thrives on its lawless past.

The high point of any tour, of course, is the O.K. Corral, rebuilt like the rest of the town after the 1883 fire, where for a dollar—fifty cents for children—the visitor may enter and follow a deviously designed passage to the spot where the famous battle actually took place, ninety feet west of the original corral. Crude Cellotex representations of the combatants have been erected there for those whose imaginations are not equal to the task. C. S. Fly's boardinghouse and photograph gallery have been restored, and inside the boardinghouse a picture of a woman who is not Big Nose Kate marks the spot where she is said to have witnessed the fight through the window in the room she shared with Doc Holliday. Elsewhere in town, plaques identify the locations where Virgil Earp was ambushed, Morgan Earp was killed, and Curly Bill Brocius shot Marshal Fred White. The hardware store where the bodies of Billy Clanton and the McLaurys were laid out before burial sells T-shirts with Wyatt Earp's likeness silk-screened on the front. It is possible to eat a plate of chicken-fried steak on the site where Johnny Ringo, Frank Stilwell, and others crouched waiting to empty their shotguns at Virgil Earp as he crossed Fifth Street from the Oriental toward the Eagle Brewery, but it is not recommended. Tombstone cuisine is not what it was in 1881.

On noncelebration days the town closes at five, a far cry from early days of all-night revels and piano music spilling over every batwing door from dusk until daybreak. When the sun goes down the ghosts that walk the machine-cut boardwalks must wonder if they are not haunting the wrong place. Yet it is only then, when the daytime dandies who clomp around in Tony Lama boots and Calgary Stampede Stetsons are drinking Coors in nearby Sierra Vista, and shadows have enveloped the gaudy facade of Big Nose Kate's Saloon, that one can feel the ghosts' presence.

A pair of stately oaks standing near the corner of Third and Fremont, where Billy Clanton and Tom McLaury died, are the only living witnesses to the fight that did not start or end anything, but that was merely one skirmish in what some experts have termed the first true gang war in American history. Next to these, separated from the scene of the battle by a flimsy clapboard fence, is a playground. The children who play there are tired of hearing about Wyatt Earp and Doc Holliday and want only to use the swings and the slide. Of all of Tombstone's many friendly citizens, they are the only ones consistently living in the present.

POSTSCRIPT

TOMBSTONE WAS YESTERDAY. At this writing the minister who officiated at Big Nose Kate's funeral is still living, and many who knew Wyatt Earp personally are in good health. For this reason the history of the events that took place in Cochise County between March 1881 and July 1882 is constantly in flux, and as old-timers die and discolored letters and diaries surface from trunks stored in attics and basements, forgotten facts continue to come to light and discredit long-held assumptions with the inevitability of changing seasons.

Bloody Season, therefore, is not, nor is it intended to be, the last word on the circumstances surrounding the thirty-second-long engagement that has come down to us as the Gunfight at the O.K. Corral. In the interest of clarity, some of the complexities of regional politics in the 1880s have been toned down, and some of the peripheral figures, such as Wyatt Earp's gun man friend Texas Jack Vermillion, have been eliminated because their participation was minor and ephemeral and would only snarl further an already tangled skein. Much of the dialogue is the author's invention. Personal memoirs seldom recall the exact words spoken by a given person at a given time, only their drift, and in all cases where the conversations have not been taken from existing quotes they have been constructed upon these summaries and crafted after the fashion of the individuals' speech patterns as recorded elsewhere.

The author offers no apologies for these and other presumptions, because the book is fiction based on fact and is not intended as pure history. At the same time he has attempted to tell the story of the Earp-Holliday-Clanton-McLaury feud with as much accuracy and objectivity as is possible after all this time. It should be noted that the issues were as confused when the smoke was still turning in the lot next to Fly's boardinghouse as they are now after a century of tampering by dime novelists, Hollywood directors, and self-styled revisionists who imagine that by making a hero of Ike Clanton and a villain of Wyatt Earp they have done something different and startling. Everyone involved lied about the events; the challenge now is to decide who was lying about what, piece together the few points of agreement, and apply common sense to the others to form a logical picture. This task, performed for the first time by Justice Wells Spicer a month after the fight and by hundreds of others many times since, can only increase one's respect for the pressures faced by that jurist when lives, including his own, depended upon his verdict.

Some cherished icons have fallen in the course of this assembly. Gone from the fight are the romantic funeral-black skirted coats of the Earps and Holliday, often seen in movies and book jacket illustrations—Wyatt and his brothers had on mackinaws that brisk day, and Doc wore gray—and firearms enthusiasts will search in vain for Wyatt's storied long-barreled Buntline Special; the best research indicates that the gun never existed. The Earps's whorehouse interests on the circuit should shock no one in these exposé-conscious times; perhaps more disturbing is the lack of evidence to dispute Big Nose Kate's assertion that Doc Holliday had never killed anyone before the Tombstone fight. It is a hard thing to give up a hero, harder still to relinquish a scoundrel.

The author gratefully acknowledges the valuable assistance of Earp historian Glenn Boyer, editor of *I Married Wyatt Earp* (University of Arizona Press, Tucson, 1976), who provided copious material from his files, including Wyatt Earp's long-lost autobiography; and of his colleague, Alford E. Turner, editor of *The O.K. Corral Inquest* (Creative Publishing Co., College Station, Texas, 1981), for taking an hour out of his busy schedule in Tombstone to clear up the question of when Big Nose Kate left that city. Together and separately, they have unearthed most of the new information concerning early Tombstone that has appeared in recent years, and they are still digging. They are responsible for much of *Bloody Season*'s accuracy. The author himself is to blame for its shortcomings.

Finally, words are not adequate to thank Dick Wheeler, to whom this volume is dedicated, for suggesting the book and for providing much helpful research to get the project started. He is a living Muse.

Wyatt Earp is not dead. Like Custer on his hill he stands tall and terrible in that dusty lot on Fremont Street, and no amount of unwanted truth or iconoclastic rhetoric will topple him. "Not a bullet touched me," he wrote of his myth-enshrouded shoot-out with Curly Bill's gang at Iron Springs, and he might have been speaking of all the fictions to come. *Bloody Season* is an attempt to touch him, his friends, his enemies, their women, their time, and their place.

Loren D. Estleman
Whitmore Lake, Michigan
April 1, 1986